ILANA'S
Wish

ANNETTE LYON

A NEWPORT LADIES BOOK CLUB NOVEL

ILANA'S *Wish*

Covenant Communications, Inc.

Cover image: *A Life Preserver Hanging on a Dock Handrail* © Brian Caissie; Getty Images.

Cover design copyright © 2014 by Covenant Communications, Inc.

Published by Covenant Communications, Inc.
American Fork, Utah

Printed in the United States of America
First Printing: April 2014

20 19 18 17 16 15 14   10 9 8 7 6 5 4 3 2 1

ISBN-13: 978-1-62108-463-1

To my third grade teacher, Sandie Mixa.

The first adult not related to me to say I had talent as a writer. I've never forgotten your encouragement.

Acknowledgments

As I LOOK BACK ON the journey that has been The Newport Ladies Book Club, I marvel at where it's taken me and how much I've grown along the way. Thanks especially to my coauthors, Julie, Josi, and Heather. I've learned a lot from each of these ladies, and without them, the series, quite simply, wouldn't exist. Without them, I also wouldn't have consumed nearly as much trail mix over the last several years—or had nearly as much fun.

No matter how in-depth a writer tries to research on her own, sometimes there's nothing like talking to someone who is an expert on the subject. So a huge thanks goes to Jenny Smith, pharmacy tech extraordinaire, who put up with my never-ending questions and volunteered just the right details I needed for Ilana's story to be real and accurate. Any remaining mistakes, of course, are mine.

I wouldn't survive or get anything done in my writing life without my accountability partner and twin from another existence, Luisa Perkins. I am beyond grateful for what she brings to my life every single day. And a special thanks to Robison Wells, the little brother I never had, for his friendship and constant support.

I am grateful for the team at Covenant for taking on a totally different kind of project and seeing it through—it's been a long and challenging trip, and I appreciate all of the work they've done to make this series a success.

Finally, a special thanks to the readers who have championed each of the eight book-club ladies and cheered the entire series on. From idea to completion, the series has taken almost six years, something I don't think any of us realized would happen when the four of us first discussed the project over breakfast in 2008.

We couldn't have done it without you, our readers!

BOOKS IN THE NEWPORT LADIES BOOK CLUB SERIES

Set #1
Olivia—Julie Wright
Daisy—Josi S. Kilpack
Paige—Annette Lyon
Athena—Heather B. Moore

Set #2
Shannon's Hope—Josi S. Kilpack
Ruby's Secret—Heather B. Moore
Victoria's Promise—Julie Wright
Ilana's Wish—Annette Lyon

For ideas on hosting your own book club, suggestions for books and recipes, or information on how you can guest-write about your book club on our blog, please visit us at http://thenewportladiesbookclub. blogspot.com.

Chapter 1

As I WALKED DOWN THE long Exhibit Hall B corridor, I compared my clipboard to an e-mail on my phone, a message from The Long Beach Wedding Show owner about two last-minute exhibitors. The show would open tomorrow morning at nine o'clock, and the floor wasn't anywhere near set up. I had to tell the display company owner, Chuck, where to add the two additional booths. His workers would set those up—and then they'd charge the exhibitors their firstborn for additional chairs and tables. The union workers were the only ones allowed to carry vendors' products to the floor or even put plugs in outlets.

I pursed my lips while studying the floor plan. The only real place to squeeze in last-minute vendors was at the back side of aisle three—not the best spot. I hoped the other businesses there hadn't started setting up yet; they might have to start over, depending on how Chuck worked the extra booths in.

This kind of thing was exactly why I tried to get my shows to turn in their final floor plans two weeks in advance, but I'd made an exception in this case. A *bigger* show meant more vendors, higher attendance, and a bigger splash, making my chances of a promotion at the convention center even better.

Halfway to Chuck's station at the back of the hall, I brushed my curly hair away from both sides of my face. It was driving me crazy; I should have pulled it into a ponytail this morning. Even though my hair looked great in the mornings after I styled it, by lunch, the Newport Beach humidity made me look not unlike Napoleon Dynamite. And we were already *way* past lunch *and* dinner.

But doing my job right meant such sacrifices. This show would be one of the most complicated I'd ever coordinated, yet the client had tentative plans to do two or three a year, so this first show needed to do well if Ethan and I were to pay off his medical school loans as well as our medical bills.

Or rather, *my* medical bills from three tries of in vitro, followed by a year of nonstop bleeding. As if infertility hadn't been bad enough, an emotional anvil had dropped on my head with my OB's declaration that I needed a hysterectomy. I had that surgery three weeks ago, and now I couldn't get pregnant no matter what. Ethan wanted to apply for adoption, but I wasn't ready for that—didn't know if I ever would be. I had yet to grieve the loss of my dream to have a baby growing inside me, to give birth to my own flesh and blood.

For that matter, I needed to recover from the hysterectomy, and the recovery wasn't happening as quickly as I thought it should. I'd assumed that by now I'd have bounced back, my surgeon's prediction notwithstanding. I could hardly move for the pain, yet here I was, walking a huge event-hall floor. This wedding show was too important to miss. I'd been working on it for months, and the payoff would be big. No way could I trust it to another event manager, especially when that meant saying good-bye to a pretty obvious promotion. I'd rest next week when the show was over.

Chuck's setup crew had just about finished putting up the booths; I was glad they weren't totally finished because this new order would have annoyed them if they'd already put away the aluminum poles and stacks of drapes. As I headed past a worker on a ladder, he lost hold of an eight-foot aluminum pole, which fell to the ground. I yelped and scrambled out of the way, only to slam into a six-foot table in a booth and twist my ankle. The worst of the pain, though, was my still-healing abdomen; it felt like I'd pulled a stitch inside or something.

"Uh, sorry, ma'am," the man said—or rather, the boy. Now that he'd scrambled down the ladder and was standing at eye level, he didn't look old enough to shave. Which was pretty much the only reason I didn't lay into him.

"Remember, Ilana," Ethan kept telling me. "You basically had someone go in and rip out your guts. Your body needs rest." At the time, I'd laughed—he was a doctor, but he wasn't using medical speak. Right now in the exhibit hall, I hated the fact that he was right.

Ripping out my guts felt accurate. It was too late for me to attempt to get any rest today. I closed my eyes and breathed through my mouth, hoping the pain would recede.

The bottle says Vicodin lasts four to six hours. Liars. A glance at the clock at the back of the hall confirmed my fear: I had an hour before I could take another dose.

I shouldn't have come in today. I should have passed this show on to Tony like Ethan begged me to do. But overestimating my strength turned out to be awfully easy when my body had no outward evidence of surgery—or gut rippage. I sat on the table with one hand on my ankle and the other holding my middle. The boy eyed me, eyebrows raised, waiting for a response. Only then did I realize I hadn't answered.

"It's okay," I said as I realized the table I was sitting on belonged to the Elegance Photography booth. I rotated my ankle to work out the twist and felt how weak I still was, like I'd been trampled by a rhinoceros. I probably looked like it too.

Worse, for the first time since my surgery, after weeks of lying around feeling like an ugly couch potato, I'd given in to vanity and put on a pair of killer hot boots with three-inch heels, which I'd bought yesterday as retail therapy.

I'd worn them because they were awesome and because heels made me look more professional and put together than, say, more comfortable but utterly hideous Crocks. From my spot on the table, I looked over the setup so far. The Long Beach Wedding Show had picked patriotic colors for the booth drapery. Maybe I could have understood if it were in honor of President's Day, but in January? I'd tried talking the owner into using plain black—a classy color that would match whatever vendors used in their displays, many of which would likely have a lot of ivory and pastel colors, but no. She'd insisted on paying tribute to our country and armed forces. In January.

Worse, she hadn't picked classic red, white, and blue; these colors were more of a cranberry red, a yellowish off-white, and an electric blue. The table skirts alternated red, white, and blue every three booths. It hadn't even looked good on paper; in real life, it was hideous. The vendors' products were sure to clash. Elegance Photography, if their reputation was any indication, would swath the booth in fabric, likely covering every inch of the patriotic drape. Maybe other vendors could camouflage their booths too. One could hope.

My headset crackled with a voice. "Hey, Ilana?" It was Chuck. "I've got the forklifts taking vendor loads to booths. That okay?"

I pushed a button on my earpiece to answer. "Do aisles one and two first," I told him. "The poles and drapery look pretty much done, but

I've got an order for two more booths at the back of three that your guys will need to add. Oh, and go ahead and send the carpet in."

"Already on it."

Good. We were running behind, mostly because Chuck's men had shown up a full two hours late. Now I had vendors calling every two minutes asking when they could start setting up, and others were already in the hall, waiting at the sides until they had the go ahead. I'd worked with Chuck for many shows, so he was a friend, and I didn't feel the need to dance around the situation like I did with other companies. Besides, he'd already apologized several times for his guys' tardiness.

I heard a female voice in the background, followed by Chuck asking, "Oh, hey, which booth is Chrissy May Candies in?"

I double-checked the floor plan and pushed the button to answer. "One-oh-one and one-oh-two—the end cap between one and two. May as well bring theirs in first." I clicked off my headset and pulled out my cell to call Chrissy May. I hesitated for a second, suddenly remembering the call the other day from Ruby at book club, inviting me out to lunch. I'd promised to call back when I found a day that worked, but then I'd hung up and never given it another thought.

Ruby was the organizer of the book club I'd joined back in November. The one I'd attended all of twice—November and December. I missed January's meeting thanks to the Home and Garden Expo. It had seemed as important as the wedding show . . . at the time. Now I wished I'd just gone to the book club, even if it had meant sneaking out of the show for a bit. Ruby was sweet and older than my own mother, and I had absolutely nothing in common with her. She was a mother and widow. She wore bright, flamboyant colors. She made her own pillows and jam. I preferred black business clothes and bought most of our apartment's accessories from IKEA. Besides, my work schedule had been difficult; it wasn't like I'd had time for lunch with anyone.

I sighed and found Chrissy May's number. One ring later, she answered, and I let her know that in a few minutes, she could set up her booth. As soon as I got the words out, I saw Chrissy May herself walking toward me from a side aisle.

She clicked her phone shut and said, "We're still up front, right?" She approached with a bulging neon-green purse over one shoulder. She probably weighed at least twice what I did, and she had two inches of gray roots at the base of a dingy-brown dye job.

"Ilana?" she said, marching toward me. "Ilana, did you hear me? I want to be sure I get the end cap at the front like you promised." Her high-pitched voice grated on my nerves. Why was she asking me if I'd heard her when I'd confirmed her booth moments before? And why wasn't she talking to the show owner? She was the one who'd given me the final floor plan; I had nothing to do with those decisions.

Get a grip. Be kind. I'd skipped dinner so my blood sugar was low; I was running on cappuccino and whatever remained of the Vicodin. Yet my stomach still ached, in more ways than one.

I'll never, ever have a baby now. The thought smacked me out of the blue again. How long would it do that? Would I ever go a day without that thought shooting through my very soul?

I nearly burst into tears—again—because I no longer carried the organ needed to make a baby. I took a deep breath and smiled in an attempt to fake a good mood for Chrissy May. She was a regular, high-paying client—she'd rented out an end cap for three shows already this year. I needed to be nice. She was sweet, if a bit of a handful.

"Hi," I said, certain my smile was tighter than Kenny Rogers' facelift. "You're right up front, next to the concessions, just like we talked about. Same spot as in the Christmas Gift Show in November. One of Chuck's guys is bringing your stuff around on a forklift any minute."

She put a pudgy hand to her chest and sighed dramatically. "Oh, I'm so relieved."

"Watch out for the forklift," I said, walking backward as a hint that I was leaving. "Operators don't always pay attention to the people around them."

"Oh, I hope they don't break the toffee," she said, looking around for the forklift as if it were a predator. As my distance from her increased, she spoke louder. "Oh, and the candy boxes—they could get crushed. And the ribbon . . ." She seemed ready to burst into tears.

"I'm sure your things will be fine," I called, although I wouldn't trust the forklift guys with a dog I hated. But Chrissy May always packed her things properly and then some—I was quite sure she'd packed everything in triple layers of bubble wrap. Even an idiot operator wouldn't be able to cause problems.

Chrissy May hurried off toward her booth to preside over the forklift once it arrived. As she left, I pictured her packaging—pink and purple polka dots with brown bows. Next to red, white, and blue drapery? I shuddered. Poor Chrissy May.

I headed for Chuck's station at the back of the hall to finally give him that new booth information and to make sure what I'd marked on my clipboard matched the reality of which vendors had already checked in. I made a check mark in the delivered box next to Chrissy May's Candies. For trade shows with simple setups, like business conventions, where the displays consisted mostly of pamphlets, posters, and stand-up signs, setup happened the morning of the show because it took all of twenty minutes.

But this was a wedding show, which meant hours of elaborate preparations. My heels clicked on the floor as I consulted the floor plan on the second page of my clipboard. There was still so much to do tonight. Setting up the midway would be a nightmare—it would display dozens of wedding dresses on mannequins. Then there was the end cap of aisles three and four, with a display of no fewer than five chocolate fountains, and the wedding cake competition at the back of the hall— with twenty-eight cakes entered but not to be touched. Oh, and a grand piano, where a hopeful wedding musician would play, business cards perched on the edge of the piano. For his sake, I hoped his music would carry across the hall instead of being sucked up in the vast space, but I had my doubts. I considered getting him a mic and a stand and pumping his music into the PA system for ambiance, but that was a decision I'd leave for tomorrow morning—and for the pianist, as he'd have to fork over the cash for the mic and outlet.

My headset beeped again, and Chuck's voice came across with urgency. "Ilana, I've got someone from Rockefeller and Sons Catering here."

I didn't remember a vendor on the list by that name, and Janette, the wedding-show owner, had not mentioned them to me when she'd given me the final list. "I don't think we have a vendor by that name." I *knew* we didn't; I would have remembered a pretentious name like *Rockefeller*. No way would some dinky caterer I'd never heard of be related to *the* Rockefeller family. And I bet the "and sons" part was made up.

"Don't see them on the floor plan you gave me either," Chuck said. "Are they one of the two last-minute booths?"

"No, those are for an invitation printing company and a florist."

"He's pretty insistent he paid for a ten-by-ten, and he's ready to set up. You'd better come back to talk to him." His voice lowered. "He says he needs to report to the management how poorly he's been treated."

I tried to run a hand through my hair, but my fingers got tangled in the curls. "I'll be right there." I headed toward Chuck's station while navigating my cell phone to Janette's number. She could confirm whether this guy had a contract with her show.

Halfway to the back of the hall, I had my eyes on my phone, ears attuned to my headset, boots clicking away on the smooth concrete, when Chrissy May's voice overpowered it all with a call from her booth. "Ih-laaaaah-naaaaah!"

Chuck's voice buzzed in my earpiece again. "So what do I—"

"Hold on just one second, Chuck," I said, turning around to Chrissy May. "Do you need something?" I called, walking backward, hoping that whatever it was could wait until after I'd dealt with the Mr. Rockefeller caterer dude. Everyone seemed to need me at the same time, all the time. Chrissy started talking fast about something I couldn't make out from fifty feet.

I was about to ask her to wait five minutes when a deep voice behind me yelled, "Comin' through!"

Something moving fast smacked my calves. I flailed, cell phone and clipboard flying, and the next thing I knew, I was facedown on the floor. I instinctively looked over to see what had knocked me off my feet—a big roll of bright red carpet, which came to a stop six feet away. Stars of pain burst into my vision, making me clutch my left arm.

Crud! My funny bone! The immediate shock of pain in my elbow was eclipsed shortly after by my abdomen feeling like a fire had erupted inside me.

With the position I'd landed in, sprawled across the floor, I had the fleeting thought that I was glad I'd worn slacks today—no skirt to provide an extra view.

Chuck's carpet guy glanced my way. "Sorry," he mumbled as he kicked the carpet roll again, sending it thudding open three more times. With each thump, a blow of pain went through me.

A stupid carpet roll had knocked me over.

Get back to work, I commanded myself. The pain in my arm would pass. It would. I put my left arm out to help me stand, but the moment it bore any weight, I collapsed. I landed face-first on top of it, my cheekbone hitting the floor. A new wave of pain shot through me. I couldn't get up. *This is more than a bump on my funny bone. Now what?*

I sat there for a moment, waiting for the white-hot heat in my middle to subside. When it did, the sharp stabbing in my elbow took over. Feeling faint, I looked around for aid. Carpet Guy had kept going, but Chrissy May flew toward me. She hit a bump in the carpet and almost tripped too but regained her balance with two hops and kept running. She dropped to my side. "Are you okay?"

After weeks of being on the receiving end of Chrissy May's whining and worry leading up to the wedding show, I never thought I'd be so grateful to see her face. "I can't get up," I said, trying not to clench my teeth from the pain. "I can't use my left arm."

"Here, let me help you." She went behind me and pulled me up by my armpits—not the most graceful way of rising to my feet but definitely effective, and it didn't hurt my arm. Much.

I stood there, trying to get my bearings as my head swam.

Chrissy May eyed me. "You look faint."

I *felt* faint. Trying to think made me feel like my brain was swimming through smoke, and I didn't think it was because of the post-surgery pain meds. All I could think about was that Chuck needed me to talk to the angry caterer. "Where's my cell? And . . . my clipboard?"

Chrissy May grabbed a chair from a nearby booth and dragged it into the aisle. "You sit here. I'll find your things. Don't you worry one bit."

"Thank you," I said, sinking onto the chair with relief. Something was definitely wrong with my arm; I couldn't move it without sharp pain shooting through it. I hoped for a pulled muscle or a simple bruise.

"You should go see the doctor right away," Chrissy May said after gathering my stack of papers that had flown off the clipboard and reattaching them. After placing the clipboard on my lap, she held up my phone. Fortunately, the screen hadn't shattered. "Anyone you'd like me to call?"

"No," I said with a weak shake of my head—which I immediately regretted because it made my vision swim and the pain intensify. I felt ready to pass out. And puke. I held my limp left arm with my right hand. "I'll make an appointment with my doctor later. I can't leave right now."

I held out my hand for the phone and tucked it into my pocket. I still had to deal with the surprise caterer plus all the other vendors and the cakes and dresses setup and getting the piano delivered and tuned. I also had to make sure the hall would stay cool enough for the cakes so the icing wouldn't droop—and then, somehow, smooth out the ruffled feathers of the chocolate fountain people, who would freak out if the room wasn't warm enough for the liquid chocolate to fall in pretty sheets. I had to keep my focus. If I could keep all of the balls in the air a little bit longer—and if the show's attendance was good and the vendors got lots of business—that promotion would be mine. And if that was going to happen, I absolutely couldn't leave.

Now my head ached along with my arm. How would I get through all of that? I wouldn't be out of here for another four or five hours.

"Can I get you anything, dear?" Chrissy May said again.

"Do you have any ibuprofen?" That wouldn't interact with the Vicodin. At least, I didn't think it would; ibuprofen didn't have Tylenol, which I knew was a no-no with Vicodin.

"Sure do." Chrissy May was about to scurry off, but then she stopped and turned back. "I *really* think a doctor needs to see that arm. You sure you're okay? I don't know that you're safe to drive."

She had a point about driving.

But I couldn't exactly be replaced right now, even if someone else took me to an ER. I didn't want to worry Ethan at work; his night shift at the ER had already started, and he didn't have much seniority as a surgeon in the last few months of his residency. Plus, I didn't want to show up at my husband's workplace only to have him worried about seeing me in this condition—and I'd get a lot of "I told you so."

"I'll see how I'm doing half an hour after I take the ibuprofen," I said.

And I would—I'd see how I felt. Not that feeling like crap would change my plans. But as Chrissy May handed me a water bottle and two Advil, I sure hoped that an hour from now I'd be feeling a whole lot better.

Chapter 2

SOMEHOW, I MANAGED TO KEEP working. A few minutes after I took the ibuprofen, Chrissy May helped me take off my boots—something I couldn't do one-handed. Then I headed to the back of the hall to deal with Rockefeller and Sons Catering. My entire body seemed to throb with pain. Chrissy May hovered near me. She found a can of Dr. Pepper, which I downed quickly, figuring it might help me stay me on my feet. I decided she was nothing short of an angel at that point.

When I reached the loading dock, a thirty-something man with a receding hairline and a scrawny build—and a ticked-off expression—waited for me. He glanced at my bare feet. I refused to let him cow me or make me feel less than a professional. This was my turf, not his.

"Mr. Rockefeller, I assume?" I said, holding out a hand in an attempt at civility.

He tilted his head and eyed my hand. "I've been waiting here for half an hour."

No way had I been sitting on the chair after my fall that long, but I wasn't about to quibble. I checked my clipboard as if confirming what I already knew, looking over the floor plan as well as the final list of vendors that Janette had e-mailed earlier that day. "I'm sorry, but you're not on the floor plan, and I have no record of your contract. I can't let you on the floor without confirmation of payment and approval from Janette."

"I paid like two weeks ago for a double-wide booth!"

Yeah right. All of the end caps were taken, and we had no other double-wide booths at this show. Janette had insisted on that, saying that double-wide booths along the length of the aisles looked amateurish.

I flipped the papers back down on the clipboard. "I'm sorry, but you'll have to leave and talk to Janette about your arrangements."

"I'm not leaving until—"

"I'll have security escort you if I have to, Mr. Rockefeller." I held up my cell phone to emphasize the threat. My head swam as his face reddened. He spun on his heel and took off.

I breathed a sigh of relief. We had pathetic security tonight. If this guy had been much taller or stronger, I might have worried about him trying to push his point.

After he stormed off—and I sent our one security guard to make sure the guy was really gone—I put Chuck and Janette on a conference call to finalize details on the midway setup and to warn her about Rockefeller. The big dock doors were still open, which made me shiver in the cool January air. We spoke for a good twenty minutes, and instead of the Advil and Dr. Pepper helping, the pain only increased to the point that by the end of the call, I was staring off into space, taking short breaths to cope as Chuck confirmed everything with Janette and I tried not to pass out.

By the time we hung up, the pain in my arm had increased until I could hardly breathe without flinching. Chrissy May had been right; I did need to get to a doctor right away. At this hour, that meant the emergency room—assuming I could drive myself there. I doubted any urgent care clinic was still open after ten.

Chuck sat at his stand and scanned the list of vendor supplies. "So what time do you want me to be here in the morning?"

As I opened my mouth to answer, my vision went black. My body collapsed. I was still conscious, or mostly so, but I couldn't see or hear anything, and I couldn't move. It was as if I'd become a rag doll. I became aware of someone holding me from behind; they must have caught me on the way to the floor. Whoever it was lowered me to the ground.

Slowly, I came to myself and opened my eyes, staring at the ceiling of the event hall and trying to breathe evenly as I again became aware of the pain shooting through my body from my arm. I shuddered, catching my breath, which made my arm move, sending out even more pain.

Whoever had caught me was gone; I lay on something hard and uncomfortable—not the floor. People bustled about me, and I was vaguely aware of a uniform or two, but everything looked blurry. I tried to focus my vision; everything seemed outlined in silver, like something out of a B science-fiction movie.

I blinked several times, but it didn't clear my vision. "What . . . what happened?" I managed. My throat felt so dry that speaking scratched it.

A male voice responded. "You passed out."

I'd figured that much out, but I couldn't vocalize more questions. I turned my head in the man's direction. He wore a dark jacket with an emblem that confused me for a second until I realized it was a medical shield. This guy was an EMT. Those were the uniforms I'd seen.

"What are you doing?" I rasped, then winced at the pain again. No more moving, I vowed.

"We're taking you to the hospital," he said as he secured straps around me.

A stretcher. That's what I was lying on.

I almost asked why he thought I needed to go to the hospital; my mind was so muddled that nothing made sense. "I was already there for my surgery." I made a weak move to get off the stretcher. "I have to stay here. The show starts . . ."

My voice trailed off when I realized no one was listening. The EMT had stood and was talking with a colleague and Chuck. I made out something he said about catching me as I fell. Maybe that was why I didn't break my nose or get a head injury on top of everything else.

I groaned; my voice sounded weak and disjointed, almost like an animal keening in my ears. *Oh, my arm.*

"When did you eat last?"

I hadn't noticed that the EMT had returned. He was crouched down, waiting for an answer.

"I don't know . . . a few hours, maybe?" I couldn't remember at all. Did the Dr. Pepper Chrissy May gave me count? Before that . . . I had no idea.

Great job keeping yourself from wearing out.

Ethan had warned me to take it really easy today—after he realized there was no way I'd stay home. "Get yourself a table by the loading dock and stay there," he'd said, almost begging. "Let people come to you with problems."

I'd sort of promised I would, but then people kept hitting me with issues and wanting me in different places, and I thought I could handle it. And maybe I could have if I hadn't worn three-inch boots. And if the carpet guy hadn't tripped me and sent me into an elbow dive onto the concrete. Chuck should fire the guy.

The stretcher lifted, and I was being carried out. "Please, I have to stay . . ." But I couldn't say it loud enough, and part of me felt glad that

I was horizontal and off my feet completely. Where were my boots? I hoped Chuck or Chrissy May—someone—had taken care of them. They were expensive.

"Is there anyone we can call? A family member?"

I sighed and closed my eyes. "My husband." I'd landed in the very situation I'd wanted to avoid. Ethan worked at Pacific Hospital of Long Beach—the closest hospital to the convention center. "Can you take me to another hospital? Like Norwalk? Or Providence Little Company in San Pedro?"

The male EMT exchanged looks with someone on the other end of the stretcher, a female EMT I hadn't noticed before.

The woman answered. "Is it an insurance concern? I'm pretty sure Pacific takes most major carriers."

Insurance wasn't a concern, and I knew Pacific would take good care of me. I shook my head, which was a big mistake. More pain. "It's . . . could we just go somewhere else? Please?"

They probably thought I was incoherent. The man spoke next but to his partner. "Ready, one, two, three, up." They raised the litter, making my stomach lurch and pain jolt through my arm. The collapsible wheels locked, and I was pushed down the ramp of the loading dock to the waiting ambulance.

Neither of the EMTs seemed to care about my concern. "Please?"

They spoke to each other in a few exchanges that I understood as my vitals, thanks to the fact that I'd lived with a doctor and medical terms for several years. As they loaded me into the ambulance, I started to panic, realizing I was, indeed, heading to a hospital. My mind tried to catalog everything I needed to remember. My purse was in my office. My phone was . . . I had no idea where. But I should call Ethan. If these guys insisted on Pacific, I'd want to warn him, and if I couldn't get to him beforehand, he still needed to find out.

Then again, showing up at Pacific could well be the easiest way to tell Ethan about the accident, like ripping off a bandage. Except that I always took bandages off as slowly as I could. I closed my eyes in an attempt to block out the interior of the ambulance and all the paraphernalia that, frankly, scared me.

The drive seemed to last forever, which gave me hope that they were going to one of the hospitals farther away. But when the ambulance stopped and the back doors opened, I saw not "Norwalk" or "Providence" written on the building but "Pacific Hospital of Long Beach."

My stomach twisted. I hated this hospital. This was where I'd had my fertility treatments and hysterectomy. All of my dreams had died under that roof. I could have been perfectly happy to never lay eyes on the place ever again. Just the sight of the building brought back a wave of emotion, the same one I'd felt when I'd curled up on my hospital bed, sobbing because my hopes of motherhood were gone, shattered forever. Ethan had sat by my side, holding my hand and stroking my hair, murmuring, "It's all right, babe. It's all right."

But nothing was all right, and we both knew it. Things would never be right again. I still felt only part female—I no longer had one of the distinctive body parts that identified me as a woman. I'd failed at the one thing I was supposed to be able to do—bear a child. Even if no one else knew my uterus was missing, I did, and I felt the loss like a hole in my belly.

The female EMT—whose name was Margo, I assumed, reading the embroidered lettering on her jacket—took off the blood-pressure cuff, folded it, and began tidying things up in preparation to leave.

I stared at the red emergency sign, knowing Ethan was somewhere beyond the doors. I needed to come clean with the EMTs before we got inside so they didn't inadvertently ask my husband to work on his own wife. But I couldn't work up the nerve.

Margo chattered on. "We'll get you right in. Assuming no one is ahead of you in triage, we should be able to get you right back into a bed. We can get all the paperwork filled out later. I didn't hear anything big happening on the police scanner, so I don't think we need to worry about a wait."

The stretcher jostled me as they brought me out of the ambulance. Confession time. I was annoyed at myself for not saying anything before, but I'd sort of hoped it would resolve by itself. "My husband's in the ER—Dr. Ethan Goldstein. Please . . . please tell him I'm okay."

Ethan had told me of some of his harrowing experiences from work, most of them happening during his first month here, which was years ago. He'd gradually stopped sharing the details of his shifts because I'd started getting nightmares, but he often railed about gangs, drugs, motorcycles, and people who didn't wear seat belts, so I could guess what kinds of emergencies he saw most often.

I tried to blink back tears, but they escaped my eyes anyway and trickled into my hairline. I sniffed.

"I'll tell him, sweetie," Margo promised, her voice softer than it had been. "Now, let's get you inside and fix you up."

Chapter 3

After a nurse named Tammy took my vitals, Dr. Lindsay, the other ER doctor on shift, came to check me out. I didn't tell him I was Dr. Goldstein's wife, just let him do his thing. I assumed he'd been told who I was.

He examined my arm—which had me nearly screaming in pain— then set it down gently and said, "Let's get that thing x-rayed." He picked up a clipboard and jotted down some notes—an order, I assumed.

The sight made me think back to the convention center. What had happened to *my* clipboard? Had Chuck called the manager at the center to get someone else to fill my shoes? Had he stuck around? And was the show ready to open in the morning?

When would I get released? I had to be there. I had an urge to just tell the doctor to give me a cast and shoot me up with some morphine or whatever they had and send me on my way. Seven o'clock in the morning would come awfully fast.

Dr. Lindsay's next question interrupted my thoughts. "On a scale of one to ten, ten being unbearable, how bad is your pain?" He said it so casually, without looking at me as he jotted notes on the page. He might as well have been ordering a side of fries. But as far as ER situations went, mine was pretty mundane. This was pretty much the fries of the ER.

When I didn't answer right away, he lifted his eyes to me, brows raised. "Your pain, one to ten?"

I grasped at what to say. It felt like a trick question. I wanted to ask him to define "unbearable." I *couldn't* bear the pain as it was. But was it a legitimate level ten, totally worse than any other pain could be? Probably not. Getting an arm cut off by a chain saw would be worse. What answer could I give so he'd order something to give me a little relief?

"An eight? Maybe nine?" I said with a tone that sounded how I felt—as if this was a test. Did I get the right answer?

He nodded and clicked the top of his pen. "I'll get these orders taken care of, and we'll get you fixed right up. I'll send someone to give you something for the pain too." He smiled what had to be his practiced bedside manner, and then he left, nearly bumping into another person in scrubs coming into the curtained-off area. "Oh, sorry, Goldstein," Dr. Lindsay said. My attention perked up, and my heart leapt to my throat as his voice went on. "I've got this one."

"I appreciate it," Ethan said. "Just thought I'd check on my wife."

Dr. Lindsay parted the curtain with one hand and looked back at me. "Your . . ." He glanced from me to Ethan. "She didn't mention that."

I waved awkwardly with my good arm. "Um, thanks for your help." And to Ethan, "Hi, honey."

Ethan stepped through the curtain, then tugged it shut before rounding the bed to sit on my right side.

"So I guess the EMT only told him to work on me, not who I am . . ." My voice trailed off.

Ethan looked ashen, his brow drawn low. I immediately felt guilty for not letting him know. I'd wanted to spare him the worry, but of course, he'd eventually find out. He held my good hand in both of his. "Hey, what happened?"

I tried to put on a happy face, even though Ethan could see right through it. He'd seen this same happy face for years, whenever a pregnancy test came back negative and almost constantly over the last week since my surgery. We'd been married too long for him to mistake it for actual happiness, but it was the best I could do. "Turns out your wife is the world's biggest klutz." I nodded toward my limp arm. For something so useless, it sure controlled my every thought and breath.

Ethan patted his cell phone hanging at his belt. "I just got off the phone with Callaway. He's on call tonight, and he'll be here soon to take my shift so I can be with you."

"What about Moore?" He was the attending physician over Ethan.

"He's fine with it. He may be a taskmaster, but even he draws the line when a spouse is hurt."

"But you don't—"

"Hey, *you* don't," Ethan interjected. "Enough of playing Wonder Woman. You wore yourself out today. You're *not* a klutz. Anyone would be tired and worn down after major surgery. I told you to stay home for the weekend."

The frustrated part of me wanted to bend to the part that wanted to curl into his arms and cry. I *did* want him by me tonight. But I also had a job to do so we could reclaim our lives. "I can't miss this show." I wanted to go on about how my surgery was weeks ago and how I was just *fine*, but we both knew better. If I'd been fine earlier today, I sure wasn't fine now.

He brushed aside a lock of my hair and gave me a kiss. His touch calmed me. "You need to rest. I'll be back in a few; I have to work until Callaway gets here."

I nodded and squeezed his hand as he stood. He left, drawing my privacy curtain closed. A few seconds later, I made out his voice talking in medical terms, and after that, a big ruckus burst through the door—some new emergency, no doubt. Ethan called out orders, and people scurried to comply. Whatever was wrong with that patient—or patients—was worse than my situation. I'd been knocked down the triage ladder and would likely have to wait awhile for my x-rays. I begged the universe for someone to come with a syringe of a painkiller while I waited.

I wouldn't call it a prayer; I hadn't said a real prayer in years.

My three years of intense appeals to heaven while trying to conceive didn't count because God hadn't answered those prayers, even though they'd been made from the deepest place in my heart. He and I were no longer on speaking terms. Even so, the pain in my arm was more than I could take, and I couldn't help but plead to whatever power did exist to send me a little relief while I waited.

Please. I can't handle it.

The fluorescent lights hurt my eyes. I covered my eyes with my right hand, my left arm still lying useless. I tried to breathe evenly and relax in a pathetic attempt to cope with the pain. My hand dimmed the glare of the lights, but their high-pitch whine now drove me crazy, like a mosquito buzzing near my ear that I couldn't swat. Tears stung the backs of my eyes, but I held them off. Ethan would be worried enough without my breaking down completely tonight.

My cell chimed with an incoming text. Apparently I hadn't left my phone somewhere back at the hall. I had yet to get out of my street clothes and into a hospital gown, so I reached into my slacks pocket and pulled out the phone. At this late hour, I couldn't imagine who was calling me besides Chuck or Janette or my boss, Alexander, an immigrant from Russia who charmed the women he worked around and flirted with them mercilessly, even though he was married to a bombshell who could have been a super model. Flirting was all about the business for him. If it increased the success of our events and the likelihood of scoring new events from show owners, so be it.

Cringing, I unlocked my phone, figuring the text was probably from Alexander. I didn't want to be told how much was riding on the wedding show. I knew.

I looked at the screen. Not from Alexander. It was from Ruby. I wished more than ever that I'd found a way to get to January's meeting, if only to get to know the other ladies better. They were different from me in a lot of ways—some older, some younger, everyone in a different life situation. Not a one Jewish like me. We had one Catholic, a Mormon, a Greek Orthodox, and the rest probably other variations of Christians. Yet being around them was refreshing. Well, except for the time someone asked Daisy if she was pregnant, and she flat-out denied it, as if a baby were some kind of disease.

True, she already had kids, and her youngest was almost out of high school, but I would have given a lot to be in her shoes. At the time, I'd wanted to tell her how lucky she was, to appreciate her body's ability to make a baby. At that point, I'd still been hoping that one day it would be me announcing a pregnancy. And there was Daisy, getting pregnant without even trying.

Another woman in the book club, Paige, looked like the classic frazzled housewife, except that she was recently divorced. She seemed sweet. She was younger than I was and already had two kids. I envied her motherhood but not her single status.

I eyed the privacy curtain in the direction I'd last heard Ethan's voice and wondered if something like divorce could ever happen to us. Our relationship had definitely changed over the course of the fertility treatments. I missed the carefree couple we used to be. We used to go on cruises or vacations all over the world just because we could. He used to say it was because we wouldn't be able to do those things after we had kids. My hand went to my belly. We'd never have kids now. We'd both turned so serious, and we weren't talking about our next trip. I wondered if we'd have another.

I shook myself out of thoughts of the mothers in book club and of my and Ethan's future and clicked Ruby's message open. Why was she sending me a text late at night?

Hoping you can make it to book club next week. We sure missed you at this month's meeting. Lots to catch you up on!

Maybe she was up with insomnia and didn't realize that normally, I'd be asleep at this hour. I hit reply, but my right thumb hovered over the keypad. What to say? I'd read the book for January—*Silas Marner*—and had loved it. That may have been because, when I read it, I was still hoping to have a child to treasure like Silas had. The truth was already hanging over me at that point though: months of bleeding had pointed to one thing, but I'd lived in denial, sure I could avoid surgery. You couldn't pay me enough to read *Silas Marner* again. Not now.

I also liked *Silas* better than the previous month's selection, *My Name Is Asher Lev*, which was distinctly Jewish. I hadn't darkened the door of a synagogue pretty much since my marriage. Reading that had just made me feel guilty. I hadn't been particularly excited about discussing an overtly Jewish book, even if it was Potok. Oh, I'd discussed it at the meeting anyway, adding my own perspective as a Jew, and thought it went over well. But on every page, I'd heard my mother's voice whispering about what I should be doing, how I didn't always keep the Sabbath—a prospect almost impossible for me when shows were virtually always Fridays and Saturdays—was I still kosher, where were her grandkids?

Ethan and I hadn't told anyone about the fertility treatments, especially Mom. I didn't want to get her hopes up. I couldn't make myself tell her about them now, but she'd probably need to know that grandchildren would never come through her only daughter—that we'd given it our best shot but had failed.

Answer Ruby, I commanded myself. I was almost done reading *The Help*, the book for February's meeting. I could go. I didn't have a show to coordinate that weekend. And yet, could I get myself to go back? At December's meeting, several of the others seemed to be close friends already; the book club had started a couple of months before I'd joined, so I'd missed out on a lot. I worried that going back would be awkward. I finally found some words to reply to Ruby with.

I've been under the weather, I typed back, code for "recovering from surgery." *We'll see how I'm feeling next week!* Code for "I have no intention of going, but I won't be mean by saying that."

I was about to click send when Ethan returned. "Who are you texting?"

"Ruby." When the name didn't register, I added, "The lady who started the book club I joined awhile back?"

"Oh, right," he said, coming in and turning the phone in my hand so he could read the interaction. I fully expected him to applaud my decision not to go. I needed to rest, right? He'd be on my case even more now about how I needed to let my arm heal.

Instead, he said, "You should go."

I pulled the phone back, trying to send the message, but he resisted and tugged the phone away. I protested. "What about my needing to rest?"

"You also need to have fun and relax in other ways than lying around. When was the last time you hung out with friends?"

We both knew I *didn't* hang out with friends. How could I when everyone else had their free nights on the weekends, right when I was my busiest? Besides, they were all parents or were expecting babies, and finding babysitters apparently wasn't always easy.

That was an excuse, and I knew it as well as Ethan did. I also knew exactly when my last nonwork outing was—December, for book club.

Why hadn't I done anything fun since then? *Things were busy with Chanukah and Christmas and New Year's . . .*

Except that we didn't visit family for Chanukah or even do much beyond getting a menorah out of storage for decoration. And true, Ethan and I didn't celebrate Christmas in the traditional sense, but we still attended Christmas work parties, exchanged gifts with some extended family—Ethan's sister who married into a Christian family—and the like. But I hadn't done a lot of festive celebrating of late. My hesitation only made his point.

Ethan took a step back and started clicking away on the keyboard.

"Hey," I said. "Give that back."

He waved me off with one hand and grinned as he typed with the other for a few seconds, then tapped one final time with a flourish. "There. Sent!" He tucked the phone into the pocket at the back of his scrubs pants. "You're going."

I was about to protest when someone else in scrubs pulled the curtain open and stepped in—a twenty-something guy with Ryan Seacrest hair. "I hear we need to x-ray your arm and give you something for the pain."

"Elbow, but yeah," I said, trying not to get too eager about the painkiller part.

He handed me a small paper cup with a pill in it and a plastic cup of water. I glanced at Ethan. "Not a shot?"

He shrugged. "Don't look at me. I didn't place the order. But that looks like Percocet. My guess is that you'll be flying pretty high in about twenty minutes."

I hoped he was right—not so much about flying high but about the medication working, and soon. I quickly popped the white tablet into my mouth, then downed it with the water. As I handed the pill and water cup back to the nurse, I eyed the clock so I could start the twenty-minute countdown.

The nurse threw the garbage away and asked, "Do you need a wheelchair?"

"No, I can walk." *I think.*

Ethan supported me with a hand around my waist. Immediately, a lightheaded feeling washed over me, so I grabbed Ethan's arm. He steadied me, and I breathed evenly until I could keep going. Why had I freaked out so much about coming to Pacific, about wanting to hide this from Ethan?

Because I'm proud and too independent.

As we followed the nurse down a hallway, I remembered how I'd felt seeing the hospital sign when the ambulance doors had opened. I hadn't dreaded Pacific because of Ethan. I'd dreaded it solely because of the bad things that had happened to me here. Because my dreams had come crashing down around me like shattered glass.

No more bad things. I can't handle anything else.

By the time the x-ray results were back, the Percocet had kicked in, and I was loopy and giggly. Ethan had to repeat what Dr. Lindsay had told him: that the x-rays didn't show a clear break, although my elbow "acted" broken, whatever that meant. Ethan hadn't been able to see a break either, but he wasn't happy with the x-rays.

Ethan leaned over and brushed my hair back. "in his shoes, I'd have ordered a new set. Something is wrong in there," he said, pointing at my elbow.

In the end, I was discharged with a sling, a bottle of painkillers, and the quasi-comforting words, "You probably sprained your elbow or pulled some ligaments."

Or had he said tendons? As we drove home, I tried to remember but couldn't, but then, my mind was too fuzzy to remember the difference between a ligament and a tendon right then anyway. Later, I could ask Ethan what Dr. Lindsay had said.

And as he drove, the brain fog from the painkiller hung around me, but the pain was nearly gone. It still seeped through the medication a bit, and I instinctively cradled my bad arm as I closed my eyes, trying to relax, trying to let myself sink into the fuzzy, warm oblivion of the medication.

But every few minutes, thoughts of the wedding show crept into my mind. The show would fall apart without me there. How many more hours until the doors opened? No way would I be able to get there at seven o'clock for final preparations; that was only five hours away.

I groaned. Ethan reached over and stroked my thigh in an effort to comfort me. He probably thought I was groaning from physical pain.

Let him think that. I didn't want to talk about how the next few hours could ruin my career.

Chapter 4

SEVERAL DAYS AFTER MY FALL, I was still miserable—I was on heavy painkillers around the clock, and my elbow was swelling and getting worse, not better. The next book club meeting was around the corner, and I debated staying home because I was such a wreck.

Even though I'd attended book club only twice, I decided to go, mostly because of Ethan's goading but also because he'd sent Ruby that text as if it had been from me, promising that I'd show. At least I was able to spend those two days finishing the book instead of working the wedding show. Finding the silver lining of the whole situation wasn't working out so well, but I was sure trying.

The book kept me from thinking about how the show was surely tanking, how Tony, a junior event coordinator, had taken over my show and run with it—or sunk it. How vendors were mad about all kinds of things and blaming me for it. I avoided my phone because too many angry e-mails and texts made the physical pain harder to bear when there was not a thing I could do to fix the problems at the convention center.

The latest word was that Rockefeller and Sons planned to sue the convention center over breach of contract. Tony sent me a few texts assuring me it was nothing to worry about, that the caterer didn't have a leg to stand on with his claims that he'd supposedly lost thousands of dollars in business by being denied entrance to the show in spite of supposedly signing a contract. The tricky part was that Rockefeller had a signed contract as "proof," but the question was whether he'd downloaded it from the wedding show's site and forged Janette's signature in place of mine or whether it was a legitimate contract.

I also avoided my phone because the ladies from book club would periodically text or e-mail, and while I appreciated their efforts, which were almost certainly a result of Ruby's intervention, they sort of made me feel like a charity case. Even so, I opted to go to the next meeting, which was exactly a week after my accident. I figured that even if Ruby had prodded them into contacting me, they probably wouldn't have done so if they didn't care at least a little, right?

On the night of book club, Ethan drove me to Ruby's house—with my arm and my meds, I was in no condition to be behind a wheel. Without reading to distract me, I found myself checking my phone constantly for updates. Today was the last day of the show. It would close during book club, and the final verdict on things like ticket sales and vendor success would start trickling in over the next few days. I had worried, not entirely without cause, that any positives from the show would be attributed to Tony's efforts, even though I'd been working with it since they'd first contacted me for an estimate ten months ago. Without a doubt, any negatives would be attributed to me. I knew that both would happen as well as I knew that in a few hours, my pain meds would wear off and I'd be miserable again. I knew because *I'd* gotten a promotion two years ago after swooping in to rescue a show that another coordinator, Ryan, had dropped the ball on. I'd gotten credit for all the good things, and he'd been fired for all the bad. The tables had turned in an awful way.

Nearly halfway to Ruby's, I was within an inch of telling Ethan to take the next freeway exit and turn the car around. I wanted to crawl into my bed and stay there until the pain—physical, emotional, all of it—went away. The pain from my arm. From my hysterectomy. From the constant ache of wanting to hold a baby; my arms sometimes actually hurt from the yearning. From the worry over my job.

All of it. But I didn't say anything to Ethan and instead let the car take me to Ruby's house. Lying around wouldn't distract me from any of the pain, but it *would* remind me all too much that I was alone.

Come tomorrow, I'd need to find another book or something else to keep me occupied until I could return to work, where I was rarely alone. Between shows, I typically made countless phone calls, attended meetings, conducted hall tours with prospective show owners, attended other conventions in the area, billed clients, and so much more. As soon as I got back to work, I wouldn't have time to think about the pain. Being alone felt dangerous right now; it left me too close to depression and morbid thoughts about how my life and future were over. My identity as a future mother was gone.

I hoped book club would keep my mind off my loneliness and my pain, at least for a couple of hours.

I sighed, then took stock of our surroundings, realizing we were almost there. "Take the next exit," I told Ethan, then guided him the rest of the way.

As he pulled into Ruby's neighborhood, he nodded toward my sling and then looked at my face—and likely the pain etched there; I needed another dose of Vicodin, or I wouldn't last through the meeting. Good thing I had the bottle in my purse. I was getting pretty good at opening the childproof top with a bum hand.

"I'm more and more sure that the x-rays missed a break—a big one," Ethan said.

My brow furrowed. "How could an x-ray possibly miss a big break?" Isn't that what x-rays did—found broken bones? I could see how the wrong angle might miss a hairline fracture but not anything significant. But I wasn't the doctor.

"The x-ray images are like a slice of your arm," he said, moving his hand in a horizontal line to demonstrate. "If the direction and depth are wrong, entire breaks can be missed. I've seen it before. Not often, but sometimes." He shook his head. "I'm getting you back in for a CT scan with the best orthopedist at Pacific first thing tomorrow. If it's broken, we need to get it taken care of properly."

Somewhere in my pain-induced haze, it occurred to me that tomorrow was Sunday—surely not a typical workday for a specialist—but Ethan probably had enough strings to pull that he could get me in anyway.

With the pain ratcheting upward, I dug through my purse for my water bottle and prescription. I found the pills, but then I glanced at Ethan and decided to wait on taking another dose, opting to just take a sip from my water bottle. Ethan might give me a funny look if I took another pill so soon; it had been only two and a half hours since my last dose, which was why he was driving me in the first place. But the pain just wouldn't quit, and the nurses had told me to keep on top of it, to not wait to take more until it was too late to knock it out. Finding a balance between the advice of the nurse at the hospital and the concern in my husband's eyes was proving trickier than I'd expected. I'd take a pill at Ruby's. For now, I sipped from my water bottle and settled my purse on my lap as Ethan pulled into the driveway.

"So how do they set a broken elbow?" Just the thought of it was painful enough.

Ethan glanced askance my way, then shifted the car into park. "Depends. You'd probably be put out when they set it, so don't worry about that. But if the break is bad . . ." His voice trailed off.

When he didn't continue, I wouldn't let it go. "If it's bad . . . what?" Having a doctor for a husband had serious perks. Yet knowing worst-case scenarios could be a serious con.

"If it's bad, you'll need surgery." He looked my way again. "Ready?"

He glanced at the distinctive brick and decorative wreath, a different one from the Christmas wreath Ruby had had on her door the last time I'd been here. This one was just as elaborate and just as Ruby—big, with plastic light-up hearts that pulsed like a heartbeat, for Valentine's Day, I assumed.

Ethan snorted. "That thing looks like it belongs in a Tim Burton movie."

I stifled a giggle and tried to get back to the more important topic. "What'll they do in surgery? You know, if it's a bad break?" I had an uneasy feeling about my elbow. I'd end up in surgery; I just knew it. The hearts on the wreath kept pulsing. I couldn't take my eyes off them.

Ethan deliberately put the car into reverse, as a hint for me to get out, surely. "Then . . . they'll set the break with pins."

I swallowed, feeling sick at the prospect. Ruby's door opened, and she came out, looking at me expectantly. No more putting this off. *And once I'm inside, I can take another pill.* I reached for my purse and my copy of *The Help*. As I opened the car door, I mentally grasped at the only straw left me. "Is a CT scan as painful as the x-rays were?" I swear, after that tech got done with me, my arm could have qualified for Cirque de Soleil.

Ethan leaned forward and kissed me briefly. "No worries. CTs are painless, I promise. The worst part is getting the contrast injected. Some people think it feels like they're wetting themselves."

I rolled my eyes. "Sounds delightful." I adjusted my sling for the hundredth time that day—the thing pulled on my neck constantly, making the muscles ache—and I took a deep breath and got out of the car. "Wish me luck."

"Knock 'em dead," he said.

Chapter 5

RUBY CONTINUED TO WAIT FOR me at the door as I walked up her landscaped footpath. She wore a peach top with silver accents that somehow totally fit her but would look ghastly on almost anyone else. She gave me a crushing hug, during which I turned to the side to avoid my bad arm being touched. I caught Ethan's wave out of the corner of my eye and smiled back weakly. He looked like he was laughing as he backed out of the driveway.

"My goodness, what ever happened?" Ruby said when she saw me.

I shrugged. "I broke my elbow at work," I said. It was the most likely scenario, even though my own doctor hadn't come up with that theory yet. "I might be facing surgery. They won't know until the swelling goes down."

Ruby tilted her head with concern. "I'm so glad you could make it."

I could tell she meant the words, and for some reason, they touched me. "Me too," I said. Coming tonight was a big deal, but I was already glad I'd made the effort.

As we headed inside, Ruby said, "How awful that you have to wait. Has the pain been terrible?"

It had been awful, but I didn't want to talk about it. I managed a small smile. "Nothing that a few pills can't manage," I said.

Ruby rattled off the names of the women who'd already arrived—Olivia, Tori, and Athena—as I followed her inside.

Somehow, I couldn't help but think that if I had to injure myself, it should have left me with a better story to tell. Like how I'd broken my arm while skydiving. Or by pushing a small child out of the path of a speeding semi. Something far more interesting than being knocked over by a stupid roll of carpet.

As we headed inside, Ruby's warmth relaxed me, and suddenly, I was glad to be here. The house alone was friendly and familiar, exuding a cheer I needed, and Ruby's crushing hug had made me feel appreciated. I found myself excited to see the other ladies inside.

After Ruby closed the door behind me, and after she'd turned her back to lead the way to the family room, I quickly dug in my purse for the orange-brown prescription bottle and slipped out a Vicodin. I popped it into my mouth and quietly washed it down. No need to draw attention to my medication.

I reached the family room behind Ruby and sighed, grateful that in another twenty-five minutes or so, I'd feel better. I was so glad I had medication to make a night like this possible without my sitting there trying not to burst into tears.

The family room had a couch, a love seat, and a few chairs for more seating during the meeting. I recognized Livvy and Athena right away from a past meeting, although they both looked better than I remembered. Livvy seemed more polished and put together, and she had a new haircut—or maybe a color. Athena wore a rose-colored top—a soft touch for someone who used to exude professionalism. A gorgeous black woman sat beside Athena on the couch. I thought I recognized her, but I was pretty sure she'd attended only the last time I'd come, and I didn't remember her name.

I sat on the left side of the love seat, next to Livvy, where others would be less likely to bump my bad arm. With a smile, I addressed the woman whose name I didn't remember. "I know we've met before, but what was your name again? I'm Ilana."

She nodded. "I'm Victoria, but people usually call me Tori."

"Nice to see you again, Tori." I looked to the others. "Livvy and Athena, right?"

"Right," they said in unison.

Livvy asked about my arm, and I promised to tell the story when everyone was here. I didn't want to recite it over and over, but I did tell her it happened at work.

"Remind me what you do again?" Livvy asked.

"I'm an event manager at a convention center," I said, avoiding naming specific events or even which convention center I worked for. Tony had taken over the wedding show, but it hadn't gone well. I almost certainly wouldn't be getting the promotion, and I could well lose my job. Simply put, I didn't want to talk about what I did for a living. I'd rather talk about the plate of treats on the coffee table—something I guessed

Ruby hadn't made because the plate still had plastic wrap over the top. Yet Ruby's house was filled with delicious smells of something still baking.

Fortunately, Livvy started chitchatting about a recent cruise her family had gone on, changing the subject altogether. The doorbell rang, and Ruby bustled off to answer it. I heard two voices in addition to Ruby's and wondered which book-club members would be arriving together. Ruby appeared a moment later with Shannon, whom I'd also met in December. She was the pharmacist and Ruby's niece. The only reason I remembered her profession was the fact that she wore her scrubs. The girl with her looked young—late teens or early twenties. She wore thick eyeliner, almost like she was trying to be sure people would notice her eyes. I couldn't help but think she'd be prettier with less makeup.

They came in without introduction, although I was quite sure, thanks to Ruby's group e-mails, that no one new had joined the group, so I had no idea who the new young woman was. Livvy and I stopped our small talk to say hello as Shannon and the girl sat across from us. They said nothing beyond basic greetings, so I wondered if Shannon had forgotten some of our names too.

Livvy must have noticed, and in her typical kind way, she broke the ice. "I'm Livvy, and this is Ilana," she said to Shannon's guest.

"I'm Keisha, Shannon's stepdaughter," the girl said with a nod toward Shannon. They looked comfortable and happy, more like mother and daughter than step. Keisha looked around the room. "I love your flowers," she said, running a hand through her long hair.

Ruby settled on a chair. "Oh, you all know Shannon's my niece, right? So that makes me Keisha's great-step-aunt. I think." She chuckled to herself.

After that, I could feel others eying my sling, and it was obvious that no one wanted to ask about it outright, but Keisha must not have felt the same reservation, because she bluntly asked, "What happened to your arm?"

I looked at the sling, shook my head, and looked back at Keisha and Shannon. "Stupid accident at work," I said. "My elbow's broken."

At least, Ethan still thought it was broken, not sprained, which was why we were going back in for the CT scan.

"Ow," Keisha said, wrinkling her nose. "Does it hurt bad?"

Horribly, especially at night. But I wasn't going to say that. "Not so long as I keep on top of the pain with medication," I said. "They're talking about surgery, possibly, so I go in again this week to get it checked out."

Which was a half-truth, as "they're talking" meant my doctor husband and his hunch.

"That totally sucks," Keisha said.

I laughed at that; she took the words right out of my mouth. Livvy smiled too, and the mood in the room relaxed; Keisha looked comfortable and at home. I felt more comfortable too, whether because the Vicodin was kicking in or because I was happy to be here, I wasn't sure—and didn't really care. I was just glad I'd come. And we hadn't even started talking about the book yet.

Livvy turned to Keisha. "So," she said, leaning forward. "Where do you work? What are your plans now that you're living in the Golden State?"

Keisha crossed her legs and leaned back with a relaxed foot bob. "I'm looking for a job right now, but I'm going to enroll in cosmetology school. I think I'd really like that."

As she went on, I looked around the room and tried to place who was missing. The young mom—Paige. I sort of hoped she wouldn't show up; every time she mentioned her two young sons, my heart felt like a dagger had been shoved into it. And that was back when I'd still had hope of conceiving.

The doorbell rang again, and a moment later, Ruby returned with the person I'd just been thinking of—Paige, who was likely a couple of years my junior, divorced, and a devoted mother. Her boys were her world—the very world I wanted but could never have.

Please don't talk about your darling little boys tonight.

My arm throbbed. Apparently the Vicodin *hadn't* kicked in. I reached over and rubbed my bicep and shoulder for relief, not that it helped much. I certainly couldn't rub my elbow.

"Um, Ilana?" Paige said with a wave when she saw me. She pointed at my arm as she found a chair. "You okay?"

"I will be," I said, forcing a smile.

Ruby clapped her hands together, making her jewelry jingle, and said, "I guess we're all here."

Athena looked around as if we were missing someone. "Is Daisy still on bed rest?"

Oh, yes. Daisy. The one who got pregnant by accident. Someone else I was relieved not to face tonight. Not now, so soon after my hysterectomy. I could handle her *or* Paige but not both, and if I had to pick one, I'd take Paige. I understood her. Daisy hadn't wanted her baby, but I'd give a limb to have one. I wasn't sure I could be entirely civil if Daisy walked into the room right now.

Ruby nodded at Athena's comment and frowned. "I offered to have us go to her place like we did last month, but she said she'd moved and her new place was too small." She turned to look at Paige as if confiding in her. "I didn't want to pry by asking too many questions."

Paige spoke up, apparently more up to date on Daisy's situation. "She got her own place a couple of weeks ago, close to where her first ex-husband and daughter live. She's still on partial bed rest, but the baby's doing well. She's able to work from home half-time now."

"Did her life turn a 180 or what?" Tori said. Everyone's heads bobbed in agreement. "But she's okay?"

"Yeah," Paige said with a smile and a nod. "I think she's doing really well. She said to thank everyone for the phone calls and prayers. She says she's felt every one."

What would that feel like—to believe that prayer worked, that God existed? To *feel* others praying for you?

I had a hard time believing Daisy really *felt* individual prayers. She probably just felt better at the knowledge that people were praying for her.

I hadn't done much praying since I was a girl when I went to temple with my parents. Years ago, my father wore his prayer shawl and said morning prayers with his *tefillin*, but over the last few years, my parents had grown a bit less orthodox in their worship, which was fine by me; the more relaxed they got about our religion, the less they freaked out over me eating a cheeseburger or dating a Christian.

They were still pleased when I decided to marry a Jew, though Ethan was about as devout as I was. At times I wondered if my parents would have preferred a wedding without the canopy—even a mixed-religion marriage—if it meant I personally still lived my faith.

I didn't see the point of following all the rules when I didn't believe there was a God in the first place. Religion was a bunch of pretty bedtime stories, nothing more.

"I'm glad to hear Daisy's doing okay," I said and surprised myself when I realized I meant it. Even if Daisy was unfairly fertile, she hadn't been dealt an easy hand. In the last few months, her picture-perfect life had gone down the drain.

"Well," Ruby said. "Daisy chose the book, but since she isn't here, I guess I'll lead the discussion. What did everyone think?"

As the others discussed the book, I mostly listened. I tuned out when they talked about the scene with the miscarriage—I'd had several, and it wasn't something I wanted to think about.

Then Ruby turned straight to Tori, which made me cringe. Sure, I thought, look to the black woman for opinions on a book about the repression of black women. Maybe she wouldn't mind, sort of how I didn't mind discussing *My Name Is Asher Lev* in December, even though I could tell some of the others had worried I might be offended.

Ruby rested her chin on her hand and asked Tori, "Have you ever felt persecuted?"

Here it comes.

Tori crossed her legs. "For me personally, I haven't experienced racial prejudice in the US," she said. "Maybe because I'm in the entertainment industry, it just hasn't been an issue for me. I find it much harder to be a woman than to be black."

Ruby tried again. "You've experienced prejudice for being a woman?"

I was tempted to ask Ruby if she had any plans to let the discussion take a natural course around the room. I loved the book and had plenty I wanted to discuss—now that we were done with the miscarriage scene— like how fast the nation had changed. It boggled my mind that the Mississippi of *The Help* was the same one in which a poor black girl grew up to become Oprah, one of the most powerful women in the world. The history gave me hope that people—from individual attitudes to cultures and yes, even to the world—could change. Really change.

I didn't quite believe that such dramatic change was possible in the Mideast between Jews—my people—and Arabs. That area of the world had been fighting for centuries, if not for millennia. But the book gave me a glimmer of hope. Regardless of my spirituality or lack thereof, Jews were still my people. I wanted peace and happiness and safety in Israel as well as in the Arab countries, where so much turmoil had churned for so long.

"Oh, yes," Tori said, raising her eyebrows.

I had to rewind the conversation I'd vaguely heard to figure out what she was replying to. Then it came back: about being discriminated against as a woman. Tori went on, and I tried to focus on something besides the pain throbbing throughout the left side of my body. Tori's smooth, coffee-colored skin worked.

"But most of the top spots are filled with men, and most of the decisions on who *fills* the open positions are *made* by men. And a lot of women fall victim to unprofessional ways of furthering their careers, if you know what I mean."

I shuddered at that—a small movement that sent a jolt of pain through my body. I grimaced and hoped no one noticed.

Athena spoke up next. "It wasn't until junior high that I really understood what racism meant," she said. "There was a group of kids in my school who decided to make me their target."

She went on about being bullied as a teen because she wasn't American apple-pie white, but Greek. I couldn't help but nod. The taunts, the name-calling, it all felt familiar—even though, looking at Athena now, I could scarcely believe *she* had ever been an awkward teen. She could have been a runway model. Sure, I was relatively thin, but I was also only five foot five, with unruly, curly dark hair. Hardly model material.

When she ended her story, I added my own. "I had similar experiences." I pointed to my nose, which, while not large, was classically Jewish. "I suppose if I'd grown up in New York or something, it would have been different, but I grew up here in California, in an area with very few Jews."

Several memories assaulted my mind, particularly the time in ninth grade when my best friend's mother realized I wasn't Christian and forbade her daughter from speaking to me ever again. I told them about the experience, eyes tearing up. I shrugged with my good shoulder. "We went from having regular sleepovers to never making eye contact. She even took different hallways at school so she wouldn't run into me." I tapped my copy of the book. "Prejudice against black people has come a long way since the sixties. And in a lot of ways, prejudice against Jews is much better than it was during World War II—but there's a long way to go in both areas."

I stopped there before letting my emotions get the better of me, which tended to happen easily of late. The constant physical pain kept my emotions hovering barely under the surface. I almost went on about how I'd planned to be the perfect Jewish mother, to make my own daughter proud of her heritage, to give her tools to combat the prejudice, but the words caught in my throat. Of course I wouldn't be doing any of that. So I stopped and cleared my throat, then sat back, signalling that I was done talking.

Paige added some insight about religious persecution, relating some harrowing stories from Mormon history. I hadn't known it had gotten so bad for Mormons. No wonder they left the borders of what was the US at the time and settled in what became Utah.

Ruby interrupted my thoughts by turning to her niece. "Shannon, what did you think?"

Shannon sat up straighter, as if the question had startled her. If memory served, she'd never read any of the book-club titles, and she'd started coming solely for her aunt's sake. "Uh, I liked it." Shannon cleared her throat and straightened her scrubs pants. "It's been a really long time since I've read a novel; I don't like much fiction." She bit her lip and flushed a bit as if she'd just confessed something embarrassing.

If she didn't like reading—didn't like novels—why did she join the book club, even to be nice to her aunt?

"I really liked this one though."

I hoped so. She clutched the book in her lap as if it were a life preserver.

"Great to hear," Ruby said, leaning over to pat Shannon's knee as if she were eight years old.

I hoped Shannon would eventually feel more at ease at book club. Even though this was only my third time attending, I already felt at home. A silence descended over the room, and I debated whether to jump in and start a new discussion, but Paige spoke up.

"Even today, people have really screwy prejudices."

"Even with Mormonism?" I asked.

"Especially with Mormonism," Paige said with an emphatic nod. "A few years ago, my in-laws had their home vandalized with death threats in spray paint. It was scary." She tilted her head and added, "When you think about it, everyone in the world wants to be accepted and loved. I think if more people could look at others who seem different or strange—really look at them—they'd realize we're all more alike than we are different. A mother in Afghanistan loves her children just as much as I love mine."

Her words warmed me—except the mother part; that part made me ache. But her point was sound; just about all prejudice could be attributed to misunderstanding or fear of the unknown or different. I hadn't thought of it that way before.

As talk of prejudice wound down, Ruby asked about favorite characters and plot points, and that's when Keisha added her two cents. "I thought it was totally sweet that Johnny still loved his wife, even though she couldn't have kids."

Shannon beamed, clearly happy with Keisha's contribution. Yet I sat there, frozen. Did Ethan still love me as much as he had when we both thought I could bear children?

Livvy agreed about Celia and talked about how she could relate to her desire to be the perfect housekeeper. "It's something I've been working on lately," she said. "I can't be perfect, and all I can do is my best, right?" Her copy of the book had a ton of little colored flags sticking out of the side, marking significant passages. She flipped to one of her favorites—one of the last pages, a scene I'd read with tears in my eyes.

The conversation gradually wrapped up, for which I was grateful. I knew I'd end up crying if it went on much longer—someone else was bound to mention motherhood again. Ruby excused herself to get the dessert. Paige and Livvy started to stand to help, but Ruby shooed them away and told them to stay put, saying it would only take a second.

Shannon ignored her aunt and followed her into the kitchen, almost as if escaping the room. The others chatted while I leaned against the loves eat, enjoying the feel of the painkiller finally kicking in and washing over my body like a warm wave. The slightly fuzzy feeling made me sigh with relief.

A few minutes later, Ruby returned, revealing a chocolate pie in her hands. *She didn't!* We all laughed at the reference to the big prank in the book.

"The chocolate pie was the best part!" Keisha said.

"Speaking of chocolate pie," Ruby said, "would anyone like a slice?"

I wanted chocolate pie—but somehow, thinking about what it meant in the book made me wary, even though I knew Ruby would have made a delicious—really chocolate—pie.

Shannon came in a second later carrying a tray with several dessert plates holding what turned out to be red velvet bread pudding and ice cream. I could feel my waist expanding just looking at it.

"So that's the amazing thing we've been smelling," I said, taking a plate. I inhaled. Bliss.

Shannon delivered cups of chilled water to everyone, then disappeared into the kitchen again. The dessert was as delicious as it smelled, and I was ready to ask for seconds until I realized Shannon hadn't returned.

Paige opened a pocket calendar and asked, "Will our next meeting be March 5?"

"Yes," Ruby said. "Does that still work for most of us?"

We confirmed the date as Shannon entered the room and then sat by Keisha, no dessert plate in hand. Ruby tried to catch her eye, but Shannon seemed to be avoiding her. I hoped she'd come back next month and give us another chance to be her friend.

Someone asked what book we'd be reading, and that's when Ruby's eyes lit up. "Why don't you choose one, Shannon?"

"Oh, that's okay," Shannon said with a polite smile. "I'm not nearly as well-read as you guys are."

"Oh, baloney," Ruby said with a wave of her hand, complete with a fresh manicure.

Note to self: get a fill on your nails.

"You have a PhD. Surely you're as well read as anyone here. Just choose a book for us to read, something you'd like to share with us."

"Really?" Shannon said, looking around the group as if begging for rescue. "I don't know. I don't read much fiction."

Athena shrugged and asked if Shannon read any nonfiction.

"Mostly only for work." Shannon seemed to think. "Well, there is one that might be interesting."

Ruby smiled and asked about it. Shannon hesitantly went on, keeping her gaze down. "Well, *The Help* kind of reminded me of it since it also involves a black woman in the 1950s. It's called *The Immortal Life of Henrietta Lacks.*"

It didn't sound remotely familiar. By the looks of everyone else in the room, no one else had heard of it either, except for Paige, who smiled. "I read a review about it," she said, nodding. "I tried to check it out at the library once, but it had a few holds on it—that was almost a year ago though. I heard it was really well done."

Shannon smiled back, looking a bit more confident. "It *was* really well done." She went on with more energy in her voice. "It's about a woman who had cervical cancer. The doctors biopsied the tumor and discovered that her cells reproduced continually, which opened the floodgates of medical research."

She was more relaxed than I'd ever seen her, explaining how this woman's cells had changed the face of medical research from the polio vaccine to cancer. They'd even been in space. Shannon took a breath as if the speech had used all her energy.

Wow. Shannon had said more in the last sixty seconds than I'd heard her say in all the hours of book club she'd attended before—combined.

"You're such a nerd, Shannon," Keisha said with a laugh.

Tori laughed too. "We love nerds," she said, smiling widely.

"I think it sounds great," Athena said.

Shannon was studying a spot on her pants, seemingly to avoid our eyes. Athena asked for the title again, and when Shannon repeated it, I wrote it down as well, asking how to spell the woman's name in the title so I could download it right away.

Shannon looked preoccupied, as if her mind was suddenly elsewhere—maybe at work. Ethan often drifted off like that after a tough day in the ER. Paige stepped in and gave us the title. "The author had a weird name though. I can't remember what it was."

"Skloot," Shannon said automatically. "Rebecca Skloot."

As she spelled it, I typed it into my iPhone notes, my thumb shaking a bit from the pills and my eyes the tiniest bit blurry. I had to blink to clear my vision, then correct the spelling several times. With next month's title picked out, everyone chatted about other things. I found myself enjoying the moment, even if my mind was a bit loopy. At least I wasn't in pain.

I texted Ethan to tell him he could come get me now, then pulled out my Kindle to see if I could find the book and start reading it already. Somehow, I couldn't wait for next month.

Ruby walked Shannon and Keisha to the door, and when she returned, she began clearing dishes from the coffee table. "Ilana," she said in a syrupy voice. "Do you need help with anything this week? With your arm, I'm sure regular chores are almost impossible."

I tried to picture Ruby puttering around our small apartment, chattering on while I tried to rest. She meant well, and she was a sweetheart, but for the time being, I wanted privacy more than anything.

"I think I'll manage. My husband is pretty much spoiling me." Even as I said it, I winced inside, remembering how she'd invited me to lunch. I'd never gotten back to her about that, and now I was turning down another show of friendship. She had to think I didn't like her or something. I'd have to find a way to fix that.

Fortunately, she gave no hint of being upset. Instead, she chuckled. "If anything comes up, will you let me know?" She paused in her plate stacking and looked right at me. "Day or night."

I swallowed, wishing I had the guts to say yes. I really could use help. I couldn't do dishes. I had a hard time brushing my hair and even getting dressed. Putting on a bra by myself was a total joke. I couldn't keep the place clean. But my pride and desire for keeping things to myself got in the way.

"Thanks for the offer, Ruby," I said instead. "But I think it's covered."

As I fumbled to slip the Kindle back into my purse, the others offered to help too, making me dig my heels in further. I would not be a charity case. I smiled tightly and said thanks but no. I glanced at my watch. When would Ethan get here? Five minutes ago, I was having fun. The whole tone had shifted, and I didn't like the spotlight on me.

Chapter 6

FANTASTIC. THE MENTAL SARCASM WASN'T enough, but Dr. Root's office wasn't the place to start swearing.

Ethan held my hand, but I felt numb, and Dr. Root refused to make sense in my head. Some of it I'd expected, based on Ethan's predictions of what the CT scan would reveal: *Fractures. Major surgery. Screws. Pins.* But the last part sent my mind spinning.

"If you're faithful with your physical therapy, you can expect up to an 80-percent return in your range of motion and strength in your left arm." His cheery tone seemed to indicate that he was giving me *good* news. "Good thing you're right-handed, huh?" Dr. Root chuckled, maybe trying to lighten things up. It didn't work.

My arm would *maybe* return to 80 percent of what it used to be? That wasn't funny. This was my life we were talking about. He smiled expectantly, but I couldn't return it. Granted, I wasn't a baseball star who needed to be able to pitch, but I still needed my arm, and more than 80 percent of it.

As Ethan and Dr. Root kept talking, I sat in the exam room chair, my mind looping around the facts about my stupid body and how it didn't work.

Then again, why do I need a fully functional arm? It wasn't like I'd need it to hold a baby. One strong arm was enough for the boring things my life was relegated to now. With 80 percent, I could do laundry carrying the basket on one hip. I could easily load the dishwasher. Cooking would be relatively simple. Scrubbing a toilet. Answering the phone.

I could still do my job well enough, provided I didn't fall on any more concrete floors. No more high-heeled boots for me. No more walking backward during setup either. An 80 percent arm could carry a clipboard. As long as the labor union guys did all the lifting and hauling and I did the general directing, things should be fine.

So why did I feel like a black hole was swallowing me?

Ethan and Dr. Root consulted a calendar on the computer and scheduled my surgery for the following morning. I was aware enough to realize that Ethan really did have to have crazy good contacts for me to get in so fast.

Throughout the appointment, Ethan wrote notes about all the things I needed to know, as if he could tell I couldn't focus enough to remember any of it. I glanced over and read items like not eating after ten o'clock tonight and what to expect post-op and from physical therapy. I looked away, not wanting to read the rest right now. I trusted that Ethan would remember it all; I could always read the list myself after the surgery.

Eighty percent.

My phone beeped with an incoming text. I already held it in my hand, with the calendar page up, but as Ethan and the doctor were doing all the talking and had the calendar and dates already figured out, I closed that app and checked the text.

It was from Alexander.

25% of vendors returned dissatisfied reports. 3 were "treated rudely" at setup & show. Rockefeller refuses to back down from suit.

Why was he sending me this? I was already getting the angry e-mails. Didn't he know that no show went without a hitch? No matter how much anyone did before, during, and after, someone would find a way to be dissatisfied and take things personally. Sure, the feedback this time sounded worse than usual, and that wasn't fun. But that brought me back to wondering why Alexander was telling *me* this information in the first place.

I hadn't been there during the show. Vendor complaints about attendance numbers would be more Janette's fault for not getting the word out. None of that would have been under my control even if I'd been at the show every minute.

The doctor and Ethan were still talking, now using medical terms with too many syllables and Latin roots. I clutched my phone, mentally going through other possible causes for vendor complaints, things I'd taken the hit for in the past but had avoided of late because I'd learned how to coach show owners beforehand on how to make their event a success. Sometimes I coached individual vendors during shows about how to improve their profits.

Like never hiring teens to man a booth, as they were typically unassertive, so they didn't approach attendees and were more likely to mess around on their cell phones the whole time. Or how clear signage, with pricing and products—and a show special—could increase or even double potential sales. And other stuff, all things that seemed obvious to people who spent their lives at trade shows but that new vendors didn't know.

So sure, if they'd made any of those mistakes, they'd be disappointed, but they had only themselves to blame—or Janette. It had been *her* show. I was just the coordinator for the convention center.

Except, how had Tony handled the show? It didn't sound like he'd worked with the vendors' concerns. Had he been on the floor most of the time, or at least available by radio or cell phone? Had he helped attendees find what they were looking for? Had he cleaned up any random messes that cropped up? Those were things a coordinator did. Things I viewed as simply my job but things Alexander used to say set me apart and closer to a raise.

Now I stared at his text. It sure looked like he blamed me for a bad show. He couldn't think Rockefeller would push through with suing the center. The guy was all hot air and empty threats. Right? Alexander had to remember how I'd worked hard on a lot of hugely successful shows in the past. I was the senior coordinator, while Tony was new, with only four months under his belt. If things fell apart, it was because Tony didn't have a clue what his job was.

Instead of replying to Alexander, I typed out a text to Tony to ask about the show—especially to confirm Alexander's stats and find out what the atmosphere at the convention center had been since the wedding show ended. For days, I'd tried calling and texting both Alexander and Tony to get updates, including on the last day of the show and the day after, but both men had continually dodged me. I could conjure a dozen innocent reasons for why they wouldn't reply; tradeshows kept you busy. But I couldn't help but always come back to the most negative possibilities.

If Alexander was flipping out, the threat of a lawsuit from Rockefeller must have sent him into panic mode. My boss never did manage panic well; he tended to spout off in Russian, speaking so fast that at times he didn't stop for a break, except to gasp for air, then spitting as he let the air out with his next words. Watching him talk like that took all my effort not to laugh—which would have nearly been grounds for dismissal.

My thumb hesitated over the little keyboard as I thought, *My raise had better not go elsewhere. Like to Tony.*

I kept my text to Tony short and professional. *Give me a report on the show—all stats.*

As soon as it sent, another text arrived from Alexander. I cringed, bracing myself as I opened it. The text was long.

I understand you will be out of the office for some time. You have 4 days of sick leave & 2 emergency days left for the year.

I stopped reading right there, furious. I knew I had at least five sick days. Was he seriously counting the night I was rushed to the hospital as a sick day? He'd deducted the show days from the total for the year—and it was only February. I'd already taken off time for my hysterectomy. I was burning through my time off. I returned to the text, and my brow furrowed.

Rockefeller will withdraw the suit if we comply w/ his demand to release the employee who wronged his company.

That meant me.

And a final sentence: *Please call ASAP to discuss your future.*

I stared at the message, which was so long it took up several colorful speech bubbles on my phone. He couldn't mean what he was saying. We'd had people threaten to sue before, but no one ever went through with it. Taking someone to court cost a lot of money. The convention center could fight a suit, but would they bother doing so if the cheaper and easier option was to fire me?

If they do, I could sue for wrongful termination. As if I had the money, energy, or time to pursue litigation.

Shock and a wave of fuzziness washed over me as Ethan and the doctor chatted. I was distantly aware that they were talking about their personal lives, like golf handicaps and the car Dr. Root hoped to buy soon.

I looked back at Alexander's text. We were to "discuss my future." What did that mean? Was I getting fired or not? A sinking feeling in my stomach told me I wouldn't be going back to work. I gripped the arm of the chair, worry and hurt squeezing my chest, and I was suddenly grateful for having a refill on the pain meds Dr. Carter had prescribed after my hysterectomy. I'd already run out of the prescription from the ER visit. The meds from my surgery kept me sane.

After I had my surgery tomorrow, Dr. Root would give me a new prescription. I hoped I'd heal quickly and be back to my normal self, with no more fuzzy brain on meds.

Dr. Root and Ethan turned their conversation to something about a convention they'd both attended awhile back. I typed out a rapid-fire reply to Alexander.

Am I fired? As soon as I hit send and watched the progress bar, I wanted to take the message back. Maybe Alexander was just venting. He'd said we needed to "discuss" my future. Maybe that meant I still had a future with the center.

Not a minute later, my phone vibrated, and I looked down at the reply from Alexander.

We have no choice. Sorry.

Awfully short for an Alexander text. I clicked the button on my phone to turn off the screen, my stomach churning with a painful combination of emotions. A moment later, another text came through. Against my better judgment, I swiped the screen and read it.

You need to come in to fill out paperwork and remove your personal effects.

My heart sank to somewhere in my shoes, and I slipped my phone into my purse, unwilling to hear from either Tony or Alexander anymore today. I had no job. The convention center had no use for me, even though I could probably sue them. I could probably sue Chuck's company too for negligence, as well as for pain and suffering because it was his carpet guy's fault that I was in this position to begin with. But I wasn't that kind of person. I couldn't do to Chuck what Rockefeller and the center were doing to me.

What did any of this mean for my future career? The tradeshow business was small enough that this could get me blackballed. Word would spread that I'd been fired to save the company from getting sued, that I'd dropped the ball, and that my last show had bombed. No way would I be able to get a similar job anywhere in the area. No one would want to hire me after this. Even if they didn't believe the inevitable rumors that would circulate and paint me in a bad light, the facts themselves didn't look great.

Ethan and I couldn't move either, pretending for a second I wanted to find a similar job elsewhere. He was four months from finishing his residency.

"Ilana. Ilana, you okay?" Ethan's voice pierced the protective mental bubble around me. He felt far away as I looked over.

Dr. Root gestured toward the examination table. "You look a bit faint. How about you lie down for a bit before you leave? Get the blood back into your head."

"No, no, I'm fine." I shook my head, even though my words were a total lie. I refused to crawl onto his table; if I got up there, I'd cry.

No, I'd stand up and walk out. If I passed out on the way to the car, Ethan would catch me. He'd take me home—away from here. I needed to burrow under my covers and cry there.

Ethan said our good-byes to the doctor, and in a few minutes, I some-how found myself successfully seated on the passenger side of our Taurus without having passed out. During the drive, little made it through the fog of my mind, except the fact that I was fired. I had no job. The world had crumbled all around me. I had no job. No womb. No arm.

I wanted to scream at the heavens, but obviously, no one up there paid attention to what was happening with me. That, or they enjoyed cosmic jokes at my expense.

It wasn't that I worried about how we'd live. Ethan's salary was enough to keep us in our apartment and fed, and he'd make much more when he finished his residency—a bright spot at the end of a long tunnel. We'd done the math long ago and knew I could stay home with children when he was a full-fledged surgeon making real money.

But now there wouldn't be any children. My eyes burned anew; I closed them tight and turned my face away from Ethan so he wouldn't see any tears trickling down my cheeks. For possibly the thousandth time, I tried to grasp that there would be no staying home to care for babies. I wouldn't feed them, bathe them, wouldn't watch them learn to walk. I wouldn't wait to hug any children when they first came home from school.

I rubbed my forehead with my good hand. I'd have to find another job to pay off my medical bills—and stay sane. But for the foreseeable future, I had nothing to do but sit around, waiting for surgery, and then after that, I'd sit around some more, waiting for my elbow and all the soft tissue in my arm to get better. I had weeks—months? years?—of physical therapy to look forward to.

I'd have to find another industry to work in, because my dream of staying home and caring for a family was shot now. I'd have to settle with wearing smoking-hot boots to a new job instead of rocking my baby to sleep while I wore sweats.

Now what? Turn into June Cleaver for Ethan? No. He wouldn't want that any more than I would; he cooked at least half of the meals we ate together, but he wasn't home for most dinners anyway, thanks to his hours. He cleaned the apartment as much as I did. He liked his clothes folded and hung a certain way, so he did his own laundry—at least, when he wasn't pulling back-to-back shifts and coming home so bleary-eyed that all he could do was pass out for a day.

My future lay before me like a gray carpet rolled out, stretching into the horizon, the same bland emptiness forever.

At our building, Ethan helped me up to our apartment. I tossed my purse onto the nightstand when we got into our room, then crawled into bed, where I leaned back on the pillows Ethan had piled up for me. He kissed my forehead and tucked me in as if I were a little girl.

He left for a minute then returned and held up a can of my favorite Progresso soup. "Interested?"

"Yes, please," I said weakly.

He gave me a thumbs-up and walked out. When he returned a few minutes later with a warm bowl of soup on a tray, he carefully set it on my lap, but his face was a mask of worry.

"What's wrong?" I asked.

"I was just paged. Multicar accident, and they need me at the hospital . . ." The concern in his eyes warmed me; he didn't want to leave, but we both knew he had to.

"I'll be fine," I told him. "Come home when you can. You'll be with me all day tomorrow, right?"

"Right." He'd taken the next day off; he wasn't even on call. But to get that time off, he needed to be on call tonight. Having him with me for the surgery was worth having him gone for part of my evening. He leaned down and kissed me. "Thanks, babe. I'll call when I can." He left the room, closing the door behind him with a soft click. I let out a deep sigh, staring at the ceiling. I was glad to be home and grateful for how tenderly Ethan had cared for me. And how he hadn't pushed me to talk about the surgery. He knew me well enough to let me think through things first.

I wanted to roll onto my side and curl into a ball, but that wouldn't work with my arm. For now, I had to rest at an angle; lying flat on my back hurt too much. Ethan had placed other pillows beside me to support my arm, which was currently out of its sling, thank heavens. For the time being, the sling wouldn't pull on my neck and back muscles.

It was only a few minutes later that my cell phone rang. *Shoot.* I'd forgotten to silence it, and I couldn't call out for Ethan to come answer it for me. I grunted and sat up to see who was calling, fully ready to ignore the call if it wasn't someone I really wanted to talk to. I pulled my phone out of my purse on the nightstand and checked the caller ID. The name threw me. Was it really Ruby Crenshaw?

I answered it. "Hello?" Why was she calling? Book group wasn't for weeks yet.

"It's Ruby. How are you, dear?"

Time to play act. "Just fine, considering I go into surgery tomorrow." I half giggled, a sound Ethan would have recognized as a nervous way to hide my real feelings—and perhaps to keep myself from crying.

"Oh, wow. It's that serious?"

"It's a rather minor surgery but necessary." I hoped that was right; Ethan had acted like it wasn't a difficult or unusual surgery. "I probably won't even have to stay overnight." All kinds of serious procedures were outpatient nowadays though. I really needed to read over Ethan's notes to know what was going on. Where did he leave them?

"That doesn't sound too invasive," Ruby said.

Except that it's invading my entire life. But that's not what Ruby meant, and she didn't know about my other surgery. If I could keep that a secret from the book club forever, I would. I didn't want or need their pity.

"Yeah, all those robotic machines make everything so easy now," I said.

Easy? My mind raged at the word. Nothing about my life was easy right now.

"Can I drive you to the hospital?" Ruby asked.

Sweet thought, but that wasn't necessary. "My husband will be taking me and staying the whole time." I almost added, *Hey, there's a plus to not having kids. If we were parents, Ethan would have to split his time and find a babysitter.*

But why was Ruby offering in the first place? I hardly knew her. Being newly widowed must have sent her nurturing instincts into overdrive. Maybe she needed to find someone else to take care of now that her ailing husband wasn't around.

She said it was wonderful that my husband could be there for me, which made me regret my words—that wasn't the most thoughtful thing to say to a new widow. She paused for a second, as if thinking, then said, "What if I bring the both of you dinner tonight so you can just relax and not worry about anything?"

Her persistence was commendable. "All right," I said. "That will be fine."

"Do either of you have any allergies?"

"Nope. No allergies," I said.

"Do you eat only kosher?" she asked.

"As far as my mother is concerned, I do," I said and found myself holding back a laugh—a real one. That felt good. I felt a twinge of guilt admitting that I wasn't kosher, so I glanced at the ceiling and glared as if God could see.

Not that you care what I put in my mouth if you don't even answer prayers.

Aloud, I assured Ruby. "You don't need to worry about cooking kosher for us. Ethan and I will eat anything you bring."

"Super," she said. "I'll be there around six."

After she hung up, I wondered whether I should call her back to say that it might be only me eating tonight and to not bring too much food. But Ethan would be hungry when he got home, and if my suspicions were correct, he'd appreciate one of Ruby's home-cooked meals as much as I would, even reheated.

I replaced the phone in my purse, then paused when I noticed the bottle of painkillers inside. I glanced at the nightstand clock, trying to remember when I'd taken my last dose. I needed to sleep, and if I couldn't eat or drink tonight before surgery, this could be my last chance for relief all night. Even if another dose would be a little early, I reasoned, I'd still be staying within the recommended daily total, and I wanted to take the pills before eating Ruby's dinner to be sure they got into my system quicker.

I grabbed the pill bottle, chugged down a pill with my water bottle, then leaned back and found myself drifting off to sleep, remembering vaguely that Ruby would be showing up soon and hoping I'd be awake enough to answer the door.

Chapter 7

RUBY'S LASAGNA WAS THE BEST I'd ever had, but it was her snickerdoodles that I kept going back to; I had to put them in a cupboard to stop eating them in order to fast for my surgery. I went to bed feeling relatively good; the pain wasn't completely unbearable, and I'd had the best meal at home in some time.

But two hours later, I lay awake, staring at the bedroom ceiling in the dark because the pain had woken me up. I had to focus to keep my body from trembling enough that it would wake up Ethan, who'd been home from the hospital for only an hour or so. By the light of a streetlamp outside, I could barely make out the shape of the light fixture and ceiling fan above us. Tears made tracks down the sides of my face and dripped into my ears. Ethan had done so much to help me over the last few days, and he was exhausted—as he always was anyway, working so hard at the hospital. We had a big day ahead of us tomorrow with my surgery; I wanted to give him as much rest as I could.

And yet.

I closed my eyes, hard, sending more tears down the tracks. I gingerly turned my head to see the clock on my nightstand, to find out how many more hours I'd have to suffer like this. I couldn't take any more pain meds; I couldn't so much as have a sip of water until after the operation. If I could have been beamed over to the hospital, to the anesthesiologist, and put under right then, I would have been.

Every movement, even breathing, hurt, with the possible exception of blinking. The slight shift to look at the clock jolted the rest of my body like a domino effect, inevitably shooting a red-hot poker of pain from my elbow to the rest of my body. I closed my eyes and waited for the shock of it to fade a bit. I felt ready to throw up, but even if I could go to the bathroom, I had nothing inside my stomach to come up except acid. It burned in my throat, but I swallowed it down and tried to breathe smoothly.

Again, I tried to see the clock, finally managing to get my head tilted to the right angle. 4:58. Finally. I'd spent so much of the night in pain, wanting to avoid the slow movement of the clock, but I couldn't help but check it regularly anyway as it had ticked slowly—excruciatingly slowly. But the long night was almost over; the alarm would go off in two minutes. When I'd gone to bed, I'd actually thought I'd have a hard time getting up at five, which I'd need to do to get to the hospital in time for my check-in.

I leaned back against my pillows again, waiting for the alarm and for Ethan to turn it off himself. I could have sworn I waited fifteen minutes for those two to pass. *Soon*, I told myself, *the alarm will wake Ethan, and he won't know I've been up most of the night. During surgery, I'll be unconscious and unable to feel the pain. And when I wake up, they'll give me something strong—maybe a morphine pump?* It was worth dreaming about. All I wanted was an escape. From all of it.

My right hand came down to cover my face as the muscles contracted in pain, both physical and emotional. I forced myself to breathe evenly and get a grip. To stop crying so Ethan wouldn't know I'd been falling apart as he slept.

When the alarm went off, I pretended to wake up as Ethan jumped out of bed, instantly alert. I had a suspicion that was a skill residents developed when they worked long hours, catching minutes of sleep in the staff beds at the hospital while knowing they could be needed at any moment. I'd seen him jump awake like that enough times that it shouldn't have been odd, but it still startled me. One second he was snoring every few breaths, deep asleep, and the next, he was vertical, clapping his hands together, eyes wide open, and saying, "It's time! Let's get rolling!"

He scurried to my side of the bed, and only then did I realize he'd slept in a pair of scrubs. I had a vague memory of the shower running last night as I fell asleep. Typical Ethan—planning ahead so he could jump out of bed and be ready for me. He probably wouldn't shave either, which was fine by me. I liked his stubble. He used to wear a goatee when we were first dating, and I always wished he'd grow it back.

He turned on the lamp on my side of the bed, then leaned down to give me a kiss. When he drew back, he studied me and furrowed his brow. "Oh, hon. You're not doing too good, are you?"

I shook my head—and instantly regretted it. The wince must have been obvious because he simply said, "Stay right there. I'll bring you anything you need so that when it's time to go, you'll only have to get up and move around once." He knelt by the bed and rummaged about for something.

"Twice," I managed, my voice cracking.

Ethan's head popped up. "What? Why?"

"I have to pee." At that, I managed a pained smile. It was funny. At least, I thought so.

"We'll make that part of the one trip if we can," he assured me. "No making you hurt more than absolutely necessary. I wish we had a wheelchair." He reached forward and cupped my cheek in his hand. "I'll make sure they get you comfortable, okay?"

I leaned into his hand and closed my eyes, feeling a hair of relief for the first time in hours. "Thanks."

* * *

The next couple of hours dragged by. All I wanted was relief, and instead, I got hours of waiting, unable to take so much as a sip of water. I hung on to Ethan's left hand as he filled out paperwork on a clipboard with his right. A nurse put on my identification bracelet and wheeled me to a room to change in. The basic check-in procedures so far today were all the same as when I'd arrived for my hysterectomy. Oh, how I hated this building. I felt weak, and I could tell I was pale, partly from not eating or drinking anything, but mostly from the pain. If I didn't get relief soon, I'd crumble into tiny pieces, shattering like a china dinner plate.

Ethan helped me get undressed and into the robe left at the foot of the bed for me. He folded my clothes and put them in a bag he'd brought along for that purpose, then helped me get onto the hospital bed to get settled. We waited there some more, Ethan clicking through channels on the TV mounted high up. He stopped periodically, waiting for me to tell him whether I wanted to watch the show. Nothing caught my attention, so I just shrugged each time. Finally, a nurse came to bring me back. Because Ethan worked at the hospital and was well respected, he was allowed to come back with me to a second room, where the anesthesiologist prepped me—something I was intensely grateful for. No way could I have handled it if an orderly had put me on a bed and wheeled me *away* from my husband through the metal double doors like had happened with my hysterectomy.

That day, when I was wheeled away from Ethan, the moment he was out of my view, a piece of my heart wilted—the piece that belonged to the parents we were supposed to become. Waking up from that surgery had been ugly.

This time, I couldn't think clearly; the physical pain muddled everything almost as much as the Vicodin did. For a brief moment, as we waited in the prep room, Ethan holding my good hand, I was almost glad that the physical pain this time was so overwhelming; I couldn't devote much time or energy to thoughts of my last surgery, not when I was consumed with coping moment by moment.

The anesthesiologist finally arrived and greeted us. He managed to distract me by asking lots of questions as he put in my IV. I glanced across the room to a bed with a girl who looked to be in junior high and wondered what surgery she was going in for.

The world slowly faded away.

When it gradually came back into focus, I lay in a different room. I blinked slowly, my eyelids feeling heavy. My whole body felt heavy.

Ethan appeared in my view and brushed some hair from my face. I closed my eyes and let his touch soak in.

"Ilana? Are you awake?" He smiled down at me as I opened my eyes again. "It's all over. You did great."

I weakly raised my right hand with a thumbs-up and found myself smiling at the oddity of how people always said the patient did great, when they were unconscious and couldn't *do* anything. The thumbs-up was all I could manage. My eyes were so heavy that they closed again. So tired.

Ethan kissed my temple. "Rest as long as you need to. I've got the doctor's instructions for when you're home. I already got your prescriptions. Whenever you're ready, we can get you home. But take your time. We can stay as long as you need to."

"Thanks," I murmured this time and slowly succumbed to the fog again.

A noise pierced the fuzz in my head, but I couldn't place it. Not until Ethan held up my phone so I could see the text that had just arrived.

"Remind me who Ruby is," Ethan said with a confused smile.

I had to let his words sink in before I understood them, and then I needed another moment to form the words to explain—slowly. "The book-club lady," was all that came out. What drugs was I on? My voice sounded far away, and my tongue felt thick, hard to move.

"Oh, that's right," Ethan said. He looked at the text again, then turned the phone screen so I could see it. "She's asking if we need dinner again. I'm tempted to say yes just to get another gourmet meal."

I laughed, or tried to. At least I wasn't in pain, so I was quite happy to be tired and out of it.

"Mind if I answer her?" Ethan asked. "I'll be honest. We don't need dinner, but thanks."

"Go ahead," I croaked. No way could I compose a coherent text, let alone navigate a touch keyboard.

Ethan typed away, chuckling to himself a couple of times as he stopped to read the screen. Ruby must have texted him back. If I'd had the mental and physical energy, I would have snatched the phone to see the conversation. Maybe he was asking her for more lasagna after all.

He sent another text, clicked the screen off, and pocketed my phone. "There," he said. "I flattered her as a cook but assured her we're doing fine."

I smiled and sighed. "Love you, babe."

Chapter 8

FOUR DAYS POST-SURGERY, I WAS supposed to be able to take care of myself, or so Dr. Root had said, but I wasn't there yet, not even almost. Yet Ethan couldn't take more time off work. Plus, he had a lot of shifts to make up—such was the life of a resident. Even though I was still utterly miserable, I put on a strong front and insisted he go to the hospital, that I'd be fine.

Truth was, the pain was still so bad that I found myself watching the clock. The second I hit the four-hour mark, I took another painkiller. If I waited too long between doses, the pain intensified. I now knew exactly what Angie, my nurse at the hospital, had meant by keeping on top of the pain.

The one real downside to the medicine was that I was starting to get headaches between pills. Ethan had warned me about those. He had called them rebound headaches.

He didn't report to work until afternoon, but before leaving, he made sure I had a light lunch—toast with raspberry jam and peach yogurt. Then he collected a bunch of items he thought I might want or need, to the point that our bed and my nightstand were cluttered with books, chargers, my iPad, my phone, and three remote controls, along with several snacks and my water bottle.

He stood back and surveyed his work, clearly not wanting to leave me.

"I'll be fine," I said, forcing a smile onto my face. I didn't feel fine, but he needed to go, and I didn't want him to worry. I gestured toward the mess on the bed. "You've got me covered."

He nodded slowly, eyes narrowed as if trying to figure out what he'd forgotten to bring besides the kitchen sink. "You sure? Anything else you can think of? I know—floss. Those raspberry seeds in the jam always get stuck between your teeth." And off he ran to the bathroom, returning a moment later with a container of floss.

I decided to throw him a bone—besides, it was nearly time for my next dose anyway.

"Could you hand me my pill bottle?" I could reach it myself, but it was something he could do for me.

He opened his mouth but then paused as if unsure what to say.

"What?" I asked.

"It's just that if you aren't really careful, you could train your body to depend on pain meds."

Sure, I thought. As if I *wanted* to live in a constant blur. "Says the ER doctor frequently faced with addicts faking injuries to get pills."

He smiled. "Point taken."

"Even so," I added. "I'll be careful. Promise."

"I know you will."

"In fact, I'll hang on a bit before I take my next dose. The pain isn't too bad yet."

"See? That's what I'm talking about," Ethan said. "I don't know why I thought of it; you've only been on it a few days."

Well, four since my elbow surgery, but I'd been taking them for a full month since the hysterectomy. But he probably didn't realize that, and I wasn't about to bring it up and worry him over nothing.

He leaned down and gave me a kiss. "Have a great day, beautiful."

"You too, Dr. Goldstein," I said and winked.

Not three minutes after the apartment door closed, I reached for my Vicodin bottle. "Stay on top of the pain," I whispered, quoting Angie.

My head pounded too. Had I taken her advice too much to heart? I shook the prescription bottle and peered at the bottom. Only four pills left. Four. Maybe I had overdone Angie's advice.

Fine, I'd totally overdone it. More often than not, I'd waited only three hours instead of the recommended four to six. And once or twice, I'd taken one and a half pills at once, hoping to increase the effect, because as long as I stayed in a slightly hazy world, I didn't feel my arm pain or the muscle aches radiating from it, and my mind didn't wander to my lost job or my lost chances of bearing a baby. The pills made everything a bit easier to bear.

I figured that once my body healed from all of my medical drama, I'd be strong enough emotionally to handle the rest. I just couldn't bear it all at the same time.

But now I stared at the bottle, stunned that I had only four of the oblong tablets left.

Those won't last me long. Nights are worst, and I'll have most of the night alone. No, no, no.

I gently sat up and reached across the nightstand for my purse, which I set on my lap. After that movement, I had to breathe Lamaze-style while waiting for the sharp pain to ease a bit. My arm still didn't appreciate any sudden movement. Or any not-slow movement. If I was being completely frank, it hated *any* movement.

When the worst of the ache ebbed, I fished inside my purse, one-handed, for the pain meds left over from the hysterectomy. Victorious, I pulled out the bottle, but even before I could check how full it was, I knew. No sound of tablets tumbling against the plastic wall meant the bottle was empty. I shook it as if I didn't believe my eyes or as if I could shake a pill into existence.

I tried not to curse, but one word came out anyway. How could I have used every pill from my original prescription from Dr. Carter, *plus* the refill, and all but four tablets from Dr. Root's prescription?

The idea of going through the night without a way to find relief sounded like my personal version of a horror movie. Dr. Root wouldn't be seeing me until my one-week post-op visit—three more days. I bit my lip, thinking. Maybe he'd give me a refill early if I asked for one. I had just undergone pretty big surgery, and I'd been misdiagnosed early on, which meant more swelling and damage before the operation.

Shoving my purse to the side with my foot, I grabbed my phone and dialed his office. After two rings, an answering machine clicked on saying that any messages received after 2:00 p.m. would be answered the next business day. I hung up, hands trembling—I couldn't wait a full business day. I needed to find a way to get through this night without my husband or any medication stronger than ibuprofen. I'd have preferred both, but as that wasn't an option, I *needed* more medication.

After a moment of indecision, I made a new plan and dialed Dr. Carter's office. Maybe my OB/GYN's office would answer. The receptionist picked up—one bit of success—and I tried to sound polite and friendly.

"Hi. This is Ilana Goldstein. I underwent surgery with Dr. Carter not too long ago."

"Of course. What can I do for you, Ilana?"

I doubted the woman remembered me, but I went along with it. "Could I speak with a nurse, please?" The nurses' station was where patients made prescription requests. I closed my eyes and mouthed, "Please, oh, please, oh, please."

"Actually, Dr. Carter's right here," the woman on the other end said. "He's between patients. Would you like to speak with him directly?"

"Um, sure." I hoped my voice didn't sound *too* eager. I didn't know any doctor who took patient calls like this, but maybe I was an exception because he'd operated on me.

"Hello?" Dr. Carter said.

"Hi, Dr. Carter. It's Ilana Goldstein." My fingers gripped the phone like it was a life preserver.

"Oh, hi, Ilana. How are you feeling?"

"Not so good, actually," I admitted. "I'm still in a lot of pain. I had a fall the other day at work, which made everything worse. I think I tore some stitches inside or something. I was wondering if you could call in another prescription refill for me. To the same Walgreens."

Shoot. Shouldn't have mentioned the pharmacy until after he said yes.

"Hmm." Why did Dr. Carter sound so uncertain? I just wanted a few pills, and I really was in a lot of pain. It wasn't like I was some druggie. My heart thudded as I waited for his reply. "Let me look at the calendar here. Your surgery was what, about three weeks ago?"

"Right," I said. Close enough. We were coming on a full month since the surgery, but one week wasn't that big of a difference. I didn't dare mention that I'd had longer to recover than he thought; that could give him reason to say no.

"Most women feel quite a bit better by this point. You'll still have some soreness for two or three weeks before you're fully recovered, but you should be over the worst by now. Over-the-counter meds should be able to handle whatever's left."

"I know, but I overdid it afterward," I admitted. "You and Ethan warned me to take it easy, but I stupidly went back to work way before I should have—I was on my feet a lot, wearing really high heels, working late hours . . ." I let my voice trail off, hoping he'd hear my pain.

"Hmm," he said again, but this time I grew a little hopeful. I could tell he was listening—feeling sympathy?

"Anyway, I tripped and fell, and I think I tore something." That was the truth, as far as it went, although the pain in my lower abdomen, which

I truthfully had felt a *lot* of, wasn't the reason I needed a refill. For all I knew, that pain was still around, just overshadowed by my arm.

"I'd prefer to have you come back in before I do that," he said. "There may be something more going on. We'll do an ultrasound to see what's happening in there. Are you free tomorrow?"

That was a generous offer; usually he was booked out at least a week. I hedged. Even if I had pulled something inside, it had probably healed by now. An ultrasound wouldn't show anything. But if I showed up with a sling, he'd know I had another reason for pain. The visit very well might *not* end with a prescription. "I don't know," I said. My shaky fingers combed through my hair. "I mean, I guess I can come in. I don't think it's anything serious though. But could you call something in to get me through the night?" I needed relief, and I couldn't reach Dr. Root. This was my Hail Mary pass.

After a pause, when Dr. Carter didn't answer, I said, "Just a few? To get me through the night until I can see you in the morning, of course."

"I suppose I could do that," he said. "But I want to see you first thing in the morning. I have some rounds to do at the hospital, but I should be in the office at nine thirty. Can you be here then? I'll delay my other appointments to get you in."

"Um, yeah. Sure," I said, although I dreaded going. "Walgreens, then?" I repeated.

"Walgreens. The one on file?"

"Yep," I said.

"I'll call in six tablets," he said. "That should more than get you through the night."

Six. But I knew it wasn't just to get me through the night; it was to get me through the next three days. Unless somehow he did find a reason to give me a refill in the morning.

Not wanting to risk that, I tried another tack. "Could you call in something else too—just in case it's not enough tonight? The pain is always so much worse then, and Ethan's gone at work. Even something as mild as, say, some Tylenol 3?"

I could hope the codeine in Tylenol 3 would be strong enough. In truth, I was tempted to ask for Percocet; I'd heard it was stronger than Vicodin, but if he didn't feel good about giving me more than six tablets of that, what were the chances he'd give me something stronger when I was supposed to be improving?

Dr. Carter's pause on the other end elongated. He finally said, "Let's talk about that tomorrow."

"Okay." Message received; he wouldn't be helping my pain any further. I hung up and swore. I wouldn't bother telling Ethan about the appointment. I wouldn't be going, and I didn't think Dr. Carter would have the nerve to charge me for a missed appointment when it was made on his suggestion and well after the twenty-four-hour cancellation window. In the morning, I'd call his office and plead illness—justifiably—when I couldn't go.

I threw the phone across the room, muttering about doctors and their stupid policies. If I changed my mind, Ethan could take me to Dr. Carter's in the morning. But that would mean preventing him from going to sleep after a difficult night shift. He needed his sleep.

But I did too.

In the meantime, I decided to call the pharmacy so they could let me know when the six pathetic pills came in, and then I'd go get them— driving extra carefully in case my last dose hadn't worn off and my reflexes weren't as fast as normal. This was going to be a long night.

But to make the call, I first had to get out of bed—oh, so slowly— and hobble across the room to retrieve my phone. I chastised myself as I stumbled through the pain. No more throwing it even if I was ticked off.

An eternal hour after I left a message with the pharmacy, they called back. I'd been holding off on taking more pills, trying to make them last. The result was that by the time the phone rang, my whole body shook with pain. I answered right before it went to voice mail.

"We have your prescription ready, Mrs. Goldstein," the tech said.

"Thank you so much," I said cheerfully. In spite of the agonizing pain, I did feel cheerful; relief was in sight, even if I was talking through gritted teeth. "I'll be right there."

I hung up and tried to decide whether to attempt changing into something nicer than the sweats I wore but quickly discarded the idea. I was post-surgery and in a freakish amount of pain. Who cared if I looked miserable? I *was* miserable. No makeup, hair flat and greasy. I'd dare someone to care because I sure didn't. Besides, getting a shirt on or off was a production that, at this point, required Ethan's help.

I slipped on some flats, grabbed my purse and keys, and shuffled toward the apartment door. I cursed at the place as I walked out, wishing yet again that we lived in the *house* we'd always dreamed of, the one in the suburbs with a yard where our children could run and play. Instead, we'd settled on this little apartment in an attempt to save money for fertility treatments, with every plan to buy a house when, not if, we had children—and *children*, plural. More than one. Not zero.

I walked out and pulled the apartment door shut, hard, and walked to the elevator. After punching the down button, I impatiently fingered my keys. Another door opened down the hall, making me turn my back toward it. I didn't care too much if strangers at the pharmacy saw me, but neighbors who knew me were something else. I hoped the person wasn't a friend.

"Hey, Ilana! How are you? I haven't seen you in forever!"

Diane. Probably the best friend I'd made in the building—if you could call anyone in the building my friend. I hadn't reached out to anyone here because I'd assumed our stay in this apartment building would be relatively brief.

Of my neighbors, Diane was the person I'd been most *friendly* with. She seemed nice, and she'd helped me out more than once, like last summer when my car had needed a jump. I'd helped her a few times too, like signing for packages and watering her plants when she was on vacation.

But now I wished I'd at least have put on a baseball cap to cover my hair. Maybe that would have kept me incognito too. "Hey, Diane," I said over my shoulder and turned away again. *Please make her take the stairs.* She was a health freak and exercised a lot, so it wasn't a total pie-in-the-sky wish.

The skies weren't on my side today.

Diane walked around to face me, coming between me and the elevator. "You okay? I haven't seen you in a while, and now there's that sling. What happened?" She touched the sling, making me flinch.

For half a second, I wished she'd be mean so I'd have an excuse to cut things short, but I knew that was the pain talking, so I bit my tongue. She leaned in, looking genuinely concerned. I gestured toward my bad arm. "I had a bad fall at work and broke my elbow pretty bad. Just had surgery. I'm heading to the pharmacy to get a prescription right now."

"Oh, that's awful," she said. "You know, I could go get it for you. I'm heading out to grab a few things from Walgreens anyway. Is that where it is?"

Bless you. I had to force myself not to slump with relief against the wall. She'd save me from having to leave the building at all. Now I could shuffle back to bed and rest. "That's exactly where it is," I said, managing a weak smile. "Are you sure you don't mind?"

"Not at all," she said.

I dug into my purse for some money, but she waved it away. "Pay me back when I bring it to you." Her brow furrowed. "You look like you're in a lot of pain."

"I am," I admitted. Did I look that bad? Probably. No way to know how much of that was from pain and how much from being completely unkempt. "The doctor called in just a few pills for tonight. That's what I was going to pick up. I have to see him tomorrow before he calls in more." I conveniently left out the fact that I wasn't talking about my surgeon. She didn't need the details. Instead, I took my iPhone from my purse and went to the picture of the CT scan, where a half-moon-shaped bone was clearly broken and separated from where it belonged, along with several other bone fragments, which were scattered about. "This is what they fixed. It took a CT scan to find it; the x-rays didn't."

She took the phone from my hand and gaped. "Are you serious? They didn't see *that* in an x-ray? It looks horrible!" She fished around in her purse for a second for her keys, then held up a finger. "Hold on right there. I've got some painkillers left over from when I had gall bladder surgery. Do you want one? It'll tide you over until I get back."

"Really?" I said, trying not to register surprise on my face. I'd always pegged Diane as the kind of person who toed the legal line. "That would be *wonderful*." I hadn't meant to lean on the last word so hard, but her offer felt like a dose of pain meds all by itself.

"I'll be right back," she said, then trotted off to her apartment. While she went inside, I leaned against the wall. My pills would last me a little longer, and I didn't have to go to the pharmacy myself. Driving would have both hurt my arm and wiped out my energy.

Diane returned, holding out what looked like manna to me—a familiar orange-brown bottle with a white cap. "Looks like I had more than I remembered. I thought there were two or three left, but look, it's almost a whole bottle. Probably a couple dozen." She pulled the bottle back to look at the label; I held my breath as she went on. "It's four or five months old. I don't ever take this stuff because it makes me throw up. You're welcome to have the whole bottle." She held it out again, shaking the tablets that would provide me with an escape from pain. The sound might as well have been a heavenly choir. She had more than twenty pills. I could easily last until I saw Dr. Root again.

I reached for the bottle, forcing my hands to move slowly, to not look too eager. I read the label—the very bottom said *Refills: 1*. I wondered if Diane would be willing to refill it for me if I needed it. Maybe I could call in the refill and pick it up for her the way she was picking up mine . . .

"Are you sure you don't mind?" I asked.

"Absolutely," she said, pushing the elevator button again; it had arrived and left while she was gone. "I'm glad I could help. So, I'll head to the pharmacy and grab your prescription right now, and then I'll slip it through your mail slot so I won't bother you; I'd hate to wake you up or make you get out of bed when you're feeling so miserable. You can pay me back another time."

"Th-thank you." My eyes felt near tears; my throat swelled with gratitude. "Really. You have no idea."

"No problem." She reached out and patted my shoulder—my good one this time, thankfully. "Can I grab some groceries for you while I'm out? Bread? Eggs?" She leaned closer. "Chocolate?"

A smile worked its way onto my face. I clutched the pill bottle in one hand and my car keys in the other. "I could use some chocolate."

"And I'll grab one of those take-and-bake pizzas too so you and Ethan don't have to worry about dinner." The elevator opened, and she went inside before I could tell her that Ethan worked tonight and wouldn't be eating dinner at home. But I did need food, something besides toast and yogurt. I could really use some chocolate. Besides, I wasn't about to keep Diane from doing a good deed when it would be so gratefully received. She tilted her head in thought. "I guess I'll have to ring your bell after all if I'm going to give you a pizza. That won't fit through the mail slot, will it?" She laughed at the idea.

"You're wonderful, you know that?" I said as the elevator doors started to close.

"You'd do the same for me!" she called, waving as the door shut completely.

I hurried back to my place, fingers fumbling with the keys in my eagerness to get a glass of water and down a pill—or two. When I got inside, I'd have to check the dosage. If the pills were only five milligrams, I'd take two. My hands could hardly function; they shook from fatigue, anticipation, and pain, but finally, the right key slipped into the lock, and the door opened. I slammed it shut behind me, flipped the dead bolt, and hurried to the kitchen. I didn't bother with filling a glass with water; instead, I opened the fridge door, grabbed a gallon of milk, and drank straight from the carton as I downed two pills. Only after I returned the milk to the fridge and closed the door did I remember that I hadn't checked the dosage on the tablets.

Ten milligrams.

Oops. But that would give me a lot of relief. *I'll finally get on top of the pain.*

I crawled into bed, pulled the covers up, and propped my Kindle on another pillow so I could read easily while lying down. I'd downloaded the next book-club pick, the one about Henrietta Lacks, the poor black woman whose cancer cells had changed medical and scientific history. I'd read a few reviews of the book—all glowing. Would I be able to get through a story about pain and suffering while recuperating and feeling so awful myself?

You don't have cancer, and you never have to worry about where your next meal is coming from, I chided myself. *Stop being a baby.*

But I was in pain. A lot of pain. Maybe not cancer pain. Not pain that would lead to death, like Henrietta's cancer, which had grown to the point that when they autopsied her, her organs were filled with cancer that looked like white pearls. It had grown all over every organ. I was so much better off than she had been. I had good medical insurance and care with the best doctors. Henrietta had faced far worse things.

Yet I was miserable.

I tried to read, but my mind wasn't following the words. I kept comparing myself with Henrietta so I'd feel better, until I remembered one big difference that was like an arrow to the heart: Henrietta had been a mother several times over. Even after she'd originally been treated for her cancer, she still had one more child.

Why did motherhood and children seem to crop up *everywhere*?

I closed my Kindle. Maybe I wouldn't attend the meeting next month, not if I hadn't finished the book. I didn't think I could finish it right now. But I wanted to go back. The other ladies might not care that I hadn't finished it. Or I could pretend I'd read it—not that I could find CliffsNotes for it, but I could skim and research it enough to figure out the gist.

I reached for the remote and turned on the evening news. Only then did I realize how late it was. Dr. Carter had probably been ready to leave for the day when I'd called. I was lucky to have caught him at all—and doubly lucky to have run into Diane at just the right moment.

I was grateful that evening programming had started; I'd spent too much time lately watching daytime television. I'd worked during the day for so many years that I had no idea when the lineup had switched from soap operas to talk and game shows—but no more *Oprah*. At least the current fare kept me distracted. I clicked around and found *American Idol*, so I watched that with the volume turned low so the music wouldn't be too abrasive. I figured the judges could distract me until the Vicodin kicked in.

I could tell almost the minute it did. And I moaned.

Relief.

Chapter 9

THE NEXT MORNING, I WOKE up when Ethan collapsed beside me in bed after work. His weight shifting the mattress and his sudden warmth beneath the blankets were enough change to wake me up. I opened my eyes and realized it was morning. I'd slept better last night than I had in some time.

It was probably the best night's sleep I'd had since my fall. That wasn't saying a ton, granted. I'd still woken up twice, once because the painkillers had worn off completely, after which I'd had to wait for more to kick in to fall back asleep, and a few more times when I tried shifting positions in my sleep, only to wrench or bump my arm, making my eyes pop open in shock.

I did feel better overall, though my arm and every muscle even remotely connected to it—along my shoulder, neck, and down my back—hurt too, as if the extra strain knocked out muscles one after another like dominos. Maybe I could get Ethan to massage my shoulders and upper back later, after he'd gotten some rest.

I slowly sat up and got my phone from the nightstand, intending to play a game or something to while away some time. But the first thing I saw when I clicked it on was the day's schedule—something I'd gotten out of the habit of seeing.

10:00—Dr. Carter

I stared at it for several seconds before remembering that I'd entered it into my online calendar. Why, I still couldn't say exactly. A glance at Ethan proved that he was out cold and would be for hours yet. Maybe I *would* go to my appointment after all to get another prescription.

I got up and very slowly pulled myself somewhat put together—meaning, deodorant and, very gingerly, fresh clothes in the form of jeans and one of Ethan's baggy T-shirts that I could put on myself. Then I finger-tamed my hair. I couldn't do much else with my hair with only one hand—no ponytails or clips or anything else. If I didn't heal soon, I'd need a shorter, more manageable haircut, but it didn't look too bad for the moment—a perk to naturally curly hair, I supposed.

I took one more tablet before slipping on a pair of shoes and heading out. The pill wouldn't take effect until after I'd arrived, so I hoped that driving there would be easy, with little traffic. Driving was one more thing I had to do with one hand.

I arrived a few minutes early, and a nurse brought me back, took my vitals, and had me wait in an examination room for Dr. Carter. Several minutes later, he came in, consulted the notes the nurse had entered into the computer, and had me lie on the table.

"Still hurting a lot, huh?"

"Yeah," I said. "It's pretty bad."

He gestured toward my arm. "That doesn't look too great. What did you do?"

I'd started to wonder why people tended to ask that. It was something I got at the pharmacy, grocery store, checking in at the doctor's office—the few places I'd gone. The question always asked what *I* did, as if I were responsible for my own injury. I decided that next time I saw someone hurt, I'd ask what happened *to* them.

"An accident at work." I grimaced. "I went back earlier than you said I should."

He made a noise of sympathy and perhaps mild chastisement. "So what happened?"

"I tripped on something and landed on concrete, elbow first. Had surgery a few days ago."

He nodded at that as he gently palpated my lower abdomen. "Does that hurt?" When I shook my head, he tried another spot. "Here?"

At a sudden stab, I sucked in my breath.

"I'll take that as a yes," he said.

Even though the pain I'd just felt had shocked me, I felt oddly relieved that it was there—a bit of validation that my pain wasn't all in my head.

"Go ahead and sit up," Dr. Carter said.

I complied, wondering if we were done. I'd expected him to do a pelvic exam or run an ultrasound. Instead, he picked up the chart and wrote on it.

"I can see why you're in so much pain. You're recovering from two major surgeries. Did your surgeon give you medication for the pain?"

"Some," I hedged, hoping he'd interpret my response as meaning the pills were gone.

He nodded. "Some surgeons can be stingy on pain meds. You've got a lot of pain to control anyway, and anything he may have given you wouldn't be enough, I'm guessing. I'll write up a new prescription for a higher dose. Don't worry; we'll get you feeling better."

He smiled and walked out to print a shiny new prescription. I sat there, ready to collapse with relief. I'd come in thinking he'd be skeptical, that he wouldn't want me to have more medication. But it hadn't taken more than a few seconds to convince him that I was really in pain. Why did that idea surprise me so much? I *was* in pain.

I left his office a few minutes later with a prescription for ten-milligram tablets of Vicodin instead of the five-milligram ones. Not seven-point-five, which I knew was the next dosage up. I learned a lot of random stuff being a doctor's wife. At the bottom of the prescription, a single mark made me smile—he'd given me one refill.

Between this new prescription, Diane's pills, and her refill, which I fully intended to use with her blessing, I would definitely survive until I saw Dr. Root and he could get me a refill too. My prospects looked brighter by the minute.

First thing, I'd get my prescription, but instead of going to my usual Walgreens, I looked up other pharmacies in the area. It wasn't like I was doing something wrong, but the idea of picking up painkillers from the same pharmacy techs too often felt awkward, as if I had to explain myself or justify my actions because I had scripts from two different doctors for the same medication. I had valid reasons, and it was no one's business. It would be easier to deal with the whole thing by using different pharmacies and avoiding the situation altogether.

My phone found another Walgreens only ten minutes away, and I figured that would work. Same chain but different employees. After dropping it off, I sat in the waiting area, antsy, until it was ready, and when I reached my car, I took a pill right away so it would start working shortly after I got home. With any luck, it would kick in right as I parked so I could go up to our apartment, put my sweatpants back on, and slip under the covers, where I could nap with my husband. That was pretty much as close to bliss as I could imagine.

Thank heavens for doctors willing to work with patients, I thought. *Wouldn't it be nice if Ethan could write a prescription for me though?*

But he couldn't. While doing so wasn't illegal, it *would* look really bad professionally. It was the kind of thing that raised red flags. He could easily have officials investigating him and his practice. I wouldn't ask him to do that for me, no matter how much pain I was in; no way would I put Ethan's career in jeopardy, not when he'd worked so hard—*we'd* worked so hard—for so many years to reach this point.

As I drove home, I sent a thanks skyward for whatever powers existed in the universe that had given me doctors who would help out. Now that I had plenty of pills, I could relax, knowing I wouldn't need to find more for a long time. Relaxing would certainly help with the pain too.

By the time these pills ran out, I'd be feeling better, or at least feeling only slightly uncomfortable—the kind of pain ibuprofen could manage. I'd be my old self again, the happy, confident person Ethan had married.

I parked and headed up to our apartment. After I changed into my sweatpants, I climbed under the blanket and breathed in the scent that was Ethan. I put my feet beside his, and in his sleep, he instinctively entwined our legs and put his arm around my waist.

I took a deep breath, feeling grateful.

Chapter 10

I OPTED TO GO TO book club, even though I hadn't finished the story of Henrietta Lacks. I couldn't finish it; I simply couldn't handle thinking about how totally opposite our lives were and how none of it seemed fair. And yes, I knew in my heart that feeling any kind of envy toward a dirt-poor black woman who'd lived in a volatile, racist society and who had died a painful death from cancer was beyond ridiculous.

I was white and had had a privileged upbringing. I had a relatively affluent lifestyle. I didn't know what it was like to *see* Jim Crow signs and segregation, let alone what it was like to live on the oppressive side of those laws.

Yet I found similarities in our lives too—at least as far as I'd read. She and I had both experienced pain. A lot of pain. A tiny part of me kept thinking my pain was worse than hers, that I had the ongoing ache of knowing I'd never be a mother, never hold a child of my own close and smell that new-baby smell, knowing that the tiny, squirming bundle was *mine*. She'd had that several times over—I'd forgotten how many kids she'd had. She seemed like a hero to me; her body could create life even as she moved toward death. Her cancer cells lived on, helping science progress in countless ways, while I couldn't conceive or even keep a houseplant alive, so maybe the universe knew what it was doing, as painful as that reality felt to me.

I drove toward Ruby's house with the partially read book sitting on my Kindle and imagined yet again what it would feel like to hold in my arms flesh of my flesh, a baby that was literally a part of me. The images filled my mind so completely that I nearly blew through a red light. I pushed the brake pedal hard and screeched to a stop.

As my heart beat in my chest—I'd stopped for the light in time to just miss rear-ending a black Nissan in front of me—another realization about Henrietta smacked me between the eyes: Henrietta had many children, but she couldn't afford to care for them. Had she been in the shoes of someone more financially secure—someone like me—she probably would have had the resources to care for all of her children or even to control her family size. Maybe pay for better medical treatment, prolonging her life so she could raise her kids. Maybe.

The light turned green, and I eased forward, thinking how in an odd, inverse sort of way, Henrietta and I had something in common—neither of us had the resources to choose the size of our families. In my case, the choice to have children at all had been stripped from me. Henrietta never had the choice to limit her number of pregnancies because she hadn't had access to something as simple as the Pill.

Did that make us more or less alike? Were our pains similar? Or was I kidding myself that we'd felt any of the same pains? Cancer surely hurt worse than my hysterectomy or broken elbow. But add emotional pain to the mix, and what was the score? As I turned into Ruby's subdivision, I gritted my teeth.

It's time to stop comparing. Only God can know everyone's pain levels, I reminded myself. *That is, assuming He exists.* If He did exist, why would He refuse to step in and help someone who so desperately wanted help—like me, like Henrietta, like her family?

I found a parking spot and tried to think of something else, but my mind again turned to Henrietta; apparently, she was never far away from me. With book club slated to talk all about her for hours tonight, I supposed that thinking of her was inevitable.

I glanced at the Kindle on the passenger seat and imagined her picture on the bright orange cover. I had no way of knowing how much pain she'd really been in.

I'd read a blog post once from someone who'd lost his wife to suicide. The man had said he'd suffered more than prisoners in World War II concentration camps. As a Jew, I'd found that idea beyond offensive; no one had any right to say their suffering came close to that of my people in the middle of the Holocaust. How dare he?

Yet, was I doing something similar, even if on a smaller scale, by comparing myself to Henrietta?

I gripped the steering wheel hard, not getting out of the car as another thought struck me. I didn't want to be a hypocrite. When I was in high school, my mother made me read *Man's Search for Meaning*, by

Viktor Frankl, a concentration-camp survivor. I didn't remember much about his short book besides the idea that he compared pain to a gaseous substance. He said that gas filled its container completely, no matter the size of the container or type of gas. He said a person was filled with pain, no matter the cause. All suffering was full and complete.

If Frankl was right, it meant my pain mattered even if it wasn't comparable to Henrietta's. I took a deep, cleansing breath before getting out of the car.

My pain matters. It's real. I matter. I had a glimpse of that idea, anyway, that whether or not there was a God out there who cared or had any idea I existed, the fact that I was alive meant I was relevant. My physical pain from two surgeries, from mending bones and soft-tissue tears, and even from the constant ache inside of knowing I'd never bear my own child was real. And stronger because it was all pain I never thought I'd face.

Eventually, I got out of the car, clicked the key fob to lock the doors, and headed up the path. As always, the pathway was lit, and a handmade wreath decorated the door. The place was warm and inviting.

With my Kindle tucked into the crook of my left arm, I rang the doorbell and waited for Ruby to answer. I could hear voices inside but couldn't make out whose they were, and I hadn't noticed which cars were parked on the street either, besides an old Dodge that looked ready to fall apart. Ruby opened the door with a flourish. She wore a purple pant-suit with chunky earrings dangling nearly to her shoulders and several long necklaces. As usual, her house smelled of baked goods, though I could have sworn Shannon was the one bringing the treats tonight.

As I entered the family room, Ruby excused herself to go to the kitchen, where she had to take care of something, with some mention of cake as she whisked away, leaving a cloud of perfume in her wake. Maybe Shannon had called to say she couldn't bring refreshments.

I stepped into the family room, where Tori, Paige, Athena, and Livvy were already waiting. Tori was just settling into a spot on the couch, so I guessed she'd arrived a minute before I had. Daisy wasn't here, and a piece of me again felt some guilty relief at that. I couldn't act strong about one more thing tonight.

Fortunately, I was able to join the light discussion about typical daily life: a new romantic comedy Livvy was watching, Paige's car trouble, Tori's latest embarrassing moment on a set—movie or TV, I wasn't sure which—and then a comedy of errors story from Paige about a trip to the dentist with her kids, from which I gathered that she no longer worked at a dental office. I managed to laugh at her story, because although it involved her kids, it was mostly about a new hygienist who didn't have the slightest idea what she was doing and knew even less about motherhood itself. That didn't sting as much.

Not too long after, the doorbell rang again, and I heard Ruby greeting Shannon. Ruby offered to take something to the kitchen so Shannon could "go sit down." My mouth watered; I hoped the "something" meant Shannon had brought a treat after all. She appeared, wearing jeans and a T-shirt rather than her usual Walgreens polo and khaki pants.

"Hey, Shannon," Paige said with a smile.

I waved my good arm and said, "Good to see you." I thought I heard voices from the kitchen, and the cause became apparent a few seconds later when Ruby entered with Shannon's stepdaughter, Keisha. Ruby took the spot on the couch that Tori had saved for her, and Keisha took a spot by Shannon.

With everyone seated, Ruby clasped her hands, crossed her legs, and placed her hands on them. "Welcome, everyone." She went on to remind us that Daisy was still on bed rest—I hadn't been reading all the e-mails that closely, but I nodded as if I knew what she was talking about.

Ruby shook her head sadly. "I offered to have it at her place again, but she was very reluctant."

That was the meeting I'd missed. Paige, Athena, and Olivia all nodded in understanding, along with Ruby, and exchanged smiles that hinted of shared memories. I suddenly felt like I had really missed out on something.

Ruby turned to Shannon, who sat across the circle. "Why don't you lead us off, dear?"

Shannon didn't speak at first, and small pink spots bloomed on her cheeks. She'd never struck me as someone who got shy speaking in front of people—she worked with strangers all day long at a pharmacy—but she looked to be at a loss for words now. After clearing her throat, she nodded and began. "I thought I'd ask if anyone had any questions about the medical events that took place."

Oooh, good move. The book had technical parts, and even with the bit I had read, I would have understood more if I'd had someone with a medical background reading it with me. Yet I understood a whole lot more than Henrietta's uneducated children had, who worried that clones of their mother were walking the streets of London.

"I think I was lost half of the time," Tori said with a laugh. "My brain can compute production schedules but not so much how the different parts of cells work. It's amazing—and terrifying—to try to comprehend how anything that small could be so destructive." She shuddered.

The whole idea of tiny, microscopic things—mutated cells—that could kill? Not my idea of light, happy reading.

"And *constructive*," Paige interjected. "Even though they were cancer cells, they spearheaded many important discoveries. I found the whole thing absolutely fascinating."

Athena leaned forward, hand poised to take her turn. "I found it so interesting to note that if any of the factors had been missing when they harvested Henrietta's cells, it might have been another failed attempt, and all the advances that have happened because of the HeLa cells would perhaps have never become a reality."

Tori laid the book on her lap and talked about how Dr. Gey, the main doctor involved with the cells, had been doubted by many in his field. As she spoke, I kept an eye on her to watch for her reaction to a story with such a big focus on black people and race relations. If I got upset over people trivializing the Holocaust, she surely wouldn't appreciate black people being treated as dispensable lab mice.

As the discussion went on, Shannon looked genuinely excited for the first time in my memory. Medicine was clearly her wheelhouse. She listed several cases of doctors and scientists who had been totally discounted in their theories but later proven right—like the guy who first theorized that blood circulated through the body and the man who believed mosquitoes could carry diseases like malaria.

Tori took a turn but again didn't touch race, which I saw as fascinating and odd all at once. "I also found it interesting that despite the eventual tragedy for Henrietta, she went to the right doctor at the right time." She shook her head and raised her hands almost in disbelief. "I don't know that any other hospital could have done what John Hopkins did back in the 1950s."

My brow furrowed; I couldn't help it. Henrietta had gone to the right hospital at the right time. The right hospital at the right time . . . for whom? She'd still died. She and her family had never gotten the care and compensation they deserved. She didn't even get the basic care a white woman in her circumstances would have had. Instead, she'd been sent away.

"I agree," Shannon interjected. "Even with all the mistakes along the way and the breakdown of ethics, Henrietta left behind an incredible legacy that has changed the world."

"But an unwilling legacy," Tori said, hand raised in protest.

Ruby tilted her head. "I think this is one of the most important books of our century. Really. It's amazing how Henrietta's contribution has led to saving millions of lives and treating even more people. Her story should be required reading in every high school."

We weren't that far into the century. That was pretty bold of her to make such a declaration. Shannon's eyebrows went up as if she too was surprised.

"I would have loved to read it in high school," Keisha said. "Of course, it wasn't published until last year."

I nodded but then caught an odd look in Shannon's eye as she looked at Keisha, almost as if she couldn't believe—or trust?—her stepdaughter's words.

Keisha asked where the bathroom was, which interrupted my thoughts. Ruby gave her directions, and I listened closely to them in case I needed to take a small break for another dose of Vicodin.

I was starting to worry that I'd never fully get the pain under control; the meds were already less effective than they'd been a few weeks ago, but my pain was as bad as ever. Would I end up on a morphine drip if I couldn't handle it?

Here I was griping, and I had to remind myself that medicine had seen huge advances—many since Henrietta's time—that gave me the hope for even 80-percent mobility.

I should be grateful for that much. If I'd sustained the same kind of injury a few decades ago, my chances of having a decent life with any mobility in my arm would have been almost zero. It had been only with a fancy CT scan that they'd figured out the extent of my break. No x-ray machine could have done that. And I doubted they'd had fancy screws and plates a generation or two ago, at least not ones as good as they had today. And my surgery had been entirely laparoscopic, something in the realm of science fiction in Henrietta's day.

Paige tapped her copy of the book and said, "I guess we never know when God has a greater plan in mind than we can see. So much good came out of the experiments with her cells years and years after her death."

Nods and murmurs of agreement went around the room, but I furrowed my brow. Did Paige really think God used humans as pawns in some cosmic game of strategy? Sure, let's have this woman—this *mother*—die, and it'll be for the greater good. I didn't like that kind of God, if one existed at all. Even if He'd made me.

Maybe I hated Him *especially* if He made me, because my body was broken on the most fundamental level it could be.

Paige's words circled in my brain, and I could have sworn the ache in both my heart and arm got worse as I tried to reconcile her idea of some big-picture God who made some suffer for the benefit of others. That's not quite what she said, but that's what it felt like.

I needed a distraction from the pain and figured that a change in the direction of the discussion would be the best way of getting it. "The development of modern medicine was a rocky road, but it had so many breakthroughs along the way." I gestured toward my blue sling. "I mean, with my arm, what they've been able to fix is remarkable when you think about it. Although, now they explain things a little more before surgery. It made me sick to think of how they didn't inform the women about the side effects of those surgeries. Henrietta had a real shock when she found out she'd been made infertile."

I wondered then how Henrietta had felt about being infertile. She'd already had five kids; had she wanted more?

And if not, did she feel a hole in her belly that made her feel like less of a woman? Had she felt like *me*?

"But getting rid of her cancer was more important than having another baby," Tori said with a shake of her head.

I found myself trembling. All of this talk of surgery and infertility, combined with how much I couldn't help but compare myself to Henrietta . . . It was all too much.

"But they *didn't* get rid of her cancer," I said quietly. My right hand wrapped around my waist as if protecting my uterus, except that it was gone.

Tori waved a hand as if dismissing my comment; I breathed a small sigh of relief, hoping no one else had noticed my emotion. She went on. "Still, I couldn't believe Henrietta said she wouldn't have done the surgery if she'd known she wouldn't be able to have any more children," Tori said.

"I mean, Henrietta was a little bit crazy to even think that. Her life was more important than having more babies. She already had five."

I pursed my lips; no way could I reply to that without yelling or bursting into tears. *I understand Henrietta, at least a little.* My eyes were beginning to water. I'd never been such a wreck at book club before. I didn't cry in public. That wasn't me. I liked to think I carried myself with an air of professionalism, perhaps a bit of elegance. A weeping ball of tears with mascara tracks on her cheeks wouldn't exactly support that.

Ruby chimed in next. "Women have to make hard choices sometimes," she said, turning from me as if she was uncomfortable with whatever emotion I was exuding.

Rein it in. I coached myself to breathe easier and hide my feelings better. I was vaguely aware that Ruby continued to speak.

"It broke my heart when Henrietta's daughter talked to the author in that first phone call." Ruby flipped through her book and read the words of Henrietta's daughter, Deborah, who had never known her mother. She'd wanted to know what her mother smelled like, whether she'd breast-fed Deborah, what her favorite color was.

What I wouldn't give to have a daughter to experience those things with—to smell her, to nestle her against me as I fed her, to share favorite colors and foods and silly dances with her at the beach. So much for reining in my emotions; I had to strangle back a sob. I looked around the circle at the other women. Paige's eyes were watery; maybe she was thinking of her own children or of her mother. The other women also looked a bit misty. I hoped they'd think my misty eyes blended right in.

I continued trying to get my emotions under control, giving my attention solely to the discussion, which seemed to have lapsed into doing math about how old Deborah had been when her mother died and how old Henrietta herself had been at her death. The hole in my belly seemed to burn like something living had been ripped out of it.

Athena typed on her Blackberry and then said, "Deborah was born in 1949, two years before her mother died."

I touched a finger to my eyes to remove the moisture threatening to turn into tears. "No wonder Deborah didn't remember her," I said.

"How tragic," Olivia, who had been pretty quiet up until now, said. "At least with my mother, I knew her . . . Of course, that means I miss her even more. But I do have the memories and the heaven reminders."

Athena wiped at her eyes, and the room grew quiet for a moment. I didn't know why at first, but then I remembered that Athena's mother had recently died. I didn't know what to say or do, but fortunately, at that point, Keisha came into the room, back from the bathroom.

She must have heard the end of the conversation because as she took her seat, she said, "Deborah sounded like a hillbilly."

After a bit more discussion, Athena looked up from her Blackberry again and said, "Deborah passed away in 2009. She never even saw the book in print."

Tori brushed her fingers through her dark hair. "At least she knew about it, and she probably read a draft. It would have been nice for her to see the book come out and to know about its success though."

"Are any of the other children still alive?" Ruby asked.

Athena scrolled through something on her phone. "It looks like two sons are."

Eventually—thank heavens, although I refused to actually thank heaven—the conversation turned to the relationship between Henrietta and her cheating husband. I could listen to that easily enough; Ethan and I had a solid marriage. The subject of being unfaithful didn't hit a nerve in the same way so many other aspects of Henrietta's life did right then.

Shannon spoke up next. "Even though Day had been with plenty of other women, you could tell he loved Henrietta very much."

I wanted to snort at that. No man who truly loved a woman would cheat on her. Ethan would never cheat on me. *At least I have that.*

"I agree," Paige said in a soft voice.

Every head turned her direction. How were those words coming out of the mouth of a woman whose husband destroyed their marriage by cheating?

Paige cleared her throat, her face reddening as everyone looked at her. Surely she knew we were all surprised. She looked down at her book, thumbing through the pages. "Remember how he took her to the hospital every day so she could be treated for pain? And when not having her children nearby upset her too much, he kept the kids right outside, under her window, so she could at least see them? I thought that was very sweet. Maybe he just didn't know another way to live."

The discussion wrapped up after awhile, but before we got to have refreshments, the talk turned to personal things. I didn't pay much attention to it until Athena mentioned something about trips and asked if Ruby had any planned.

Ruby's eyes widened, and small pink dots blossomed on her cheeks. "Well, actually, yes, I do have a trip planned. I'll be going to Greece on a two-week tour with a group of people I met at the senior center."

"You are?" Shannon said, echoing my thoughts. "When are you going?"

"We leave March 10."

I found myself smiling for Ruby's sake; a trip with fellow seniors sounded like the perfect thing for a widow living alone. But my happiness for her was soon overshadowed by my arm throbbing to the point that I could have sworn it pulsed like a light.

"How lovely!" Tori sighed. "I've heard that Greece is *gorgeous*."

"There's nothing like the Greek Isles," Athena said. "Anytime my mother heard someone say Disneyland was the happiest place on earth, she would lean over and tell me that was only because they'd never been to Greece."

I'd never felt all that connected to Athena, but suddenly, I could picture myself going on a cruise with her and enjoying myself. But arm pain cut through the fantasy, and the image faded quickly. I'd missed some of the chitchat, but I returned to the conversation, hoping I could contribute something after being little more than a bump on a log the past little bit.

"I went there many years ago with my husband," Ruby said, and in typical Ruby fashion, she clasped her hands. "It will be a nice treat to visit it again, and I should still be able to find time to read our next book—whatever that is."

Now that was something I could help her out with—reading while on vacation. "Do you have a Kindle?" I asked, ready to pull mine out of my purse to demonstrate it if needed. "They're great for travel; you can take thousands of books with you for less than a pound."

"Oh dear, I don't want thousands," Ruby said with a slightly hooded look in her eyes, as if she distrusted technology. "Just one would be good, maybe two." She lamented not knowing know how to use e-readers, and she stumbled on the unfamiliar term, asking if they were hard to use.

Shannon raised a hand and excused herself, saying she'd get the refreshments ready. I watched her go, Olivia trailing after her, and for a moment, I wondered if I'd said something wrong.

"Or you could invest in an iPad," Tori suggested, bringing my attention back around and making me feel better about bringing up the idea of an e-book. Tori explained that an iPad was like a small computer, and that on a trip, it might be the better option, giving Ruby access to e-mail and the Internet without lugging a laptop around. "I have mine in the car if you'd like me to get it and show you how it works," she said, adding that it was very user-friendly. Would Ruby see *any* modern gadget as "user-friendly"?

Paige wished wistfully for an iPad. "My boys would go crazy over it."

"The Kindle is pretty easy to learn," I said, knowing that if Ruby was scared of technology, a Kindle would be easier for her to get comfortable with than an iPad. "I could show you how to work it."

Tori asked me to show Ruby, so I pulled it out, flipped the switch, and moved seats to demonstrate. Ruby seemed impressed that I already had dozens of books loaded on it and it was so light—as if data had weight. Ruby thanked me and seemed less intimidated after pushing the buttons and not making the Kindle explode or something.

Ruby glanced toward the kitchen, where Olivia and Shannon were still working, but then she assumed her official facial expression and nodded in Tori's direction. "Tori, you can choose our next book."

After a moment of hesitation, Tori's eyes brightened. "I have the perfect book. *The War of Art* by Steven Pressfield."

As if on cue, the refreshments arrived—brownies with vanilla ice cream. I figured I could manage eating one-handed if I propped the bowl in my lap just right.

Tori went on about her book selection. "I read it a couple of years ago, but I'm due for another reading," she said as she used her spoon to break off a piece of brownie.

"It's that good?" Ruby asked as Athena looked the book up on her Blackberry and I searched the Amazon store with my Kindle.

"It's that important," Tori corrected. Her cheeks got an excited flush to them. "It's about following your dreams and not letting anything stop you."

I found the book on my Kindle and was about to click the purchase button, but at Tori's words, I hesitated. *Dreams.* I'd been following my dreams—chasing them rabidly—for years, and look what I had to show for it: a bunch of debt and a broken body.

I pursed my lips again, angry at myself for letting my emotions come to the surface so much tonight. *Maybe I should skip next month's meeting.* But even as the thought passed through my mind, I clicked the button and downloaded the book. I knew I'd read it. I knew I'd come to book club next month. But that didn't mean I'd *like* doing either.

The others agreed on the book, and Ruby confirmed it, adding, "And I'll have a full report on Greece at our April meeting."

I winced. A trip to Greece sounded like a dream too. I tried to hide the tears welling in my eyes. Ruby had had decades of a great marriage. She was a mother. She had a beautiful house. Her late husband must have set aside plenty of money because she didn't seem at all strapped for cash. And now a trip?

Would I ever have my turn to have a dream come true?

Chapter 11

Midweek, my physical and emotional pain swirled into a void so dark and intense that I thought I'd never get out of it. I took more pills than I strictly should have but knew that unless I started looking jaundiced, I wasn't killing my liver. Besides, Dr. Carter had reiterated what my nurses had counseled: the need to get on top of the pain.

I stayed in bed as much as possible, getting up only to go to the bathroom and eat. Even those simple, everyday activities were misery. Somehow, I'd become horribly constipated over the last few weeks. Maybe it was because I wasn't exercising while recovering. Maybe it was because my diet wasn't as good as it usually was; while I ate baby carrots and grapes, I could no longer make myself big salads like I used to when I had two functioning arms. Whatever the reason for the constipation, my trips to the bathroom were painful, not only on account of any movement from my arm but also because of my innards and their discomfort.

Every so often, an errand would get me out of bed, such as Friday morning, when I decided to refill Diane's prescription, just to be sure. I probably had enough pills from Dr. Carter to hold me over until I could get a refill of Dr. Root's prescriptions, but I wasn't positive—and I was absolutely not about to risk the literal agony of not having medicine when I needed it. I braced myself for getting out of bed to run to the store to pick it up. I'd need to change clothes if I was going out in public. I'd been wearing the same T-shirt and sweatpants for three days now because changing clothes, especially shirts, proved to be pure torture.

I decided to call Diane to ask if I could use the refill on her prescription and to ask her to pick it up for me too. I'd use the excuse that Ethan was working long hours. And he was. But I also knew he'd frown on my using meds technically written for someone else and probably wouldn't pick them up for me.

This was pretty much the first time I was grateful that at times Ethan was expected to pull insanely long shifts, often one after the other. He sometimes slept at the hospital, then kept working the next day. He'd call and text to check on me, and sometimes I'd wake up after a nap to find takeout food he'd left on the nightstand for me, with sweet notes, but for the most part, I'd been on my own for the last week. He was likely making up for the time he'd taken off during and right after my surgery. That, and his superiors were undoubtedly taking advantage of the last weeks of his residency, working him as hard as they could to free themselves up.

When I called Diane and explained the situation, she said, "Of course you can have the refill. I'll call it in right now, and I'll go pick it up when I'm out and about running errands at lunch. Sound good?"

"Diane, you are a doll. I can't thank you enough." Relieved, I hung up and shifted positions but instantly regretted the movement as I clenched my teeth and waited for the shock of pain to subside. When it passed, I gingerly reached for the comforter and arranged it around me, trying to get warm. No matter what I did, I seemed to always be cold lately. I used to run warm, not needing thick comforters, even during the cooler months of the year. Now I was bundled up in sweats and thick socks, with an extra blanket, and I could have sworn my fingertips were slightly blue.

I lay there, under the layers of blankets, feeling all too aware of every inch of my throbbing body. Relief. I needed it, and now. The directions on my prescription—my *prescriptions*, I corrected myself—said to wait four to six hours between pills. But I'd sometimes taken two pills at a time. And I'd taken doses two or three hours apart. Not the best habit to get into, so I decided to try spacing out the pills like a good patient.

I checked the clock on my phone. Three hours and nine minutes since the last dose. Fifty-one minutes, minimum, before I was technically allowed another.

I can do that. I can. Closing my eyes, I tried to breathe deeply to relax my body and muscles. The throbbing just got worse. After what felt like an eternity, I checked the time again. Three hours and twelve minutes since my last dose.

Hang directions, I thought, sitting up. The movement made me catch my breath; I had to hold my arm for several seconds, waiting for the worst of the shooting pain in both my arm and abdomen to subside. Then I slowly reached for the Vicodin bottle on my nightstand. I read the label again as if I didn't already know every letter and number of it.

Take one tablet every 4 to 6 hours as needed for pain.

As if one tablet came remotely close to handling my pain as I "needed" it.

I tenderly held the prescription bottle in my left hand, making every movement deliberate so as not to hurt that arm, and took off the lid with my right. Even that movement sent shards of glass through my arm.

I should have asked for a non-childproof cap.

I tapped two tablets into my palm. I was pretty sure the only reason the instructions said to take fewer than that was because of the Tylenol component to the drug, and therefore the potential for liver damage with an overdose. But I rarely drank alcohol, and I was young; my liver was probably *just fine*. If the whites of my eyes started going yellow, I'd be more careful.

As I stared at the two tablets, then looked at my arm, then back at my palm, I made a split-second decision. Forget two. I needed to get *out* of this misery, to get on top of the pain, as the professionals were telling me to, once and for all.

I tapped almost half of the contents into my palm, then set the bottle back on the nightstand. Only then did I bother counting the pills. My index finger spread them out, letting me count them more easily— two, four, six, eight, ten.

Ten? You're crazy, my mind cried. I pictured my liver crying uncle, but the idea of being pain free for even a little while quashed that thought. Ten wasn't nearly enough to pose a serious health risk—people didn't die from ten pills, I was quite sure.

I hesitated for only a second before popping a few of the tablets into my mouth and downing them with a swig from my water bottle. I repeated the action, and once more, until my palm was empty. Then I hurriedly capped the bottle and shoved it into a drawer to hide it—from myself as much as from anyone else.

Ethan didn't pay close enough attention to my meds to have a clue about how many had been in there the last time he'd seen me. But having the bottle out of sight made *me* feel better.

Ethan wouldn't see it, and neither would I.

I leaned against my pillows and flipped through TV stations as I waited for the pills to do their thing. Halfway through a talk show, I felt the familiar tingling wave come over me, only this time much, much stronger. It disoriented me for a second, but then I smiled and settled in to watch the show, for once completely comfortable, with no cares in the world.

I closed my eyes and enjoyed the hazy feeling that had no pain whatsoever and listened to the television. I drifted in and out of sleep during the show, but when the sound on the TV faded, my eyes opened in confusion. Had I rolled onto the remote and shut off the TV or something?

No, it was on. But I could barely hear it. *Odd.* Figuring I'd hit the volume control accidentally, I grabbed the remote and pushed the buttons. I upped the volume to maximum, but I still couldn't hear the people talking, so I hit the mute button. A mute symbol popped up, showing that I'd just cut the sound. I undid it and adjusted the volume settings again. The network had likely messed up their broadcast, so I changed channels.

That much thinking was about all I could do; my brain swam through a sea of warm confusion. I changed the channel to a game show. I collapsed against the pillows again, letting the remote drop to the comforter. But I couldn't hear the new program either.

Maybe something's wrong with our television.

I groaned with frustration, but my voice sounded odd to my ears. Or rather, it didn't *sound* at all; instead, I felt the vibration of a groan through my throat, but I didn't actually hear any sound. Silence had descended on the room. Alarmed, I clapped my right hand against my leg several times. I could barely make out the sound.

My eyes widened. What was happening? Was something *else* wrong with me now? Not only did I lack a uterus, but I also had a bum arm . . . *and* I was going *deaf*? Panic swelled in me, piercing through the brain fog. As my heart sped up, I grabbed my phone and tried to do an Internet search for my symptoms, but the simplest of key words took way too long to type out; my hands shook like crazy, making me hit all the wrong letters.

At some point, I gave up and let the haze take over. I stared at the ceiling, trying to quiet the anxiety, but there was no denying the terror I felt. I closed my eyes, feeling nauseated.

Hours later, the apartment door slammed shut, jolting me awake. It sounded like Ethan shoving it closed with his foot when his arms were full, which happened often. I lifted my head and registered that the lighting in the bedroom had changed. Somehow, I pieced together that the sun's movement meant the passage of time. How much time?

And then it hit me—I'd *heard* the door slam shut. My heartbeat increased as I sat and tried to hear more. I cleared my throat—and heard it. The woozy fuzz of Vicodin was still there, though fading. The feeling was more like two pills' worth.

"Hey, babe!" Ethan called. I *heard* him call. The sound of his voice had never been more welcome, and it wasn't just that I'd missed him. "I brought dinner. Hope you're hungry."

"Hey," I called back with a weak voice as I tried to psych myself into standing and going to the kitchen to greet him. Ethan worked late so often that having him home for dinner was a treat. Even better, he'd brought food, so there was no guilt on my part for not cooking.

I moved my legs to the edge of the bed, where they dangled, but before I could stand, Ethan entered carrying two pizza boxes balanced on one arm and a two-liter bottle of root beer in the other. A stack of napkins and a sack of breadsticks sat atop the boxes.

I laughed. "You think we can eat that much food between the two of us?" My mood had shot up since my hearing had returned. Maybe bad things wouldn't come in threes for me after all.

Ethan placed his load on the bed and served me a slice of combination pizza.

"Sausage, huh?" I said. "My mother would have a coronary."

He shrugged, a grin tugging one side of his face as he said, "I figured if we're combining meat with dairy, we should go all the way and eat pork. Am I right, or am I right?"

One bite, and the spices in the sausage burst onto my tongue. I moaned with pleasure. "You're right," I said. "Just don't tell my mom."

He mimed locking his lips and throwing away the key, then leaned over and gave me a hello kiss before sitting back and pouring some root beer into a plastic cup I hadn't noticed him bring in for me.

"So why the pizza?" I asked. He had to know what I meant; Ethan wasn't the kind of guy to get takeout—let alone his favorite pizza—just because. Maybe tonight it was to celebrate saving someone's life in the ER. "Have a great surgery? A patient who made your day?"

His face dropped, and his brows knitted together. "Actually, the opposite."

Shoot. I hadn't given a thought to the other reason he often turned to comfort food—when he was upset and ticked off.

He took a bite of pizza and chewed it a bit, then breathed out contentedly. "I needed that after today."

"What happened? Was it something someone said?" I wanted to know what happened in Ethan's life, but men tended to be quiet about things like their workdays, or at least Ethan was. To find out what went on at work, I often had to ask his coworkers at parties. He'd typically shrug and say that "nothing really" had happened. Which I knew couldn't possibly be true in an ER, especially when he worked so many nights. He was there when the worst cases arrived by ambulance: heinous car accidents, gang shootings, and other intense injuries that tended to show up more often at night. I prodded to know more, feeling like this was the first time since my first surgery that we'd really had a chance to sit down, enjoy each other, and *talk*.

"It was a lot of stuff one person said."

"An orderly?" I asked. "One of the nurses?" The person was just as likely to be a fellow doctor, but I wasn't about to ask that. For some reason, it was easier for him to talk smack about a fellow doctor than for me to hint at it.

"A patient this time," Ethan said. He scrubbed a hand through his hair, then rubbed his chin, where a bit of stubble had grown. I had an urge to kiss it.

"So how did a patient ruin your day?" I couldn't imagine what a patient could say that would upset Ethan. He'd faced all kinds of people from all walks and all conditions. What they said typically rolled off his back. But he was obviously upset now.

He'd set his pizza down on a pile of four napkins and begun pacing our room. "I am so *sick* of junkies thinking the ER is their personal drug house. They come in, plead some fake illness or injury, and beg for painkillers—as if I don't know what they're doing. They're so transparent."

My throat oddly tightened. "Really?" I said to show that I was paying attention. I swallowed against the knot in my throat. Why did his words make my stomach twist? I wasn't some homeless junkie on parole, looking for drugs.

"What frustrates me most is that we can't just turn them away; we still have to treat them, and that costs the hospital a lot of money. When the patient inevitably doesn't pay up, the cost ends up going to normal, healthy, honest people paying insurance. I'm sick of the fraud."

I cleared my throat, pretending that a crumb of crust had gotten lodged there. "What did this one say?"

"The usual," Ethan said. "That he was in so much pain from a back injury, yada, yada." He came over and sat on the edge of the bed, his face suddenly animated. "I was on to this guy fast, way before he had any idea. I asked about his other symptoms—specific stuff, like whether he'd felt dizzy or tired lately or whether he'd experienced a change in his digestive tract, like diarrhea or constipation, whether he'd felt extra cold of late, a whole bunch of stuff. To someone who doesn't know better, it probably sounded like I was listing off random symptoms."

"What were you looking for?"

"All of that stuff is connected to narcotics." He raised his eyebrows as if letting that sink in. "And then when he asked for Vicodin? Yeah right." He laughed sharply, like a bark. "But I'd gotten him to trust me. So when I asked if he had any other unusual symptoms, he gave me the nail in the coffin of his argument." He nodded, pleased with himself, and took another bite of pizza.

I had to set down my pizza because I was trembling too much. "And what . . . what was the final nail in the coffin?"

Ethan gave a one-shouldered shrug. "A relatively rare side effect of overdosing on Vicodin—temporary hearing loss. Turns out he'd gone deaf for almost a day in one ear, and it totally freaked him out. I so nailed him." He shook his head and gestured toward our pizza feast. "I guess in a way this is a celebratory meal. I called out a slime-ball addict on his fraud. I checked with the police, and sure enough, he's got a warrant, and right before I left the hospital, the cops arrived and took him away in handcuffs. Not too shabby for an ER doctor. Should have been a detective." He sat straighter and puffed out his chest, then laughed.

"Nah," I said. "I prefer being married to a sexy doctor."

I forced the words out. I had to look casual, unfazed. If he ever had the slightest clue—ever—that I had several of those symptoms, including that unsettling hearing loss, which, hooray for me, had been in *both* ears, he'd flip out.

Would he leave me if he knew? But I'm not some freak addict.

As he finished one slice of pizza and took his second, I glanced surreptitiously at the top drawer of my nightstand. Good thing I'd hidden the pill bottle, just in case he had seen it earlier and realized it was dramatically emptier. No way could I give him any reason to think I was like his idiot junkie patients. The cheese from the pizza seemed to harden in my stomach. I gave up on my piece and put it back into the box, then leaned against my pillows.

"Babe, you okay?"

"Just in pain. And my stomach's upset. The pizza didn't agree with me." I tried to smile. "Maybe karma's getting me back for not being kosher."

Ethan chuckled. "I think you're mixing religions there." He stood, tucked me in, and placed a kiss on my temple. "Love you, babe," he said, then quietly carried the food out.

I didn't move; I didn't dare let him know that I wasn't okay, that I was terrified he'd think I was some reject addict. I *wasn't*. Yes, I'd taken way too many pills. That was stupid. But one bad decision didn't make me an addict.

"It doesn't," I insisted in a whisper—but aloud, to make sure my hearing still worked—as a tear trickled down my cheek and onto my pillow.

Chapter 12

ETHAN WAS AT WORK AGAIN, with back-to-back shifts, so I was alone. I lay in bed all morning, feeling lazy, dirty, greasy. I needed a shower, but I didn't care enough to get up to take one. It was too much work to psych myself into getting out of bed and doing all the things to prepare for the shower, then getting in and washing up, all while babying my pathetic excuse for an arm, getting out, still favoring the arm and drying myself one-handed, then trying to comb out my wet hair with the fingers of one hand, get dressed, and everything else . . . and that was assuming I could function enough to do all of that without crumpling to the floor and whimpering from pain.

I could swear the pain was getting worse, not better, and I blamed that fact on the physical therapy and the splint, which I tried to wear most of the time but *had* to take off when the pain got to a certain point, which happened more often than not. Simply put, I couldn't stay on top of the pain anymore, but I wasn't about to try to really get on top of it like I had the other day. Losing one of my senses for hours had me terrified.

So I was back to watching the clock for when I could take another dose, but one dose didn't come close to helping anymore—forget about four hours. So I often overlapped the Vicodin with Aleve or four—or six—Advil. I hated admitting it even to myself, but the one bit of relief I did get was the way the world sort of drifted back a few feet. It didn't go away, and I was still well aware of all my problems, but it was like taking out my contacts before I'd had Lasik; everything, including my problems, wasn't in such sharp relief, with colors so bright they hurt and edges so sharp that the slightest touch felt like they'd make me bleed. Instead, the painkillers made my inner self feel a bit more like a blurry kaleidoscope—all the colors and shapes were still there but muted, blurry. Easier to look at.

I rolled over onto my right side—lying on my left was out of the question—and tried to stretch out the huge knots in my muscles that wearing the sling and then the splint had developed in my neck and shoulder. That pain was almost as bad as the elbow. And it reminded me that I needed to put my splint back on. I reluctantly reached for it, muttering, "You can do this for 80 percent. Come on."

The blinds in our room were closed, so I couldn't tell how far into the afternoon it was. The morning was long gone, a clear fact because the news shows were over. I turned the TV off but couldn't read or focus on anything. I needed a distraction, though, because my thoughts always veered back to the old topics. How I'd let down the convention center. How I'd let down Ethan because I could no longer help pay off our debt. That was a conversation we'd both avoided. I'd shown him the texts, and even if he hadn't known I'd been fired, he would have figured it out by the fact that I wasn't going to work, checking e-mail from the convention center, or doing any work from home. It was like we'd silently agreed to drop the subject until I'd recovered.

No matter how I argued with myself, I felt like I'd let down Ethan—and my parents—by not being able to bear a child.

My gaze landed on Ethan's nightstand and the cordless phone resting there, which he normally took out of the room so if it rang, it wouldn't bother me. I wouldn't have answered the phone if someone had called anyway, no matter who it was, so there was no point in having the phone nearby. Since my fall, I had communicated solely via Facebook, texts, and the occasional e-mail. Those were things I had at least a modicum of control over. I didn't do so well with thinking on my feet, talking in real time. Part of that was the haze of medication, but not all.

When I was forced to talk to anyone but Ethan, I couldn't help but wonder what they were really thinking about me. Did they pity me?

Please, no, don't let me be pitied.

For some reason, I couldn't help but stare at the phone. The little orange light at the top blinked on, then off. A pause. Then on and off. Pause. The light meant we had a voice message. I slowly made my way across the bed and reached for the phone to see who had called. Probably someone for Ethan. *Hopefully* someone for Ethan.

I scrolled through the caller ID. Ruby had called—twice. I didn't see anyone else on the list who would be likely to leave a message. I felt a surge of frustration at the idea of having to listen to Ruby's voice mail, even though I had no reason to be annoyed. If anything, she had a reason to be annoyed with me; she'd e-mailed about April's book-club meeting days ago, even asking if I'd pick the May selection, saying she'd decided that pre-assigned months might be a more organized way of keeping the club moving right along. I'd never gotten back to her.

I would be both leading the discussion and bringing refreshments. Heaven only knew what I'd end up bringing for that. Back in December, I'd been roped into helping make potato latkes because they fit well with the Chaim Potok book they'd chosen to read, and as the only Jew in the group, I was the only one who knew how to make them. But that was the only time we'd had something savory; every other month it had been a dessert. Good thing I had a couple of months to think about it. By then, I could probably bake whatever I was going to choose myself, rather than place an order at a bakery.

I pushed the button that played back the voice messages, wondering how long ago Ruby had called. There were two messages, both from Ruby. She was checking in on me with her cheery voice, wanting to see how I was doing after my surgery and whether she could count on me to come to the April meeting.

"Remember," she said in the second message, her tone sing-songy, "book group is around the corner! I can buy a copy of the book if you need it. Let me know how you're doing; I'd love to help out. Call me back!"

I deleted both messages, which said the same things as her e-mail. I stared at the silver phone in my hand. *Fine*, I thought. *I'll call her back.*

This was a big step, considering how much of a hermit I'd become over the last few weeks.

Dialing felt ridiculously hard, and my heart rate picked up as I waited for her to answer. The phone rang three times. I smiled, thinking the call would go to voice mail and I could leave my own message, but then Ruby picked up.

"Ilana?" she said.

I swallowed and girded up my loins. *It's a phone call. You used to make them every day at work.*

"Hi, Ruby. Sorry it's taken me awhile to call you back." The truth was, I'd totally glossed over the part of the recording that had said when she'd left her messages. It could have been a few hours ago or a few weeks. As she probably hadn't called from Greece, I was wagering it had been somewhere in between.

"No problem," Ruby said. The level of cheeriness in her tone felt like nails on a chalkboard. I needed something as relaxing as a getaway if that kind of excitement and happiness were the result. Ruby went on. "I'm sure you've been busy with work and keeping that husband of yours fed."

I didn't answer at first because I figured she had to be kidding. First off, this wasn't 1956. And Ethan would laugh when he heard that I was supposed to "keep him fed." Even if I wanted to cook for him, I wasn't well enough to do that yet. Ethan was taking care of me as much as he could, but I was practically an invalid. Some days I propped myself up with so many pillows to avoid the sling straining my neck that I looked like the Michelin man as I slept. Twice a week now I had grueling physical therapy that hurt so bad it made me cry. They kept making the splint straighter and straighter, and while I was glad to see improvement, every millimeter had been gained through a lot of effort and pain.

Then there was the reality that I no longer had a job. I'd forgotten that the group didn't know. "Actually, I'm not working for the convention center anymore."

"Oh? You changed convention centers?"

My stomach went sour. I leaned my head back against the pillows. "Uh, no. I lost my job." Had I seriously not told the book club about that? It seemed like a big thing to leave out; maybe Ruby had forgotten or had been out of the room when I'd mentioned it. Or had I? Maybe I hadn't. Hard to remember when my attention had been consumed by my arm the whole time. But as I thought back to the last meeting, I realized how little of my life I'd shared with them. How I'd hidden my pain and kept to myself. I hadn't talked about Ethan. Or how my mother was constantly on my case to live kosher and go to temple on Shabbat—and give her a grandbaby.

I hadn't told my own mother that I was infertile. I couldn't face her disappointment.

"Well, you'll probably find something soon enough." Ruby was trying to be my cheerleader, but her efforts fell flat. Maybe if I'd been up pounding the pavement, trying to find a new job—and a new dream—it would have worked.

"I'm taking it one day at time, so we'll see," I told her, staying vague. "I'm just working on getting completely healed."

"Is your elbow still bothering you?"

Normally, inquiring about someone's health wasn't a deeply personal probe, but with the whole hearing-loss incident and everything else, the question came a bit too close for comfort. "I still have a little pain, but that's to be expected."

Little was an outright lie, but I didn't want to reveal too much. "It was a pretty invasive operation."

I used to be one of those people who thought an out-patient procedure meant it wasn't serious, that the patient would bounce right back. I knew better now.

Yet maybe other patients in my situation recovered faster. Going in, I'd certainly assumed that a month out I'd be doing a lot better than I was. I hated where my life was. Who I'd turned into. I wanted to change but found myself pretty much living hour by hour, waiting until I could take my next dose of medication to dull the pain—all of it.

"Have you been in for a follow-up appointment?"

"Of course." I heard myself snap the words and instantly regretted it. Ruby was a sweet person with a genuine concern. I was just *so* tired and didn't want to explain things. My husband was an ER surgeon, and I wasn't stupid. Of course I'd been to a doctor. More than once, and more than one kind. "I'm still going to physical therapy. There's not much more anyone can do but wait."

Anyone, meaning me, the doctors, and the physical therapists. An entire team basically failing at returning me to health.

Ruby hemmed and hawed a bit, seeming unsure what to say. I jumped in to save her and to end the conversation because I could feel myself melting down, and if I didn't hang up soon, I might say something I'd really regret to kind, old Ruby. "I'm glad you're home safe from Greece, and I'll see you at the next book club."

She didn't reply. I had nothing else say, and fatigue wiped the slate of my brain. I hoped she'd take the hint and end the call.

After an awkward second or two, she spoke. "All right, dear. If there is anything I can do for you—"

"Some quiet and rest is about all I need," I said quickly. What I really needed was quiet, rest, *and* medication to keep me sedated enough to not want to chop off my arm with a pick ax. Before Ruby could gear up again on another topic, I said, "I've got to run. Talk to you later." I clicked the phone off and tossed it onto the comforter. I breathed out heavily and stared at the ceiling.

Had Ruby said some semblance of a good-bye? I hoped so; I didn't want to be the person who hung up on friends, but man, I was in no mood to talk to anyone, especially about the pain I was in. Pain was my world, and it made me impatient and rude. And those things made me hate myself.

Even after my arm healed as far as it would—to 80 percent or wherever—my world would still be made up of pain, but not the kind caused by broken bones and stitches. So much had to heal in my heart, but I couldn't imagine those wounds ever healing. I closed my eyes, pulled the comforter to my chin, and let hot tears leak from my eyes as I thought back to my three miscarriages and the children they still represented to me. The children who were lost to me forever.

Chapter 13

DAYS PASSED, ONE AFTER THE other. I hardly noticed what day of the week it was. I did tend to note the calendar date, as that helped me keep track of when I could refill my prescriptions. In spite of my best efforts, I took more pills than I told myself I would, always promising that for sure the pain would be better tomorrow, and I'd take fewer of them.

I'd gone back and forth over the last while with taking more than I should—although never close to the big dose I'd taken before—and trying to wean myself off the meds altogether, only to have the arm pain along with new, hideous headaches roar back like a freight train and flatten me.

Before I knew it, a week of April had come and gone. One day, as Ethan shaved, he asked offhand whether I'd read the book for Saturday's meeting.

"Yeah," I called back to our bathroom. "I have."

Yet somehow, I didn't want to go. Sure, I'd read the book, mostly because it was so short. Being laid up as I had been for weeks, I didn't have any excuse for not reading it, unless you counted the fog of medication.

But somewhere through the fog, I'd returned to reading; I could stand only so many game shows and other mind-numbing daytime television. I'd read *The War of Art* and a lot of other things. I'd even started buying audio books to listen to when my eyes felt strained or the light in my room was painful and made my growing headaches worse.

Pressfield's book was so short that I could have easily read it several times, but I hadn't. Just once. That had been more than enough, because although it had been a quick read and it had been inspiring at times, it tended to be guilt-inducing at others. By the end of it, I'd felt like a fraud and a failure and as if my dreams didn't matter. I *had* fought the war for them, and I'd lost. I would have thrown the book at the wall if it hadn't been on my Kindle. Instead, I'd held my thumb over a button, ready to delete the thing and get it off my e-reader. Had book group already met, I might have gone through with it too. But I needed to have it on hand to refer to, so I removed my thumb, turned off the device, and comforted myself with the thought that I could delete it the moment the meeting was over.

Two days later, as I got ready for that night's meeting, putting on makeup one-handed—I was getting better at that—Ethan came in and leaned against the bathroom door. "Want me to drive you again?"

I lowered the mascara wand and smiled at him through the mirror. "Tempting," I said. "We need some time together, don't we?"

He didn't get many evenings off. And here he was, home, and I was leaving. But he wanted me to go, so I was going.

"Yeah, but that's not why I offered," he said. "I'm totally fine driving if you aren't up to going so far on your own yet."

I'd driven myself to physical therapy appointments for weeks now, but the office was only ten minutes from home; Ruby lived more than a half hour away, and I had to go on freeways to get there.

"I'll be fine, but thanks." I walked over and gave him a kiss. Oh, he smelled good. I patted his shirt. "You order in and watch Vin Diesel blow something up."

He laughed and kissed me back. "I think I will."

After finishing my mascara, I swiped on a thin layer of lipstick. I gave Ethan another kiss—this one good-bye—and grabbed my purse, turning to see his lips pressed together and one eyebrow quirked as if he was reconsidering whether he dared let me make the round trip alone after all. Normally, that eyebrow made me want to kiss him like crazy. Right now, it meant he didn't trust me, and that made my insides go sour.

"What?" I said, slumping a bit.

"Are you sure about driving? When was the last time you took your pain meds? I don't want you driving on anything."

I looked straight into his eyes. "It's been *hours* since I took anything except Advil."

The truth, sort of. I'd taken several pills. My last dose of anything had been hours ago—three of them. I felt fine for driving, even though the medication was technically in my system. "Plus, I can steer just fine. I'm getting really good at doing stuff one-handed." I tried to smile widely to give him a strong sense of confidence. By the look on his face, he didn't buy it, but he didn't make a move to take my keys or stop me from leaving.

"All right," he said. "Be safe." And he waved.

I waved back and headed out the door.

Truth: I knew full well that I'd be in a lot of pain by the time book group ended, which meant I'd take a pill or two while I was there. I worried far more about driving home in crippling pain than I did about getting there in one piece while the painkillers were still semiworking. They didn't affect my driving. Not much, at least. I made a point to not drive in rush-hour traffic, and as long as the roads weren't too full, I did okay.

This time of day, I should be fine. I'll make sure I keep extra distance between me and the car ahead.

I closed the apartment door behind me and went to the elevator. As I waited for it, though, I looked down the hall at our door. I'd be able to manage the pain better at home, in bed, with my husband at my side. I was nearly out of pills and couldn't get a refill until Monday. I had enough to get me home from book club, but I had no idea how I'd survive the weekend; I'd taken too many pills this week and cursed myself for it.

I silently argued for both sides of the issue—going to book club would distract me from the pain temporarily. But would the extra exertion make the pain completely nightmarish tonight? If I stayed home, maybe I'd be able to *not* take my last three pills, which I'd planned to take at book club. That would keep me going a little longer. If I had those three pills in the morning, I could probably get through part of Sunday having nothing stronger than ibuprofen on hand without wanting to die.

Maybe I shouldn't go at all.

Or maybe it was time to find another doctor who would give me a third prescription to tide me over between the two I already had, which seemed to disappear before I had a chance to get relief. I wished I hadn't gotten Diane's refill yet and half wondered if we had another neighbor with an old bottle of pills they'd be willing to give me.

The elevator doors opened, but I just stood there, looking inside it. I'd about decided to go back home when my phone dinged with an incoming text. I pulled it out of my jeans pocket and opened the message, which was from Ethan.

Enjoy tonight. You're right. You need to go. You've been cooped up too long, and that's not healthy. You're always glad you went. Love ya.

"Yeah," I murmured, staring at the message. He was right; I did need time away with friends. But what if I ended up in so much pain that I needed Ethan to drive me home after all? That was a real possibility whether or not I took the three pills still in my purse.

The elevator doors started to close, but I stepped forward, blocking them with my body. They bumped my hip and opened again. I stepped inside, taking a deep breath. I could do this.

As I drove to Ruby's house, I eyed my purse and imagined my e-reader. *The War of Art* had been interesting in its own way. On one hand, it was intended for creative people, and I didn't consider myself a particularly creative person with a mission to make art. In a lot of ways, the book didn't apply to me. I wasn't a painter or a writer or a dancer or any other kind of artist. But it had been an interesting peek into the life of the artist mentality.

On the other hand, I still felt haunted by the feeling that I'd fought resistance, as the author called the opposition to dreams, and I'd been ground up and spit out as a result.

I arrived at Ruby's two minutes late, which was perfect; I didn't like being early to things like this. Better if others arrived before I did. Ruby welcomed me at the door with a short side hug, which was unusual for her, but she was clearly being considerate by avoiding contact with my arm.

"Oh, I'm so glad you came!" she exclaimed. It had to be hard for her to not give me a big bear hug; those were her MO. The thought made me smile. By the time I could be hugged like that, she'd be thrilled to do it. Would I still be coming then? I thought so. Hoped so. If Ethan had his way, I would be.

"Are you feeling all right?" Ruby asked.

"Of course," I said with a smile, trying not to react to the fact that I probably looked worse than a drowned rat. No makeup in the world could cover the circles under my eyes—unless it was stage makeup.

Maybe Tori could hook me up with some.

Ethan was pretty good at seeing tension around my eyes that indicated pain. Maybe Ruby recognized it too—from Phil's final illness, maybe. I seemed to remember hearing that cancer had taken him.

Ruby showed me to the living room, where Paige, Livvy, and Athena were already seated and talking.

I slipped onto a spot on the couch, which Ruby insisted I take instead of one of the metal chairs, and gave the other ladies a little wave when they looked over. I didn't want to interrupt their conversation about Ruby's trip to Greece. That was partly because I didn't want to admit that I hadn't paid attention to Ruby's e-mail updates, so I had no idea what they were talking about or who this Gabriel person was. But the other part of the reason was that the painkillers were wearing off. I was only half aware of the platter of food in front of me; one of the side effects of the Vicodin was nausea—something I was happy to experience, as I'd already lost five pounds since my surgery, even though I hadn't been working out. Not that I technically had much weight to lose.

So I sat there, acutely aware of the pain creeping back and not paying much attention to the others as they talked.

Ruby joined us and explained that Shannon wouldn't make it—something about filling in last minute for someone at the pharmacy. She finished with, "Has anyone heard from Tori lately?"

I hadn't, but that wasn't saying much; the most I kept up with were the latest seasons of reality TV shows from my bed. But Tori wasn't known for being late. Her punctuality was likely because of her television production job—I'd figured out from small talk that she worked on a reality show called *Vows*. She had to be on time or else. And she worked crazy hours. I wasn't sure how she'd found time for book club in the first place.

I didn't expect it at all when Livvy turned to me. "How's your arm? Any better?"

The question felt like she was waking me up. I sat straighter. "Oh, um . . ." I gestured toward the splint. "Still hurts. I'm in therapy, which is awful, but I'm making progress. My arm used to be at less than a ninety-degree angle." It wasn't straight in the splint, but it wasn't a right angle anymore either. "They hope I'll get at least half of my old mobility back. Optimistically, I could get up to 80 percent." My brow furrowed, and I looked between Livvy and Paige. "But I think I already told you that, didn't I?" I wasn't sure who I was addressing on that last bit. I could have told any of them.

Ruby had asked the whole book group to check up on me after the surgery, which was sweet, even if it had made me feel like a charity project. Did they really care? Their texts and e-mails seemed a bit too much like homework for me to take it all as being totally sincere. I had a feeling Paige really did care, even though I hardly knew her. Maybe it was being a mom that made her nurturing side come out. While I appreciated it, I couldn't figure out why else she'd care. Regardless, I couldn't keep straight who I'd told what to.

Athena leaned forward. "That's got to be pretty miserable, but I'm so glad you made it tonight. I was hoping you'd be here."

"Wh-why?" I asked.

"For your sake, for starters," Athena said. "But I also thought you'd have an interesting take on the book. You always have interesting comments."

Really? I didn't think I'd added much to the book club besides the occasional Jewish comment for the Potok book last year.

Livvy nodded and waved her hand in agreement. "Oh, you so do."

Paige nodded too.

Now it was my turn to quirk my eyebrow like Ethan had. What would I contribute tonight about this book? I had no deep insights into the creative arts. As the owner of a magazine, Athena had far more to say on the subject than I ever could. My mind rewound what Athena had said. Had she really said she'd liked my comments at past meetings? Maybe it was because of the Potok title. I had a memory of almost monopolizing the discussion at one point in December. That had to be it. They'd be sorely disappointed tonight; I had nothing to offer.

Right then, a set of headlights shone through the windows, and Ruby breathed a sigh of relief. "I'll bet that's Tori," Ruby said and hopped up to answer it. Sure enough, a minute later, the doorbell rang.

From the entryway, I heard a voice. "Mind if borrow your kitchen for a minute?" Tori's voice. She'd picked the book, so I was glad she was here to lead the discussion. I guessed she had aspirations of creating films of her own instead of helping others make them. Didn't just about everyone in southern California have a screenplay or four on a hard drive?

Be kind, I told myself. Tori had always been nice to me. And she was smart too. I would have bet that if anyone could get a screenplay bought or a film produced, it was Tori.

She and Ruby chatted as they headed to the kitchen with Tori's refreshments, and soon they returned. Ruby sat by me. She placed a hand on my knee and asked—again—if I was feeling all right.

"I'm fine," I said a bit curtly and winced at my tone.

Of course I didn't feel great; Ruby could obviously tell. To her credit, she removed her hand and nodded, dropping the subject as Tori entered wearing a wide smile that looked a bit too strained to be natural. Her feet were bare, and I suddenly wished I'd abandoned my boots by the door. Except that they had zippers, and there was no way I could get them off—or on again—without help. Ethan had helped me get them on.

"Hey there, everybody!" Tori said, her white teeth contrasting with her gorgeous cocoa skin. How old was she again? I thought we were close to the same age, but I was already developing crow's feet, and her entire face still looked like silk. She sat on a metal chair and placed her iPad beside her. Ruby took the cue and revealed her iPad, glowing with her new toy and her obvious familiarity with it as she tapped the screen like a pro.

She gestured toward the spread of Greek food on the table and insisted Tori take some. Tori added a few things to her plate but not much. I had to wonder what the catering was like on the set of her new reality dating show; maybe she was watching her calories tonight after eating a few too many cookies or éclairs during work.

"Thought you'd gone no-show on us," Athena said.

Tori laughed. "Yeah, well, you know how I like to make an entrance." She settled the plate of food on her lap but didn't eat any.

"It must be a side effect of working with all those egos in Hollywood," Livvy said with a grin.

Tori rubbed shoulders with important people, had stories she could tell of the most famous celebrities to grace the tabloids. There had been a time when I'd been a little important. I'd produced benefits and high-profile shows. Now I was an unemployed woman who spent her days in bed nursing her aching elbow. Arm. Heart.

"You're not lying there, Livvy," Tori said with an air of confidence—a confidence I recognized as something I too used to own. What had happened to me?

Oh yeah, you lost all your hopes and dreams and your body fell apart too.

Tears pricked my eyes. I took a deep breath and willed them away; the pain in my arm was already increasing. I'd need to be strong for the whole meeting, and thinking about what I'd lost would ruin the night.

When I'd first had the surgery, Dr. Root insisted that I'd be almost back to my old self by now, but my pain was becoming a bigger ball of wax than I'd ever expected. The emotional pain was almost worse than the physical pain, but both were numbed by my meds—something I viewed as nothing shy of a miracle, except for the awful fact that I had developed a tolerance to the painkillers. Five milligrams didn't register at all, and ten barely touched the pain.

I hated taking more than was recommended, mostly because I was probably entering dangerous territory. If the pain kept up at this level, I'd end up torching my liver. But what else was I to do? I had to cope somehow.

Tori went on about her job. "You would not believe the egos I've had to deal with recently. Those bikini-bottomed bimbos are killing me."

"I bet," Athena sympathized. She leaned back on the comfortable couch, nodding.

Ruby asked for details, but Tori waved off the chance to spill juicy Hollywood tidbits.

"Sorry, guys," Tori said, her eyes flickering with humor. "The almighty contract has forbidden me to speak of what I know. Ask me next season about what went on this season, and I'll be able to tell you some of it."

"Dang." Ruby snapped her fingers.

I smiled at that; the fake curse word sounded odd coming from her senior-citizen lips.

Too bad Tori couldn't spill any details. Hearing them would have been a fun way to distract myself from my dark thoughts and the escalating pain. The Vicodin had definitely worn completely off. I had to make a fist of my left hand and brace the other under my leg to keep myself from rocking back and forth.

"So let's get this party started!" Tori said. She wasted no time; she set her plate on the coffee table and opened the book on her iPad. "*The War of Art* by Steven Pressfield," she declared. "I'm really glad I read this book again." She paused and tilted her head as if realizing something. No one asked her why she'd paused, and I was in too much pain to think clearly enough to vocalize my thoughts, so I just listened as Tori went on.

"Really, the subtitle kind of takes away the mystery of why I was glad to have read it: *Break Through the Blocks & Win Your Inner Creative Battles*. I don't know how many of you know this, but I'm a writer. This is why I work in the film industry."

I knew it. She was one of the tens of thousands trying to make it in Hollywood as a screenwriter. *Good luck with that.* Then I caught myself. Again. *Stop being mean, even in your head. You already admitted that if anyone could make it in the film business, it would be someone as smart as Tori.*

Tori went on, her face growing more and more animated as she spoke; the forced look of her smile from before melted into genuine hopefulness as she spoke of her dream. "I don't want to direct film or produce it. I want to write it. I want to change people's lives and minds with the words I put into the mouths of good actors."

"Really?" Livvy said. "I love hearing about women chasing their dreams."

Which posed the question: why was Tori working on a reality show when she wanted to change people's lives with her own stories? I couldn't very well say that; it would sound rude. It sounded rude in my head, even though it was more from confusion on my part. I didn't say anything as Paige added her delighted surprise and the others chimed in with their hopes of Tori's success. I hoped that because I sat next to her, Tori wouldn't notice that I hadn't interjected anything. I couldn't; I felt as if my body would shatter if I so much as opened my mouth. I was barely hanging on to my sanity, trying not to moan with pain.

And, of course, that's when Tori looked at me—really studied me. Her eyebrows drew together, and I almost—almost—saw where wrinkles might develop one day on her forehead. Why was she looking at me like that? I tried to smile. I murmured something I hoped everyone would take as agreement, then added, "That's great." It was all I could do not to whimper at the end of the sentence.

Now that Tori was looking at me, everyone else seemed to as well. Why couldn't I blend in when I didn't want to be noticed? Did I look *that* bad, really? I'd run a pick through my hair before leaving. I couldn't style it much with one arm, so it didn't look as good as it usually did, but a bad hair night didn't justify their looks of concern. No one actually said anything as I forced my smile to stay plastered on my face.

"I'm really glad I read it," Tori said, crossing her legs the other direction. "And this is going to sound dumb, but the thing that struck me the most was something mentioned at the very beginning of the book." She turned to her iPad and found a spot she'd navigated to earlier. "There's a line here where it says it was easier for Hitler to start World War II than it was for him to face down a blank canvas every day." She went on about how she really wanted to be a writer, but she let her job on set take over her life to avoid the blank screen. "It keeps me so busy and leaves me such little time when I'm actively involved in filming that I can't be bothered with reaching out and achieving my dreams, you know?"

Wow. That was probably the most Tori had ever said about any book—or about herself—in any meeting. She was brave to open up like that. I wouldn't have dared. I'd rather stay in my little cocoon of an apartment and avoid people and places. I'd rather avoid ever applying for a job again so I didn't have to face explaining why I'd been fired.

Wait. Is that a kind of resistance?

Maybe. Even though I didn't have an artistic bone in my body, or my soul, for that matter. But the idea that an outside force constantly tried to keep anyone—including me—from doing what we knew in our hearts that we *should* be doing? That felt familiar. Real. Something I'd experienced every day for years and especially since my accident.

I used to face my dreams and chase them. Or rather, my *one* dream. Just one. But motherhood was denied me now, and I'd taken to letting resistance control my life so much, I couldn't even think enough to find a new dream or purpose for living. I was a pretty pathetic excuse for a wife of late too. Ethan deserved so much more than me.

I looked around the circle, and all the others were nodding. I found my head bobbing as well. Somehow, as different as we all were, we could all relate to resistance in the way Tori had described it. Maybe the others had figured it out before tonight, but I hadn't. I'd read it as a distant concept that didn't apply to me. I reached for my purse and pulled out my Kindle. I fingered the textured yellow cover. I'd have to reread the book with a different mindset. Maybe it could help me find a direction, a purpose in life beyond lying in bed and losing muscle mass while surviving minute to minute on pain medication.

Oh, the pain. Another wave rolled over me. I clenched the Kindle between my fingers.

Ruby spoke next. "There are lots of things I want to do," she said deliberately. "Maybe not artistic things, necessarily, but things I want just the same, and I let resistance get in my way. My whole life, I've let other things define me. I was the spouse who supported her husband in all of his stuff but never had a—" She stopped suddenly and flushed, to cover, I assumed, whatever she'd been about to say. She turned to her iPad and appeared to be looking for a quote she'd highlighted.

Livvy jumped in next, starting out with how just joining the book club had been a way to fight resistance. "And some of the things I thought had been holding me back were really nothing more than my own fears, insecurities, and excuses. By me taking charge of my own life, I found happiness. I found happiness in my marriage." She laughed and went on about how not even her marriage was exempt from struggles—and some days, she'd like to strangle her husband with his own tie—but the idea that she was *happy* in her marriage hit me like a brick in the head.

I'd been happy with Ethan for years. At least, relatively so, in the harried, stressful rush that had been our lives. I'd gone along assuming I was still happy with him. But was *he* happy with *me*? Our relationship was strained. Polite, helpful, considerate. He was as kind as ever. But things were strained. When was the last time either of us had confided in the other? Expressed real feelings? I didn't know if I'd told him how scared I was for either of my surgeries or how I felt empty, like a failure of a woman, an employee, a person. A wife.

Ruby sniffed. Her eyes looked glassy as she said in a trembling voice, "I'm so glad you've found happiness in your marriage, Olivia."

She must really miss her late husband, I thought. Poor Ruby, all alone.

Athena spoke up, saying that she didn't love the book, which surprised me because I thought a magazine was a creative thing and she'd relate. As she explained, my mind drifted away to Ethan's words from shortly after my hysterectomy.

If we're never parents, we can still have a good life. A happy life. A life filled with meaning. It'll just be a different meaning than we expected.

I couldn't help but think of Ruby's comment about her life being defined by others. Was Ruby's life one unlived? What dreams did she have? Had she chased them? Abandoned them? Fulfilled any of them? Maybe her life wasn't as charmed as I'd thought. I didn't want to end up her age, a widow, filled with regrets.

The pain in my body—not just my arm but every muscle, every bone—grew worse. I glanced at my purse, wishing I had something strong. But my purse had only a small bottle of Excedrin, Advil, and those few pills I'd need to get through the rest of the weekend. Somewhere in the recesses of my mind, I heard Livvy defending the book, explaining that a painting or work of literature could change perspectives and even history. I couldn't follow or add any of my two cents; I could hardly think straight. I blinked a few times and tried to refocus.

I did hear the last bit of Livvy's argument: "Art creates action in the person participating with the artist." That had to be profound in some way, but I'd have to think about it when my attention wasn't taken almost entirely by the throbbing ache pulsing through my body, radiating from my arm to every nerve ending in my toes and fingers. I could have sworn that even my hair hurt.

Somewhere through the fog, Paige put in her comments and said, "My favorite quote in the book was that resistance is directly proportional to love."

That certainly sounded profound, but it also made my heart hurt. Paige knew all about love; she had two treasures in the form of her sons, her own flesh and blood who loved and adored her as much as she loved and adored them. I'd never have that. Was my life destined to be one of resistance because I'd never experience that kind of love? My heart began to ache along with the rest of me.

The whole discussion was becoming too esoteric for my brain. There had been a time when I'd loved talking shop and digging into meanings, but tonight, all I could think of was the excruciating pain. Paige's comment had only made it worse, adding emotion to the physical hurt. I found myself rocking back and forth again—subtly, I hoped—in an effort to distract myself. It helped, but only a little.

My entire arm throbbed, and my head was pounding; I was done trying to follow the discussion. All I heard was resistance this and artist that. Half of me wanted the night to end already so I could curl up in a ball. Being on and friendly and positive took energy I didn't have. But at the same time, I didn't want to go home yet. Even though Ethan had offered to drive me here and back, he was on call, so there was a good chance he wasn't home, and the apartment would be dark and dreary. If he was home, I'd want to curl into his arms, but I knew I should talk to him and open up. But I wouldn't; I couldn't yet. Avoiding the elephant in the room was easier.

I had a sudden urge to watch an entire season of *Mythbusters*, head resting on Ethan's shoulder, with a big bowl of popcorn on his lap. But those nights seemed like they belonged to another life. Fertility treatments—especially unsuccessful ones—changed people. I knew I'd changed. So had he.

I need relief. If I could just get a few prescription-strength pills, the pain in my arm and my headache would ease. A bonus would be the fuzzy blurring of the world and the emotional pain, which was swelling beyond endurance.

I had to get to Monday. And when my current prescriptions ran out, could I convince Dr. Carter and Dr. Root to write new ones? I needed more time to heal, and then—I hoped—the pain would ease. Someone had to help me.

I caught both Livvy and Tori giving me an odd look, so I quickly stopped rocking and smiled at them. *Everything is fine*, I hoped my face said. Even though my entire left arm felt like a hot poker had been shoved into my elbow and the fiery heat radiated throughout my body.

I hated myself. I hated my body for refusing to heal. For being unable to perform the most natural of female functions. I hated Ethan for—well, I wasn't sure what for. I loved him. I did. But he was so infuriatingly *quiet* about everything. If he'd just yell or scream or punch a wall, I could relate to him more. If he'd do *anything* to show me he cared about the shattering of our dreams. He was almost *too* kind about his wife's body falling apart. About her falling apart emotionally as well. His concern about me driving on medication was the most he'd said to me in a long time.

With all the pain shooting through my body, I felt ready to throw up. Beads of cold sweat sprang onto my forehead, and I felt feverish. I shouldn't have come tonight. What had I been thinking? I'd hoped to be distracted by book club, by the discussion. To find a way to power through the pain. It wasn't working.

I finally decided to cry uncle; I had to leave the room, take a break, get a drink, and splash some water on my face. I raised a hand to speak. "Hey, um . . ." The voices around me quieted as I ran my fingers through my hair and then massaged my forehead. Paige looked concerned, and I had a horrible urge to tell her to go to her holy temple and be righteous so she didn't have to judge me. To be happy that she had two adorable kids. I'd cut off my arm to be a mother. I practically *had* lost an arm, and it sure as heck didn't give me any kind of reward like motherhood—or anything else.

Ruby leaned toward me and laid a hand on my arm. I wanted to throw it off; my body felt as if bugs were crawling all over it, and her hand was a giant beetle. I forced myself under control enough to speak, afraid I'd start dry heaving on Ruby's perfect white carpet at any moment. I needed a break—at least that splash of cool water on my face, a moment to rub my head with my one good hand in hopes of easing the pain there. Something to get me past this hump so I wouldn't take my last three pills. Maybe I'd take some ibuprofen and a couple of Excedrin tablets in case they helped. But what I really needed were a few Vicodin.

I felt like everyone could see right through me—disconcerting because I wasn't sure what they were seeing. I ran my fingers through my hair again and rubbed my forehead some more, wishing I could inject painkiller straight into my temples.

"Can I use your restroom?" I asked.

"Of course, dear," Ruby said, patting my arm. "A half bath is just down the hall past the kitchen."

"Thanks." I couldn't get out of the room fast enough, not with talk of love and the meaning of life—and the jolts of pain shooting through my body. I headed down the hall, hanging on to my purse as if it were a lifeline. I tried not to look at the others—I felt self-conscious enough without seeing their concerned expressions.

Fortunately, as soon as I'd left the room, the book talk started up again, with Paige leading the way. I didn't care what she was talking about. As I passed Tori, who sat at the edge by the hallway, she raised her eyebrows and smiled. What was the deal with everyone smiling all the time? What was this, Stepford?

Had I responded to Tori? I was vaguely aware that I should care, but for the moment, my priority was getting to the bathroom. Now. As I neared the half bath, I looked up the nearby staircase and made out what looked like the master bedroom at the top. I would have bet money that a master bath was attached. Ruby was getting on in years. A lot of seniors had aches and pains; Ruby had mentioned trouble with her joints. And her husband's cancer. How hard it was to control his pain in the end.

Maybe, just maybe, in Ruby's medicine cabinet . . .

I can't. Don't do it. You can last until you get a refill on Monday.

But I'm in so much pain. It would help calm me down. I'd be able to enjoy the rest of book club.

No. Don't even think of it.

As the argument went through my mind—almost like the classic angel on one shoulder and the devil on the other—I glanced back at the ladies to make sure they weren't watching. Quietly, I began climbing up the stairs, but I saw a flash of Tori's face and cringed, hoping she hadn't noticed that I'd gone upstairs instead of into the half bath.

Enough with the paranoia. Tori had probably been adjusting her position in her seat or something. It didn't matter anyway, as I was already moving into Ruby's bedroom. Instinctively, I flipped on the light and moved across the plush dark blue carpet toward the bathroom on the other side. In my haste, my foot caught on the edge of her wooden bed frame, and I nearly tumbled to the floor. At the last moment, I caught myself, but some of my weight landed on my left elbow, sending jolts of pain through me. Stars erupted in my vision.

After righting myself and catching my breath, steadying myself on the bathroom counter, I trained my eyes on the medicine cabinet. What if I found nothing there? What if I did? I could use just one pill, I assured myself. It would help me get through the evening so I could relax and maybe sleep tonight, take the edge off. I'd check the drawers and the dresser. I needed a pill to drive home safely; driving in blinding pain was more dangerous than driving with a slight Vicodin buzz.

With a quick tug of the latch, the mirrored door opened, revealing a classic brown-orange prescription bottle. My heart leapt with relief. I was lucky—no wasting time looking around, making the book club wonder where I was or getting suspicious. The bottle was nearly half full of white tablets. They could have been nearly anything, so I reached up on my tiptoes—I hated being so short—and pulled the bottle off the shelf.

Generic Percocet. Perfect. Something even stronger than Vicodin. The prescription was old and written out to Phillip. Ruby wouldn't miss a tablet or two when the bottle had belonged to her late husband anyway. I braced the bottle in my left hand and worked the top off with my right, something I was getting good at. The lid slipped in my fingers, and pills went flying all over the counter and into the sink. I frantically rescued the ones in the sink first; if even a few drops of water got the tablets wet, they'd make the pills dissolve. I collected three pills, then palmed them, wondering how many I should take. I tapped one more from the bottle.

I turned the sink on—low, to avoid the sound carrying downstairs— and drank just enough water to swallow all four tablets. Then I scurried to gather the rest of the pills, glancing at the bedroom door every few seconds to make sure no one had followed me. With the bottle half full again—or nearly so, minus four pills—I searched the sink and the floor and spotted one more pill on the floor beside the blue floor mat.

Phew. Glad I noticed that one. I was about to pop it back into the bottle but at the last second thought better of it and added it to the little bottle of meds in my purse. It would be my backup in case I needed it on top of my own three Vicodin. I put the bottle back into my purse, Ruby's back on her shelf, with the label facing to the right, as it had been when I first saw it, and gently closed the medicine cabinet.

I sighed heavily and tried to get my shoulders to relax; another thirty minutes, and I'd get some relief. The prospect was almost enough to feel the pain lessen. As I walked back down the stairs to the hall, I checked my watch to see what time it would be when I could expect actual relief—it was eight thirty now, so I could plan on the medicine kicking in around nine.

I can last that long. Thank heavens for friends.

As I reached the hall, I nearly ran into Tori. She looked startled to see me. I tried to erase any hint of guilt from my face by smiling as we passed. Good thing I'd reached the main floor before running into her.

I reentered the family room with a smile and a quiet "Thanks" to Ruby, then took my seat, leaned back, and willed myself to keep relaxing—a hard proposition in light of the pain. I could try to relax now, now that I *knew* relief—actual relief—was in sight. The gentle wave of medication would soon wash over my frayed emotional nerves as well, calming my anxiety, my anger, my sadness. My eyes strayed to the clock above the mantel.

Twenty-eight minutes.

Tori returned a few minutes later wearing a haunted look. Maybe she had a headache or had to take a call and got bad news from the set. Either way, she looked troubled, but I was too tired to worry about her. The other women would surely notice her distress and try to help her out. That's what being part of this book club was all about, right?

When the refreshments were brought out, I ate a donut with the rest of them. I laughed at all the right places, even though I still wasn't paying close attention to the conversation. The sheer sense of calm—the lack of excruciating pain accompanied by a stronger haze than I was used to—let me laugh and enjoy myself. I did hear Ruby talk about her trip to Greece and, instead of feeling jealous about it, decided to be happy for her. Maybe Ethan and I would go on a trip to Greece someday. It could happen.

When it was time to leave, I still felt a bit woozy; I wasn't used to this much Percocet like I was used to Vicodin. Similar medications, but this was stronger, a bit disorienting. I debated sticking around a bit to let some of it wear off so I could drive better, but no. I'd rather get home still feeling good and when I had a fighting chance of falling asleep while the medication still flowed through my veins. I'd still wake up in the middle of the night and have to stifle my groans, but if I hurried, I might be able to get home in time for a couple of hours of solid sleep before it wore off completely.

Before I could change my mind, I said my good-byes and left first, clutching my purse and picturing the pills inside.

I was so glad I'd come tonight. I hadn't expected to be helped in this way, but at least now I could muscle through tonight and the next day and reach Monday morning and my refill without going through torture first.

Things were definitely looking up.

Chapter 14

I HAD A ROUGH TIME driving home from book club; my brain felt like cotton. But I got home without getting into any kind of accident. I barely had the energy to get into my pajamas and climb into bed. I struggled against the height of the mattress and my splint. Two days ago, at my last PT appointment, the splint had been dried to a slightly straighter position, and my arm still ached with the new angle. I took the splint off and tossed it.

Just for tonight.

As I reached across with my right hand to rub the knots in my shoulder, I checked my alarm clock out of habit, calculating how long it had been since my last meds, the ones I'd taken at Ruby's house. Almost two hours. I could probably take a couple of Vicodin and be just fine—and maybe sleep all night. If I took anything else, tomorrow could be horrific. That's why I'd taken Ruby's pills—to tide me over.

I opted to take just one Vicodin so I'd have something in my system. The pain was always worse when I hadn't gotten enough sleep. As I swallowed the pill, I felt good about it; a restful night would give me the strength to get through Sunday without needing as many pills. I could tell tomorrow would be all right.

Another consideration that dangled in the back of my mind was that I wasn't sure how my body would react to the two different narcotics at the same time. Better to play it safe than to lose my hearing or discover some other freaky side effect the hard way. The last thing I needed was Ethan seeing me struggle with side effects. He had enough to worry about.

I pulled my blankets up to my chin and waited to drift off, trying to think of anything *but* the pain, but that was sort of like someone telling you to not think of a pink elephant, inevitably sending a pink elephant promptly into your head. Eventually, the Vicodin did kick in, and with the two medications overlapping, I was able to relax and slowly fall asleep.

Two lingering thoughts crossed my mind before I lost consciousness. First, how I probably should have worn my splint to bed—my physical therapist would be seriously annoyed if he knew I'd taken it off as soon as I'd come home, and I *did* want as much of that 80 percent as I could get. Second, that I should have set the pillow to prop me up because I'd wake up in a weird position with strained muscles. But I was too close to sleep to do anything about either thought.

Sometime later—I had no idea when, but it was pitch black in the room save for the lights of the alarm clocks—I was vaguely aware of Ethan coming home after being paged as the on-call resident around midnight. Somehow, he must have gotten away after the crisis was over. He kissed me on the forehead as he slipped into bed beside me. He edged closer and entangled his feet with mine. I smiled. His were so much warmer than mine, and his touch and warmth felt good. *I* felt good, even half-awake in the middle of the night. I breathed in and out happily and let sleep claim me again.

I'd set my cell phone to automatically go to do-not-disturb mode at eleven each night and to last until eight o'clock in the morning. Only Ethan's calls could come through during those hours, but when morning came, he slept beside me late, catching up on much-needed hours of shuteye after working at least an eighty-hour week, so I was quite sure I wouldn't be disturbed.

For some reason, when morning came, my phone rang and rang and rang. I pried an eye open. What time was it, and who in the world was calling me? I glared at the clock; sure enough, it was after eight—barely. The do-not-disturb mode had just turned off—the only reason the call had come through rather than going straight to voice mail.

Who would be calling me so early on a weekend morning? Maybe my parents or my brother? Maybe, with an emergency. I grunted and reached for my phone, figuring I might as well answer now that I was awake, but as I did so, I made a mental note to change my settings so calls went to voice mail after only four rings. My phone had always been set to ten because show floors were often noisy and I didn't always catch calls if they didn't ring longer than a few seconds.

My eyes were still blurry from sleep, so I only glanced at the caller ID when I answered but didn't recognize the number. "Hello." I was cranky and absolutely unapologetic about it.

"Hey, there. Ilana?"

"Yes . . ." Not a wrong number, then, and not family. I stretched my aching neck to one side.

"Hey, it's Tori . . . you know, from book club?"

Tori . . . from book club.

"Tori, right. Hi. What's up?" I cleared my throat, hoping the early morning frog was gone, and softened my tone. I'd answered as if Alexander himself were calling about how I'd messed up at work. He'd done that more than once even when I didn't lose an entire account or have a company threatening to sue.

Of course, Alexander would never again call to chew me out. As much as I hated his early morning calls, I suddenly missed them for the sole reason that it meant no job, no prospects, and one more loss to add to my list of things that had tanked.

"I was just thinking about you and hating that we really didn't get the chance to talk last night. I had some things going on with work that kept me pretty distracted."

That would explain the look on her face toward the end of the night. I'd nailed it—she'd almost certainly had to take a call or reply to a text after getting bad news.

She went on. "Anyway, I was thinking about you and your style."

My style? I used to have a style, but lately, I was a lump of T-shirts, yoga pants, and, if I was feeling particularly peppy, a cardigan. I couldn't help but sigh at another area of my life that had fallen so far.

I hadn't replied, but Tori rushed on. "Anyway, it's my mom's birthday coming up. I've been thinking a lot about my mom since we read the Henrietta Lacks story, and I really want this to be special. You always look so nice and have such great ideas about things. I was wondering if maybe you'd come with me to buy her a present. I would love some professional advice."

She stopped talking completely then, waiting for me to respond. I looked over at Ethan as if he'd be able to give me advice. He lay sprawled on the bed and was sleeping soundly, one foot still touching my calf. His hair was mussed up, and I had an unruly urge to run my fingers through it to mess it up some more.

Help her out? Me? Where was this going? I had to be missing something. I leaned against my pillow and rested my eyes. And remembered how I had only a few pills to get me to Monday. Overdoing it today would knock me down for the count.

"I don't know about today," I said, hedging. I sort of wanted to go, but leaving the comfort of my apartment felt unnerving. In the back of my mind, I could almost hear Ethan telling me that if I wasn't careful, I'd develop anxiety about going out, which could turn into full-blown agoraphobia. Even so, I wasn't ready to go out today. I needed time to get used to the idea. "Could we do it some other time . . . later?"

"Um . . . sure," Tori said. "I guess later would be okay. Her birthday isn't for a month."

I breathed a sigh of relief. I had a month before I had to give a firm answer—or find a good excuse to say no.

Tori went on. "I have to work all this week, and the hours are pretty intense, but you know, the show goes on hiatus in a few weeks. We could do it then."

"Hiatus?" Somewhere in my head, I knew that word, but I couldn't pull out the definition this close to waking up.

She explained that it was just a break from filming. I sat there for some time without replying, gently massaging my left arm. Did I want to go out with Tori? Was this a charity invitation? Or did she really want to see me?

I looked over at Ethan again. If he knew about Tori's invitation, he'd insist I go. That clinched it—at least as far as not turning her down entirely. "Okay," I finally said. "When you're on hiatus. Call me then." Not a direct acceptance of the invitation, but I hadn't turned her down either.

After a little light chitchat, she hung up, and I stared at the phone, still wondering at her calling me the morning after book club. There had to be a connection, but what?

The idea of getting out of the house did sound nice, and I'd always liked Tori—though if she could have a zit or two or gain a few pounds, I'd have liked her even more.

She thinks I have style?

I'd gathered that her schedule was too crazy to think about things like that. But the annoying thing was that her coloring was to die for; she didn't even need makeup. Sure, her hair was often pulled back into a curly bun or ponytail, but it looked like an intentional statement about simple beauty.

She thought I had style and wanted to spend time with me. I pictured Ethan saying, "Go. You need time out with a friend." That's exactly what he'd say, and he was right. I'd go, if Tori ever did call me back.

Chapter 15

ON MONDAY, I HAD ANOTHER follow-up appointment with Dr. Root. He seemed puzzled at why I still had so much post-operative pain. He ordered an additional set of x-rays and a CT scan just to be sure he hadn't missed any slivers of bone and to see if my elbow had another problem he hadn't detected earlier. I returned on Thursday to discuss the results.

"Ilana, how are we doing today?" Dr. Root asked as he opened the door and entered the examination room.

"All right, but I could be better," I said with a smile.

He closed the door, crossed to the stool, and folded his arms. "Unfortunately, the tests all came back normal."

"Okay . . . so now what?"

"I don't know what to tell you beyond the fact that your pain is certainly an odd animal. Every patient is different. Your body was already recovering from the trauma of another surgery. I'm sure the delay is because of that. It'll go away soon."

"But until then, what do I do about the pain?" What I needed was another prescription with a refill, but I worried he'd tell me to try biofeedback or acupuncture or yoga. "I can't handle it at this level much longer."

"I'll get you a new prescription for painkillers—no worries about that. We need to keep you comfortable and in as little stress as we can so your body can heal." He tapped his pen on his leg for a second as he stared at me, thinking. "I'm thinking it may be a good idea to put you on an antidepressant."

I tilted my head to one side. "Why?"

"Chronic pain can lead to depression quite easily, and based on your recent medical history, you've been under quite a lot of stress and pain. I would be surprised if you weren't also dealing with depression on top of everything else, and depression only exacerbates pain."

I nodded, agreeing with his assessment of my life—appreciating how he'd talked around my hysterectomy as "my recent history" instead of spelling it out. I'd take anything to feel better, to get out of the dark pit I sat in almost all the time, which had to mean that Dr. Root was right; I was suffering from depression.

Ethan was the only person who had managed to pull me out of my funk, and even he'd managed it only a few times. But maybe Tori would be the female friend I needed, the yin to Ethan's supportive male yang to help me keep going until the pain eased.

If I went on the antidepressant, I could hold on a little longer. "Sounds like a good idea," I said.

He nodded. "Great. I'll go write both of those up. Be right back."

Minutes later, I had two prescriptions in hand, one for a mild anti-depressant and the other for Vicodin at ten milligrams. I got them both filled, and as I drove home, I wished with every part of my soul that this nightmare would end soon. It had to, right? In the meantime, while the antidepressants built up in my system enough to work, my biggest job was to make sure I had enough painkillers until things got better.

Dr. Root had been the one to suggest a new prescription. I wanted to cheer at that fact alone. I'd dreaded having to come up with a good way to request one. If he was anything like Ethan, he kept himself suspicious of patients who asked for painkillers.

* * *

I didn't see Dr. Root or Dr. Carter for the next two weeks, but I did have two appointments a week for physical and occupational therapy.

Almost three weeks after starting on the antidepressant, I could feel a slight improvement. I hoped it would continue to get better, but as I drove to the physical therapist's office, I felt as grumpy as ever. I *hated* physical therapy.

As usual, Mark, the guy I was assigned to, had no clue about what pain meant. "Here, I'll just support the weight of your arm while it's bent, and you turn your forearm to the inside," he said. But he'd push the rotation farther than I could do it myself, making me cry out.

"Good. Now back to neutral. Hold it there for a second. And now let's rotate it to the outside." Again, excruciating pain rocked my body, but I didn't want him to think I was a wimp, so I bit back my groans through gritted teeth.

Mark went through other exercises, flexing and extending my arm in various ways and measuring how many degrees I could go compared to last time. He shook his head. "You know, you should be doing better than you are. Maybe you should come in three times a week."

"No, I'm sure I'll get better," I said quickly. "I can't afford three times a week anyway." I wasn't entirely sure whether that was true, but I wasn't going to find out. But no way would I come in more often for this guy to torture me.

His eyes narrowed as he folded his arms. "Are you doing your exercises at home?"

"Of course I am," I said and rolled my eyes. I *was* doing them. Just not every hour as he said I should.

What sane person would willingly put themselves into agony every single hour? That was nuts.

"Well, see if you can do more of them. That would really help my job. We don't want all the work we do here to stiffen up and go away when you're at home." He jotted something in my file and waved. "See you next week."

I waved back and grabbed my purse, eager to get out of there, away from this sadist. When I reached the car, I popped two pills into my mouth and downed them with some flat Diet Coke that still sat in the cup holder. But before putting the bottle of pills into my purse, I shook it. Only a couple of tablets remained. I opened the bottle and counted the pills, stunned at how few there were. Had I left some at home? Put some in a different bottle?

Or had I really gone through an entire month's worth of meds in two and a half weeks?

I swallowed, nervous. What now?

No sense worrying today. I worked hard in there and already took the pills. Therapy would make me sore and achy for the rest of the day. *I totally deserve them anyway*, I thought as I put the car into reverse and pulled out.

Right after I parked in the apartment's garage, my phone rang—Tori. Again. Ever since her show had gone on hiatus, she'd been calling and texting, trying to pin me down on a day to go shopping together.

I couldn't ever manage to just say no—not that she would have accepted a no anyway—but saying yes felt too scary. Even so, I got out of the car and answered as I headed inside. "Hello?"

"So are you up for a shopping trip?" Tori asked. "My mom's birthday is in a few days, and I desperately need to get that present."

I entered the elevator and leaned against the wall. The pills had just started their pleasant hum that blurred the edges of my reality. Part of my mind yelled that I was running low on pills again—Dr. Root's script was almost gone, and I couldn't refill it for another week. But the relief of the pills kicking in overrode my anxiety about leaving home. With my eyes closed, I sighed, enjoying the sensation of the meds, and found myself saying, "Sounds great."

"How about tomorrow? I was thinking South Coast Plaza, around eleven."

"Perfect. I'll be there," I said. I might regret it later. Or I might be really glad I went. Ethan would certainly be glad.

She suggested we meet by Bloomingdale's. I agreed and hung up with enough presence of mind to put the trip on my phone's calendar just in case I forgot. Tomorrow would be fun. I needed to focus on that fact rather than on the reality that I was going through pain meds like Pez candy.

Stupid body that needed so many strong drugs.

Chapter 16

I GINGERLY GOT OUT OF bed and managed a shower, all while trying not to wake Ethan. As long as I used my right arm to wash my hair and soap down, I did okay. My range of motion was getting better on my left arm, but not using the splint much yesterday—or last night—had probably set me back. I'd have to make a point of using it when I got home from shopping with Tori.

As I got ready, I found myself grateful that I could let my hair air dry, and it would look pretty good as long as I used a little mousse to encourage the curls. I got dressed, and as I was about to leave a note for Ethan, he woke up and saw me all showered and shined. He raised himself on one elbow, his hair askew, his eyes droopy. I loved it when he looked like a little boy.

"You look nice. Going somewhere?"

"Thank you, and yes, I am." I straightened my pink sweater and eyed my skinny jeans and brown boots. I did look good. "Tori from book club asked for my help picking out a birthday present for her mom. We're going to South Coast Plaza."

Ethan combed his fingers through his hair; now it stood completely on end. "Have fun. You guys will probably go out to lunch afterward, I'm guessing—girls' day out and all that."

"Maybe," I said, trying to remember what restaurants were in or near South Coast Plaza. I went to his side of the bed, gave him a good-bye kiss, and added, "You're off tomorrow, right? Let's do something fun."

"Great idea." Ethan squeezed my hand as I headed for the door. "You'll be back for dinner?"

"Oh, I'm sure." As fun as shopping would be, there was no way Tori and I would hang out that long. We didn't know each other well enough for that.

As I drove to the 405, I thought more about what Ethan had said. The idea of this being a girls' day out hadn't occurred to me—I was just helping out an acquaintance. Friend? I was doing her a favor. But I supposed he was right; women did more than shop when they got together; they typically went out to lunch too. I hadn't gone on a real girls' day out in so long I'd almost forgotten what they were like.

Traffic was light because it was a weekend morning, so I reached the mall ten minutes early. I got out of the car and headed toward Bloomingdale's, feeling that the day ahead looked brighter and brighter. This would be fun. Maybe it would distract me from the pain enough that I wouldn't even think about the pills stashed in my purse.

Once again, I was in the position of not having many prescription-strength pills left, so I'd put a handful of ibuprofen into the bottle as well—anything as a stopgap until I could get another refill from Dr. Carter. I felt like I was juggling time tables and schedules just to keep my sanity.

Shopping would serve as a great distraction. Not even watching Ellen's dancing could do that anymore. But when would the pain *end*? I remembered Dr. Root's observation that I seemed to be a special case. It was the first time in my life I didn't want to be "special" in any way, shape, or form. I just wanted my normal, pain-free life back. Until then, I'd continue living a life filled mostly with counting pills and hours between them and trying to distract myself from pain. If you could call that a life.

I reached Bloomingdale's before Tori, so I stood at the side of the store entrance and people-watched. Who in this mall had a pain they hid from the world? Any of the people passing me could have, and I'd have no clue. The mother pushing the double-wide stroller. The elderly couple riding the escalator. The forty-something woman coming out of Bloomingdale's with the classic brown bag with handles and "Medium Brown Bag" printed in big letters on the side. What did the bag contain? Was this a happy purchase, a celebration? Or was it more like the stupid boots I'd bought to console myself after my first surgery?

Then there were the teenagers wandering around, window shopping and grabbing snacks from the food court. They all pretended to be cool and aloof, but I knew that no adolescent was free of angst.

Any and all of them could be hiding a secret pain like I was. Looking at me, they wouldn't know I was miserable. I looked put together and classy, standing there outside the shiny, immaculate store with my nice ankle boots.

No one would peg me for someone who spent most of her days in bed because she hurt too much to get up and brush her teeth. We all had secret pains.

What is Tori's secret pain?

It was an odd question to pop into my head, but I wanted to know. Perhaps the day would come when she and I would grow close enough for her to tell me about her life and its struggles and how she dealt with them. About all I knew was that she was tired of the egos in Hollywood and had aspirations to write screenplays that would actually be produced. She wanted to be a writer, but she lived in an area swimming with wannabe writers. Every other waitress and cabby hoped they would be the one to break into the industry.

I'd heard people compare the creation of art to giving birth. Of course, that was something I'd never do.

If the comparison was apt, I had to wonder: was the pain of failing to create a viable screenplay anything like the pain I felt in the failure to create a baby?

Someday, I had no doubt, Tori would sell a screenplay. Maybe she'd win an Oscar for it. She was talented and determined and powerful.

But would my pain *ever* end? On and off, I worried that Dr. Root was wrong in his assertion that it would go away on its own. That sounded a bit too much like magic. When my body stabbed, when I could practically feel every nerve ending crying out, the emotional and spiritual pain over my loss of motherhood always came crashing after it. The one pain always followed the other.

I *needed* the pills. No ifs, ands, or buts about it.

Tori walked up wearing a fantastic pair of black jeans, a fitted black T-shirt, an off-white scarf, and big hoop earrings. I couldn't have pulled the outfit off.

"Look at you," I said. "You look fabulous."

Tori laughed, eyed her clothes, and shrugged. "I'm on set six days a week, sometimes for sixteen hours straight. I rarely wear anything nice or bother with accessories." She indicated the scarf and earrings. "Might as well feel almost like a woman one day out of the week, right? In spite of gorgeous fashion statements like this." She held up one foot, which had a blue brace on it. "You aren't the only lucky one to have an accident at work. I tripped over a dolly."

"Oh no," I said. "Are you in a lot of pain?"

"Fortunately, no. Aleve pretty much takes care of it. The medic on set gave me a prescription for something stronger if I felt I needed it, but I've been okay."

"You should totally let me borrow a few pills. Heaven knows Aleve isn't cutting it for my injury," I said, half joking. At least I hoped she'd know I was joking—yet I wouldn't turn down an offer. "What do you have?"

Tori gave me a funny look. "Lortab, but I think it's against the law to share prescriptions."

Of course it was illegal, technically. People did it all the time though.

I mentally made a note that she'd been given Lortab. That meant Vicodin—same medication, different name. Again, weird thing I knew thanks to being married to a doctor. I laughed and waved my hand so she'd know I wasn't that kind of person. She laughed along with me, which made relief flood through me.

"I haven't bothered filling it," she said. "The pain isn't that bad."

"Well, that's good." I envied her ability to control her pain with something as small as an over-the-counter remedy. It was definitely time to change topics. "So do you want to go in here first? Any idea what kind of thing your mom would like?"

Tori walked, limping slightly, into the department store, and I followed at her side. We wandered along the black-and-white checkered floor for a while. "I really am horrible at gifts," Tori said. "But this is Mom's fiftieth birthday. I need to get her something nice that she'll *like* for once."

We reached a makeup counter, where I stopped and looked around, on a mission for the perfect gift. "Tell me about your mother so we know where to start."

"Well, like I said, she's turning fifty." Tori held up her hands helplessly. "I . . . I'm seriously so bad at this stuff. She's my mom; I should know what she'd love. But she seems to have everything she wants. She's one of those people who always gets herself the things she needs so no one has a chance to buy her anything for birthdays or Christmas."

"Hmm," I said, thinking how my own mother loved digging into my life to find details—and how I actively worked on keeping up barriers so she wouldn't be able to learn those details. I shared what was shareable and kept the rest wrapped up in a secure vault. "Does she have any hobbies? Anything she loves learning about? Collecting?"

Tori's lips pursed to one side as she thought. "She loves plants, but she's pretty intense about what kinds she likes. She hates fake plants."

My mouth clamped shut again as I pondered. Then, "Does she like gardening?"

"Yes. A lot. But she already has the latest anything for her garden. She even has the accessories—gloves, shovels, knee pads, you name it."

"Perfume? Clothes?" I tried to think of more ideas. "Something to hang on a wall in her house. A cool decoration for her kitchen. Shoes." The ideas came out as a list, one after the other as I thought of them.

"Maybe . . ." Tori said, though I didn't know which idea she was replying to. She walked along the aisles, stopping here and there.

In an area where the classic checkered tile made way for classy cream tones, Tori stopped at a display of handbags. She grinned and walked over as if they drew her to them through their sheer beauty.

She stroked the side of one with a purple alligator print. "I love purses. For some women, it's shoes. For me, I could have a house full of purses and still want more." She nodded toward the purse she carried today—bright yellow with a quilted effect on the top.

"Would your mom like one?"

Tori considered. "Hmm. Maybe." She wandered around in the handbags, looking inside to check out the pockets and zippers, hitching them over her shoulder to see how they'd hang, almost like trying on shoes in front of a mirror.

She gathered four or five purses and "tried on" each. She'd gathered so many that I offered to help hold something to keep it all straight. "Oh, would you? Here, just take my purse so I don't get it tangled up with the rest."

The same moment she thrust her purse at me, she picked up a black-and-white number with a chain for the handle and slung it over her shoulder. She looked lost in paradise. This was Tori's personal Disneyland. I held her purse in front of me, smiling at how alive she looked. She tried on one handbag and then another, discarded several, went back to the racks, and picked more.

"I'll be over here," I said, indicating a chair. My energy was flagging; I needed a seat. "Can I put anything back for you first?"

"Those three there," Tori said, waving at some bags on the floor. "Thanks so much!"

I picked them up and returned them—I hoped—to where they belonged. Then I toted her loud-yellow purse with me to a chair a few feet off. Sitting felt like bliss. I silently cursed myself for wearing my ankle boots. Nothing good ever came from boots with heels, I decided.

Maybe it was time for some ibuprofen. I'd need at least four or five to make a dent. My mind went through the usual song and dance of weighing how many pills I still had against how long I needed them to last against how bad the pain was right now.

My forehead was already breaking out in a sweat, and the arm pain along with a raging headache were coming back, barreling toward me. My right hand instinctively went to my left arm to massage the pain away.

I glanced at Tori's purse in my lap. The top was unzipped, the insides clearly visible. People-watching was fascinating, but here I had a chance to see the real Tori. And keep myself distracted until she came back.

After that, I'd take several ibuprofen and hope for the best. And maybe I'd add half a Vicodin. I could spare that much. Maybe.

Without touching anything, I peered inside. A lipstick and two lip balms. A small tube of hand lotion. A purple wallet—that girl loved bright colors, no question. Her smart phone. Several pages folded in half. From what little I could see, they looked like set notes and to-do lists. A key chain.

And . . . my eyes stopped when they landed on a quarter sheet of paper. A prescription. For Lortab. This was what she'd been telling me about earlier. This was the prescription she didn't plan to fill because the doctor was overreacting and she was *fine*.

My mouth went dry. *She has access to medication she doesn't need. I don't have access to medication I really do need.* I breathed in, out, in, out, debating. *She won't miss it.*

Her purse wasn't a disaster, but it had enough messy stuff like random, crumpled receipts and gum wrappers that I suspected she wouldn't remember if the paper had actually been there if it suddenly disappeared.

As if I were part of the cast of *Mission: Impossible*, I looked around me, trying to act casual as I took in customers and workers and whether anyone—including Tori—was watching me. No one was. Yet I couldn't believe what I was doing. This went beyond taking a couple of pills from Ruby's bathroom, but I wouldn't have thought of doing this if I didn't really need the medication.

I unsnapped the opening to my purse with one hand. Then, with one quick move, I slipped the paper from Tori's purse into mine. My heart sped up so fast I went lightheaded for a minute. My hands felt cold.

"Hey, you okay?"

I jumped a bit when I heard Tori's voice. "Yeah. Yeah, I'm fine. Just got a bit of a head rush. Maybe I need to get something to eat."

"Great idea," Tori said. "Let's go to Charlie Palmer while we're in Bloomingdale's."

I stood, feeling shaky as I handed Tori's purse over—I could have sworn it felt lighter, even though a slip of paper was the only thing missing from it. "I've never eaten there. Let's do it. Did you find anything for your mom, then?"

"Nah. I realized after looking at about thirty handbags that she's never carried one in her life. Ever. It was fun for me, but I'd better get her something else. I'm sure I'll come up with an idea over lunch."

Chapter 17

THE REST OF THE DAY with Tori was pleasant enough, except for the time we walked right by a baby boutique, but we eventually landed on just the right gift for her mother. We said good-bye, and then I waited in the parking lot before pulling out and driving in the direction I knew she lived.

Eventually, I reached the Walgreens I believed was closest to Tori's apartment, assuming—hoping—that this was where she filled her prescriptions. Over the months I'd known her, she'd mentioned tiny things about running errands and whatnot, and she'd used Walgreens for those things. I could only hope this pharmacy had her insurance information. The last thing I needed was a red flag in the mind of a pharmacist or a tech if Tori didn't have insurance here; I couldn't exactly produce her insurance card or bill the prescription to mine.

I didn't go in right away; I just looked at the building and thought. Tori looked healthy; maybe she hadn't ever needed to get a prescription, so no pharmacy had her information. Then again, even a prescription allergy pill would have her coming to the pharmacy often enough for the workers to recognize her and know in an instant that the Jewish woman with the crazy hair wasn't the woman from Barbados. Or was it the Dominican Republic?

At least this wasn't either of the two pharmacies I'd been using with my other prescriptions. They'd know my face and probably remember what meds I got. Showing up with a script for someone else—and picking it up for them—wouldn't fly. Or maybe I was being paranoid.

I cringed, realizing how crazy all of it sounded when laid out like that. I was using different pharmacies just so no one suspected anything about legitimate prescriptions from actual doctors? There wasn't anything *to* suspect; I really did need the pills. But I feared my actions would look bad, so I'd gotten creative to avoid any raised eyebrows.

My fingers tightened, crinkling the paper. I was getting *really* creative now. If this worked, I'd have thirty-six new pills, plus one refill on this prescription too—technically a month apart, but I could probably get refills earlier if I paid cash.

That would be a last resort though. Paying with cash and paying without insurance were both red flags. Unfortunately, I knew these things, because ever since Ethan had gone off about junkies trying to get drugs, I'd surfed around online to see what real addicts did so I could be sure I wasn't one. That I didn't *look* like one.

Of course, I would never do some of the things real addicts did, like buy drugs on the street or order them online, all without a prescription. *Those things* crossed the line. I wasn't a junkie.

I glanced at the rectangle of paper in my hand—a prescription, yes, but not mine. *This is crossing a line too.*

But it was just this one time, twice counting the refill . . . if I even used it. After that, I'd be feeling better. I'd be okay. I knew it. How would anyone ever know?

Gathering my courage, I got out of the car and headed toward the store. *Tori. Tori. Tori.* I repeated her name over and over like a mantra so I'd remember to play the part, to answer to the name. Unless the pharmacy tech knew Tori, in which case, I'd pretend I was a friend picking it up for her.

Then I remembered: I'd have to produce photo ID to get it anyway. I *had* to pretend I was picking it up for her.

I reached the counter and handed over the paper. The tech, a thirty-something woman with a pixie haircut, looked it over. Her eyebrows went up. "You know Tori?"

I smiled, glad I'd assumed Tori would be recognized; the script was written out to *Victoria*. "Yeah. We're good friends," I said, glad I really did have a friend in Tori. "We met in a book club about what, six months or so ago now?" I nodded toward the prescription. "She had a nasty fall at work and sprained her ankle or something. I told her I'd fill this for her."

The tech, nodding, was already typing something into the computer, looking between the paper and the monitor. Why had I blabbered on like that? A normal person answers a simple question with a simple answer. I could have said plain old "yes." My little speech could have alerted her to something being wrong. I held my breath as she finished inputting whatever it was into the computer.

"It'll be ten minutes or so," she said.

"Okay, thanks." *It worked.* So far.

I turned around, facing the aisle of cold medicine and over-the-counter painkillers. *Should I wander the store, pretending I have something to shop for? Should I sit in one of the red chairs by the pharmacy?* I opted to wander the store, not wanting to be noticed or watched. I picked up a shopping basket from the end of an aisle, and as I headed toward the cosmetics section, I realized the pharmacy had a camera trained right at the spot where I'd been standing.

My lungs froze, and my breath came up short. *Breathe. Breathe. It's okay. No one ever looks at those things unless it's a robbery or something. Besides, there's nothing to see.*

With a nod to assure myself that my thoughts were the truth, I headed to the far wall, determined to buy myself a fun new nail polish.

Ten minutes later, I returned to the pharmacy, where they handed over a white paper bag with the receipt stapled to the top. I had to show them my ID, which I had ready to hand over.

I drove home in a hurry, heart pounding. With fear? With the thrill of not getting caught? And with the anticipation of relief—especially with relief over my supply lasting a bit longer.

Yes, that's what it was—anticipation.

Traffic built up on the freeway, slowing speeds sharply. The black SUV ahead of me stopped abruptly, and I slammed on my brakes just before my bumper could ram into its rear.

I sat there, shaking, my breath uneven. I'd nearly crashed. I could have died.

I need to get home. Away from the crowded street. A sense of claustrophobia came over me. *I need out, now.* Instead, traffic crawled forward, then stopped, went forward a few more feet or inches, and stopped again. I was stuck in multiple lanes of traffic that might as well have been a parking lot.

After a minute or two of creeping forward and stopping again, I found myself eying the paper bag on the passenger seat. My water bottle sat right next to me, half full. Taking one tablet now would relax me, help me get home.

Or it could get you dead in this kind of traffic. Even though I'd built up a pretty high resistance, my reaction time on Vicodin was still a little worse than without it. Six months ago, if I'd driven in this kind of rush hour on anything, I would have crashed into another car. Would have totaled it. Gotten really hurt.

But I *had* built up a tolerance, and I could focus on the road better when I wasn't hurting. Now that I was moving slowly, I'd drive better if I took a tablet. Just one. When traffic came to a standstill again, I quickly reached over, tore the top of the bag open, and tossed it aside. With practiced skill, my fingers whipped the bottle open. I purposely ignored the label with Tori's name.

I popped one pill into my mouth and washed it down with a few gulps of water. I hesitated, looking at the bottle, and opted for five more pills. The cars ahead of me moved again, so I balanced the pill bottle in one hand as I moved forward until I had to stop again. Then I quickly tapped out more, twisted the lid on, and tossed the bottle into my purse. I downed them with a single gulp from my water bottle. Gripping the steering wheel with both hands, I sighed and found myself smiling. I'd be okay soon.

The medication took longer than usual to kick in. But when it did, my reaction time was seriously impaired. Only then did I remember that while I'd driven on more than one pill, it had been only on slow roads, not the freeway. And never with six pills in my system.

Shoot.

I drove the rest of the way with my hand gripping the wheel for dear life. By the time I reached my exit, my heart pounded like a bass drum against my rib cage. As I veered onto the off-ramp—finally!—and headed toward the residential streets by our apartment building, the full strength of the medicine kicked in with its woozy warmth working its magic.

I pulled into the parking lot but had to circle it twice before finding a spot. When I did, I pulled in, but the front of the car didn't turn as fast as it was supposed to, and it bumped into a Corsica on one side. Startled, I braked, then put the car into reverse. My bumper had only nudged the other car's bumper. No harm done.

Even so, it took me three tries to get into the spot, and my parking job was pretty crooked. I got out, not caring. No way would I attempt a fourth try. Not when I was so tired and looped out.

I snagged my purse and water bottle, then stumbled out of the car and to the building doors. The loopiness had been just enough to impair my driving but not enough to take away all the pain, and I'd gotten home in one piece.

I'd probably need more medicine to get to sleep. Riding up the elevator, I leaned my head against the back wall and smiled. Good thing I had more right here in my purse. A minute later, I had my key out, ready to unlock the door, when it opened.

Ethan poked his head out, concern wrinkling his forehead. "You okay?"

"I'm fine." I had to push the words out of my mouth. I gave him a peck, then went inside, heading to the couch, where I dumped my purse and began searching through it for the pill bottle.

"Where were you?"

I paused in my search. "Shopping with Tori, remember?"

"That was this morning."

Shopping and lunch at Bloomingdale's café had taken longer than either of us had planned, true. But it was my detour to the pharmacy, combined with rush hour, that was to blame. A hand went to one hip. "I got caught in rush hour. It was a nightmare out there. Since when did you become my father anyway?" My voice sounded odd to my ears. *Stop talking; he'll know something's off.*

Ethan groaned with frustration. "I'm not trying to parent you. I just got worried. You said you'd be back around three, but it's almost dark out. And you weren't answering your phone or texts."

I'd put my phone on vibrate before lunch so as not to be disturbed. When I lifted the prescription from Tori's purse, I'd been so focused on it that I'd forgotten to turn the sound back on. I slipped the phone from its pocket in my purse. Four missed calls. Eleven texts.

I could have explained the situation—that my phone had been on vibrate and I hadn't heard it—but my defensive side had kicked in, and I fought back. "It's not like I could text you back behind the wheel."

I never text and drive, but I'll take a narcotic and drive? I silenced the thought as I slid the phone into my jeans pocket.

Ethan scrubbed a hand through his hair. "Here." In spite of his words, he came to me, and he didn't even look mad. Confused, I let him tilt my chin up to look at me. Maybe he wanted to kiss me because he was so relieved I was safe and sound. He didn't kiss me. He didn't apologize or hug me either. Instead, he studied my eyes.

"Pinpoints." The single word came out as a declaration, an accusation. He stalked to the table, kicked a chair free, and sat on it. "You were driving on pain meds, weren't you?"

My eyes tracked to the window and back to him. Had he seen my pathetic parking attempt? Before I could answer, he grunted.

"Why am I asking? Of course you were. You're on some powerful stuff, babe. You're playing with fire. If you aren't really careful, you could get addicted. In fact, you should be off them by now and could already be—"

"How *dare* you!" I almost whipped out my index finger to stab his chest with it but stopped myself in time. I was glad I hadn't found the pill bottle yet. If Ethan saw that I'd been about to take another pill—actually, two, but he definitely didn't need to know that—he'd say he was right, that I was an addict.

He's not right. I'm not an addict. I don't take pills just for fun. I take them for real pain.

I used that logic on him. "So we're talking addiction, right? Addicts take pills when they *aren't* in pain, right? I am *still* in a lot of pain, and you know it. Legitimate, horrible pain." The words came out sharp, like barbs. My vision grew blurry, and my nostrils flared with anger. "How could *I* be an addict?" I demanded. "Me? Your wife?"

Ethan stood there, staring at me as if trying to decide what to say. I could almost see wheels turning in his head as he thought. He licked his lips then said, "I'm sorry I said those things. Just . . . be careful, okay? I worry. I see a lot of scary stuff at work."

"I know." I nodded, wiped my eyes with one hand, and sniffed. "I'll be careful. I promise."

Ethan opened his arms and stepped forward. As he approached, I quietly dropped the bottle into my purse. This time he leaned down and gave me a deep, slow kiss. He pulled back and rested his forehead against mine. "I see too much at work. I guess I've started reading meanings into everything I see. I'm . . . I'm sorry I accused you of something like that. I should know you wouldn't abuse your meds."

Somehow I smiled and pressed a kiss to his lips. "I love you."

"Love you too."

"Do you want me to order in for dinner?" I asked.

His eyes lit up. "I'd love some Chinese."

"You got it." I smiled broadly. He squeezed my hand, then turned away and headed for our bedroom.

As soon as I heard the TV turn on, I dove for my purse, knocked two pills into my shaking palm, and downed them as fast as I could with my water bottle. I zipped my purse shut so he wouldn't see the bottle and then stashed the purse in a cupboard in the kitchen.

Trembling, I lowered myself to the couch, feeling a bizarre mix of euphoria and shame. I'd feel better—no, *great*—soon, but I'd basically lied to my husband. I was taking more medicine than I should. Taking meds that weren't even mine. I felt like a fraud.

I hadn't actually lied about the one important part. *I am not an addict.*

No way would I ever stoop to buying drugs off the street or anything like that.

Yet Tori's prescription bottle seemed to burn its way through my purse. Something in my head whispered that what I'd done wasn't much better than being a junkie on the street. But I *wasn't* a junkie on the street. I was better than that.

Even so, I could have sworn the pill bottle glowed, taunting me through the cupboard.

Let it. I'll take the pills anyway.

The thought felt like a victory.

Chapter 18

ONLY A COUPLE OF DAYS later, Tori called again, this time inviting me to go out to dinner with her Monday night. "I know this great little bistro you'd just love," she said.

I didn't answer right away. Why did she want to see me again so soon? It wasn't like we'd totally bonded over the chocolate cheesecake at lunch. In spite of that, I found myself tapping my phone to check the calendar. We'd had fun, and I'd enjoyed the day out.

My next physical therapy appointment wasn't until Tuesday. Even if I didn't keep putting off applying for a new job, Monday night was clear. Ethan worked the late shift then anyway.

"Sounds great," I said. "Can you send me a link to the restaurant so I can find the address?" I liked looking at the menu and programming my GPS with the address in advance. It might have looked a bit overcontrolling, but when I had so little control over every other aspect of my life, the little things counted.

"I'll e-mail you the website so you can see the menu," Tori said. "But I'm happy to pick you up. How about six?"

Dinner *and* a ride? Why was she being so friendly and helpful? Maybe she'd really enjoyed our shopping trip. Or maybe . . .

A little alarm bell went off in my head, and as the realization dawned on me, my heart rate sped up. What if she'd noticed her missing prescription—and knew I'd taken it?

"Oh, wait. Hold on," I said, as if I'd noticed a conflict with Monday after all. "Hmm. Maybe Monday isn't the best time. How about a rain check? We can figure out a better date at book club." I could put her off that long. In my heart, I really wanted to hang out with Tori. She was fun and kind and everything I wanted in a girlfriend.

"What do you have going on that night?" Tori pressed. "I was really looking forward to seeing you. I've been stuck on the set with actors who have egos the size of the Pacific; I need another break and some conversation with someone who's normal." She laughed. "I have the rare Monday night off, and I'm going to do something fun with it."

I sat back, surprised. Maybe she *hadn't* noticed that the prescription was missing. Her purse *had* been a mess. Maybe she really did want to have a night of girl talk. "I may be able to sneak dinner in," I hedged. "I'll pencil it in."

"Pick you up at six, then? That way we'll get in before the worst of the dinner crowd." Her voice sounded awfully bright.

I hesitated for just a second but talked myself into accepting. "Sounds great. See you then." I hung up, feeling an odd collection of emotions braiding themselves into a thick cord. I'd joined the book club in hopes of meeting a few women so that when I wasn't working marathon hours before a show I'd have something to do besides sit at home alone while Ethan covered his shift. Months later—now that I needed a good friend more than ever—Tori was giving me an opportunity to connect.

I could connect just as well with old friends on Facebook, I argued, biting my lower lip while staring at my phone. We'd moved to this area for Ethan's job, but it was far from family and friends. I'd devoted so much of my energy to work and fertility treatments that I'd fallen off the wagon of being a friend anyway; my old college roommates weren't contacting me anymore, not after I'd spaced replying to their e-mails or texts. I didn't blame them.

I almost called Tori back, but the thought of having a real, in-person, live friend to hang out with won the day.

* * *

Monday night, I got myself ready as best I could; my left arm had more mobility than it used to, and I could take it out of the splint more often, so doing my hair was a little easier than before. I managed a ponytail before my arm protested so loudly that I popped four Vicodin.

Tori was driving. I didn't need to avoid pills on account of being behind the wheel. Besides, this was a girls' night out; I deserved to feel good. I deserved every single tablet.

She picked me up right at six o'clock, and we headed to the bistro, with Tori oddly quiet as she drove. I thought back to past book-club meetings and to lunch last week. The Tori I'd always known was talkative and lively. The one driving tonight was deep in thought and on edge. When a car honked, she about jumped out of her seat.

"You okay?" I asked after she settled down.

She sketched an anxious glance at me. "Yeah. I'm fine." And then she flashed me a big, fake smile.

I smiled back, confused. Maybe something was up in her life. Maybe she wasn't on set right now because she'd lost her job and she needed to commiserate about being unemployed. Maybe her injury was worse than she'd let on. Which brought me back to the prescription worry. If she'd reconsidered and decided to fill it but couldn't find it . . .

But Tori never said a word about her injury or the script, not as she drove or parked or as we walked into the bistro. Not when we ordered or ate. She did break the silence here and there—thank heavens. I would have started pulling my hair out if she'd kept her mouth shut the whole time. I couldn't fill in the gaps all alone, especially when my brain worked at half speed because of the four pills. They'd kicked in, thankfully, so I was feeling pretty good. I kept up my side of the conversation, laughing, sharing stories, and relaxing. Tori never seemed to relax entirely, and she didn't open up either. Everything seemed surface level.

She paid the tab in spite of my protests. As far as she knew, I was the wife of an ER surgeon and was rich; she didn't know about all the medical bills and the still-unpaid-for med school loans. But she wouldn't let me pay. Something akin to guilt crossed her face as she signed the receipt and we stood to go.

I glanced at my watch. I didn't want to go home yet, but I had no reason to hang out with Tori any longer—not that she was the best company tonight.

At least she didn't ask about the prescription. That would have been awkward. Wordlessly, we headed back to her car and got in.

As she backed out, she said, "Up for another stop before I take you home?"

I shrugged and smiled. "Sure," I said, pleased Tori was eager to hang out a bit more—and glad I wouldn't be facing the dark apartment alone quite yet.

Maybe she'd take me to meet someone in the cast or crew. Or to a bar where celebrities hung out. I couldn't help but admire her life working on a big-time television show—one I'd seen before. Okay, I'd seen the entire season so far; I was hooked. In my defense, there wasn't much else but the TV to keep me occupied and my mind distracted from the constant pain. But as Tori drove through busy city streets and I relaxed in the glow of street lights and traffic signals, I wasn't about to admit that I'd watched every single episode. Including every one of them from past seasons that were available to stream.

I rested my head against the back of the seat, closing my eyes and not paying much attention to where we were going. I was trying to focus on the comforting buzz the meds still gave me. Tori had put on a relaxing playlist with songs by Kenny G and Enya. The music, coupled with the hum of the car on the road, almost lulled me to sleep.

Next thing I knew, the car had stopped. As Tori pulled her keys from the ignition, my eyes opened, and I tried to grasp where we were. Not a club or a movie theater or any other place I would have expected—not even a cool gallery open late or an independent bookstore, which had been my later guesses because of our book-club connection.

Instead, I made out a big, shadowy building with tall windows that came to arching points at the tops. And some stained glass. What it was didn't register; obviously, I wasn't entirely awake or functioning at full brain capacity. I had enough wherewithal to unbuckle, grab my purse, and get out of the car, hurrying to catch up with Tori, who was walking quickly down a sidewalk. She glanced back to be sure I was following, and when she saw that I was, she stopped to wait, then put on an overly cheery smile.

"Come on," she said as I came up even with her.

I paused and looked up at the building again now that I was close to it. With my face lifted to the sky, I finally noted one significant detail about the structure—it had a cross on top of it. A jolt of something—fear, anxiety?—shot through me, and I took a step back.

"I'm not Christian, remember?" I said.

"I know," Tori said. "I'm not trying to convert you or anything." She smiled bigger, but it didn't look any less fake.

I hesitated for a few seconds, trying to decide what to do. It wasn't like I could walk off and drive myself home; I was sort of stuck until Tori agreed to drive me. Unless I called a cab.

That's when I noticed a woman standing just out of view, in the dark. She looked familiar, but with the moonlight casting odd shadows, I wasn't sure where I'd seen her before. She stepped close, and light fell onto her face. Shannon.

"Okay, Captain," Tori said to Shannon. "Lead on."

The two of them had obviously planned something, but what? Had Tori invited me out to dinner as a ploy to get me to this church? If so, why? To make me believe in God?

"Hi, Ilana," Shannon said.

I couldn't answer. Instead, I glared at Tori, who looked to be trying awfully hard to avoid my eyes.

Shannon went on. "I found a place we can talk."

"Talk?" I repeated. About what? "I don't understand." My heart rate picked up. I wanted to run home and into Ethan's arms.

Shannon headed for the church doors, and Tori took a step in that direction as well, but my feet felt glued to the concrete. Someone needed to explain.

I still wanted to whirl around and run away, but the logical part of my brain asked why I had this sudden need to flee. These were my *friends*, right? Not close friends, maybe, but the only ones I'd turned to recently. They wouldn't be out to get me, to make me join some cult or otherwise hurt me.

Even so, Tori had to nudge me forward to make my shoes leave the ground and step forward. She walked behind me as I followed Shannon, almost as if making sure I'd actually go in.

I felt cornered. What were they up to? I wished I'd been more involved with the book club. That I would have joined earlier, attended the January meeting, and participated in the discussions more. Maybe then I'd know these two women better, and I wouldn't feel so weird. But I would have participated more lately if I hadn't been in so much pain that even my teeth hurt.

My pain. My surgery. Maybe they were trying to befriend me because they knew I was struggling.

With Tori still behind me, I followed Shannon down a hall and around a corner. She looked comfortable in the building, like she knew exactly where we were going.

Again, I couldn't help but wonder, where?

And why?

Chapter 19

I GLANCED AT MY WATCH and turned to look at Tori behind me. "I really should get home." An outright lie. Ethan wouldn't be back for hours yet. But the farther down the hall I went, the more my nerves turned on high alert; I could feel adrenaline kicking in, yet I still didn't know why.

Tori wordlessly took my good arm and gently led me to a room with a bench and chairs. One side had a wooden crucifix hanging on the wall. I turned my eyes away; those things always gave me the creeps. I never liked the scrawny bodies, the woeful expression that was on so many I'd seen. If I were Christian, I'd want to worship a God who was strong and powerful—even in death.

Yet the pained look in the eyes of the Christ figure on this crucifix looked a bit too familiar—I'd seen that expression staring back at me from the mirror more than once.

Shannon was already sitting; she indicated a seat opposite her for me. I swallowed and slid onto a metal chair, grateful the crucifix was behind me. I started to sweat, and I wasn't at all sure it was because of the heat in the room. I felt as if the Christian god on the crucifix was staring at my back, boring into my soul.

Shannon pulled out her cell phone and silenced it; I followed suit to be polite but wished I'd driven myself to dinner after all. I could have done it without getting in a crash.

I could still look up a taxi service, but not without looking rude. Maybe in a few minutes. I'd watch for a good opportunity.

Shannon leaned toward me and smiled, but I didn't trust it. "Ilana," she said. "I'm sorry for the trick we played to get you here."

It *was* a trick. I snatched my purse from the floor, ready to run out the door and find a cab, when Shannon went on.

"But we're really worried about you."

Friends, I reminded myself. *These are friends.* I looked over at Tori, who nodded in agreement. Her eyes were even a little glassy. They cared. Really cared about me. I couldn't quite grasp it. Or why. None of this made any sense.

I let my purse settle onto my lap and slowly sank back into my chair. "Worried about me?" I turned to Tori for answers; she was the one who'd brought me here. "What are you talking about?"

"I know you took some of Ruby's pain pills last month," Tori said. "I found one on the floor of the bathroom after you left."

My eyes widened, and my mouth dried up. But the wheels in my mind spun, coming up with explanations and excuses. It was all very logical, I'd say. I was a day away from getting my prescription renewed— at least, I'd thought I was that night, so it wasn't a lie, not really. I'd been in so much pain. And it was *one* pill.

That they knew of.

"Percocet," Shannon added. "From a prescription bottle in Ruby's master bathroom."

A pill found on the floor of a room I'd been in didn't mean I'd taken others. Where did they get off suspecting that? It may have been the truth, but it sure took some gall on their part to jump to conclusions.

But then my gaze flipped to Shannon as I tried to piece it all together. If this was about Ruby's outdated medication, why wasn't *she* here? And then it finally hit me.

Shannon is a pharmacist. She knows what pills look like. She had a professional duty to turn me in. But *how* did Shannon know I'd taken anything? If I admitted to taking a pill, they could report me to the police. Which was ridiculous. Sure, people weren't supposed to share medications, but what household *didn't* share a pill or two every so often? It wasn't a big deal.

Better play dumb. They can't prove anything.

"I don't know what you're talking about," I said, picking tiny balls of lint from my slacks. I felt my nostrils flare and my cheeks grow hot with anger—and fear. Had they told any of this to Ethan? What would happen to his career if word got out that his wife had shared someone else's prescription pills without permission? I wasn't about to agree that

I'd *stolen* them. That sounded far worse than the reality, as if I were some kind of thug.

Enough. I had to get out of there. I slung my purse over my right shoulder, ready to stalk out, but I hadn't risen more than a few inches from my seat when Tori put her arm around me and urged me back down. The pressure didn't hurt, but there was a no-nonsense edge to it—and to the look in Tori's eyes. She was serious about this. Back on my chair, I sat there, my mouth opening and closing as I tried to figure out what to say.

Shannon leaned closer, hands together as if she was pleading with me. "There's a meeting going on in the next room," she said, nodding behind me. "And I'd like you to attend it with us. Then we'll talk, and we'll take you home."

My heart felt ready to pound right out of my chest. "I don't have to stay." My voice had a tinny quality; it didn't sound like me. I looked back and forth between Tori and Shannon, begging them to just let this go. What if a cop was in the other room? Some "meeting" *that* would be. "I can call my husband to come get me right now," I said, voice rising. "You can't do this!"

Nothing I did or said ruffled Tori's calm. "You *can* call your husband, Ilana," she said. Her tone was kind, warm. I took a deep breath, hoping I was overreacting. "But we're trying to do you a favor. We could just have easily gone to your husband about this or your doctors or the police."

"You're *threatening* me?" So much for kindness. So much for friendship. "You have no proof of anything, and you're threatening me. Great. I just—I need to go." I headed for the door, but Shannon called after me.

"It's illegal to possess someone else's prescription."

Her words stopped me cold. I'd never possessed *Ruby's* prescription.

"That includes the paper script and the actual fulfilled product," Shannon went on, speaking to my back.

Tori's prescription. Oh no. No, no, no, no, no.

I slowly turned around to face them, feeling my once-hot face drain. This wasn't just about me taking some of Ruby's old pills. They knew I'd found and filled Tori's prescription too.

I felt weak as fear gripped my windpipe. I pictured Ethan sitting in a courtroom, watching a judge pronounce a sentence on me. What would that do to his career and his reputation? He'd be in our sad little apartment alone, with nothing but our debts for company. And I'd be where—in jail?

Was this kind of crime a misdemeanor or a felony? *Crime*. It wasn't that bad. Couldn't be. It wasn't like I was shooting up with diseased needles, looting department stores, or hurting other people. I didn't sell baggies of meth on the street to feed an addiction.

No. *I* had a life. *I* was educated. Upper middle-class. I'd had a great job. I wasn't homeless. I had nice clothes and a husband and . . .

And I *wasn't* an addict.

But I could still be nailed on those charges. I stared at Tori, begging her to save me from this. She probably had enough evidence to lock me up. She'd surely found out her prescription had already been filled—while I'd hoped she'd assumed it had fallen out of her messy purse or been buried beneath receipts and gum wrappers. My driver's license number was recorded in some database as the person who'd picked it up. A search would show that I was the person who had the pills.

Tori smiled at me. How could she *smile*?

Through the panic of the thoughts of crime and jail, the realization of what this all really was hit me—Tori and Shannon were trying to do an intervention. That's what this was. I felt my jaw go slack and my eyes widen. I almost looked around for the cameras, sure this couldn't be real. Tori worked for a reality show, right? Maybe this was a setup, a lame attempt to produce her own show.

Was Ethan in the other room—not at work in the ER at all—waiting to confront me?

Please, no, I begged . . . Something. I straightened, dismissing the thought of prayer yet again. Today, God, if there was one, had abandoned me. I'd get out of this on my own. Somehow.

If Ethan was home, how would I get myself out of this mess? The look on my husband's face if he heard or already knew . . .

As I gripped my purse, the knuckles on that hand went white. They waited for me to answer. I struggled to find words. I couldn't deny everything; they knew. I couldn't argue or pretend or undo my actions. My only options were to go along with whatever charade they expected of me and then find the path of least resistance—the path of least damage. And figure out a logical explanation for my actions that didn't involve crime or addiction.

Shannon walked toward the door, paused, and motioned for Tori and me to follow. I looked back at Tori, pleading with my eyes for her to get me out of this. Instead, she smiled again and waved me along in front of her. Robotic, I pivoted forward and forced myself to take one step and then another.

I'm trapped between them again. Great.

Shannon showed us into a larger room filled with rows of chairs. She stopped at the edge of an aisle, where a young man smiled a greeting and stood, making room for us to sit in the exactly three seats that were empty next to him. Shannon knew this guy. And he'd saved us seats? He looked barely out of high school; how did he know Shannon? I shot him a suspicious look as I scooted past him and sat beside Shannon. Of course, I ended up sandwiched between Tori and her, with the young man on the end. If I wanted to leave—if I needed to get out—I wouldn't be able to. My hands started shaking at the thought.

My arm throbbed, and I found myself doing the back and forth rocking motion that tended to help the pain—something I found myself doing the rare times I was in public. I didn't notice it at first, not until Tori turned my way, looked me up and down, and raised her brows. She'd noticed the movement and likely thought I was having withdrawals or whatever. I forced myself to stop moving.

A woman began the meeting of Narcotics Anonymous. I cringed at the name, even though I'd guessed that this was a support group for junkies. Against my will, I noticed several other people sitting in the room, and to my chagrin, not one was covered in piercings or tattoos. None looked homeless or in desperate need of a shower.

They looked alarmingly *normal*.

The woman let attendees know about upcoming events—as if I wanted to ever see these people again, normal looking or not—then set her note aside and spoke about a party she'd attended for work.

"You'll all be proud to know that I drank iced tea instead of wine."

The room erupted in cheers. Grinning, she raised her hands over her head like Rocky, as if she'd conquered the world.

Maybe she has. Where had she been? How low had she sunk? I wanted to hear her story as much as I wanted to cover my ears and tune out the entire meeting. After a few more remarks, the woman gave the floor to the attendees.

The young man in our aisle—the guy who'd saved our seats and had looked for all the world like an honors student—stood and headed to the front.

He must have a druggie parent, I decided. *Poor kid.*

He took the microphone and held it with confidence as he said, "Hi, my name is David, and I'm an addict."

My mind whirled. *Wait. He* is the addict?

"Hi, David," the audience said back, just like I'd seen in movies.

He grabbed the sides of the podium as if he needed the support. He scanned the crowd; I might have imagined it, but I thought he looked directly at me for a moment. "Life is hard," he said, his voice filled with pain. "And each one of us encounters things in our own lives that we simply can't handle. It's not because we're stupid or weak or less than someone else; it's simply a fact that every person in the world deals with things that are too much."

He was right about that; in the last few months, I'd faced far more than I could handle; I was crumbling from the inside out.

"And when we encounter these things," he went on, "we are offered a variety of ways to cope with them. Some people find that faith in a higher being can lift them just enough that they can keep moving forward."

Not me. Obviously.

"Some people have a special relationship with someone else, some-one stronger who can carry them through."

That had been me for a time. I'd relied on Ethan during the years we'd tried to conceive. We'd been in that fight together; we'd leaned on each other. But lately, problems and trials seemed to be heaped on *my* head, not Ethan's. I felt so alone; he couldn't understand, no matter how much he wanted to. Everything I used to define myself with was gone—my womanhood and potential to carry a child, my job, my body and its health, heck, even its ability to do something as simple as get dressed without pain or sometimes without help.

David kept going, speaking with a tone of wisdom that seemed far older than his years. "And some people find a bottle of one kind or another that takes just enough of the edge off for them to survive."

I'd found a bottle to help. Not one with wine or vodka. Rather, several small bottles, all orange-brown with white caps. I swallowed against the knot growing in my throat.

But I am not an addict.

"For me, I found a pipe. The stuff I put into the end of that pipe softened the edges of the hard things I *couldn't* handle anymore. It was such a relief to get a break, ya know, to simply inhale deeply and feel as though I were suspended above the garbage instead of sinking into it."

His voice seemed to fade into the background as my thoughts went in circles, around and around, my life over the last months coming into focus with a frightening clarity. Each pill I'd taken had given me just what this David kid had described: relief, a break from the "hard edges" of the unrelenting pain. Pain that was, now that I allowed myself to really think about it, just as emotional as it was physical. Maybe *more* emotional.

My body certainly had pain; there was no denying that. But some days—okay, *most* days—I could justify taking a pill even when my arm wasn't so bad. It always made me feel better. I could go on, take another step, and greet Ethan with a smile when he came in the door. The warm buzz, the thickness of my thoughts while on the pills numbed the sharp grief of my missing womb.

Somehow, I needed to hear what David had to say; my morbid curiosity insisted on it. His words could have been my own.

"Maybe if those people had never left me, I'd have never found myself alone with the beast," he went on. I'd missed something and mentally berated myself for zoning out. Stupid me for taking a pill over dinner. I couldn't think as clearly as I wanted to.

"And maybe I'd have never been able to truly feel the fear I should have felt in the beginning. I don't know if that's how it would have happened, though, because I chose my path, and I can't go back and change it. But I *can* change how I handle stress now and my obsessive compulsive disorder and the abuse from my childhood and the girl who broke my heart and the college I didn't get into and the grandmother I loved so much who died so suddenly when I was too young to process my emotions."

A murmur rolled over the room, and I found myself part of it. This boy had been through a lot in his what—twenty or so years? More than I'd expected. Maybe he really did know about pain. Mine was different, but his was no less real, I could tell. Behind my eyes, I felt a burning sensation. I swallowed again and took a deep breath, unwilling to cry here, in public, in front of strangers. In front of Shannon and Tori.

"I wanted to share today because today is my twenty-four-month anniversary of being clean—two whole years."

Applause exploded throughout the room, making my determination erode and tears stream down my cheeks. What had he gone through in those two years to reach this place? The thought of going without painkillers for a *week*—forget a year or two—sent fear through my body, and my hands began shaking again, getting worse and worse. I clasped them together to calm them, but it didn't work. I had little control left, so I stared at the floor, breathing slowly, trying to get myself to calm down.

I can't go without my pills. I need them. Maybe for just another month. I can't just drop them all at once. I couldn't handle that. The fear was absolutely paralyzing.

I continued debating with myself about how and when—and if—I'd be able to stop taking the pills. My tears were as much out of fear as anything else. I couldn't do this. No way. I was terrified of feeling and facing pain—any kind of pain.

I was vaguely aware of David telling more of his story, about when he hit rock bottom and nearly died. He'd done things that put him in the "junkie" category for me. It would have been so easy to write this whole evening off by saying, "See? He's a junkie, and now he's better. I'll never hit rock bottom and nearly die, abandoned in a park. I'm not a loser."

Yet his description of what the drugs did for him rang true and sounded uncomfortably familiar, and I couldn't discount that.

David quoted his mother, who had stopped enabling him and who had visited him in the hospital. Instead of begging him to stop his dangerous behavior, she said, "I think it would be easier to visit your grave than to see you like this over and over again. Maybe that's what I should be praying for."

I sucked in a breath. I pictured Ethan standing beside *my* hospital bed. He'd be wearing scrubs, a stethoscope around his neck. He'd shrug and say, "This isn't what I wanted, and you aren't the woman I married. Maybe I should be hoping for your death."

A shudder went through me. I cradled my bad arm and rocked back and forth; I couldn't help it.

Shannon reached over and gently took my left hand in hers, squeezing it lightly in support. I waited for a jolt of pain to shoot up my arm, but it didn't come. Tori reached for my other hand, and I let her take it as well.

The three of us sat there in the hushed silence that followed David's speech, holding hands. This didn't look or feel like a threat. Until that night, I'd had no idea how much they cared.

But were they right that I needed to get help? Couldn't I try to get off the drugs myself? I did need to; after tonight, after hearing David's story and his feelings and what his mother had said, I knew things had to change. I could do it on my terms though. I would.

David went on about his low point in the hospital with his mother. "I don't know why that moment was different than the times she'd begged me to get well, bribed me to get well, screamed at me to get well, but something about her apathy that day made me realize just how far I had fallen. I was in the hospital for three days, and even though I told her I was going to get clean and it was going to work this time, she wouldn't let me come home. We'd done that so many times, and I'd brought too much chaos with me, but she contacted our pastor, and he found an older man from our congregation who agreed to let me stay with him. I went to a doctor and got help for my OCD and my anxiety disorder. I started talking to my family again, and perhaps most importantly, I started going to NA meetings regularly—every day. I met people like me, not bad, evil people with no willpower and no soul—good, decent people who'd chosen the wrong way to cope with their struggles."

If I didn't change, would Ethan be the one kicking me out of my home? Divorcing me? I had to remind myself to breathe.

David had started crying; he even had to take off his glasses to wipe the tears away.

I shook my head. Daily meetings would be too much. I needed to be home in a safe place. Weekly meetings. Maybe I could handle those. Maybe.

"Thanks for letting me tell my story." He opened the floor for anyone else wanting to share their stories. He returned to his seat, and others got up to share their experiences, but I kept replaying David's words in my head.

That, and wondering what the future would hold for me. What it would be like to attend an NA meeting and be expected to say, "My name is Ilana, and I'm an addict."

To attend regular NA meetings.

No. I can do this alone. If Shannon and Tori will just let me—and not tell the cops or my husband. I must have looked like I'd seen a ghost—and in a sense, I'd certainly imagined one—because Shannon took my hand again. I hadn't noticed when she'd let go before. The meeting seemed to be wrapping up, so she turned to me.

"Ilana," she said, looking directly into my eyes. I wanted to look away; her piercing look felt disconcerting, but I tried not to look away. "You're going to be okay."

I pulled my hand away and held it with my other, again trying to stop the shakes. My whole body was shaking now, as if my fear were a palpable entity taking over my life.

Somehow we left the room with a brief good-bye to David, and we headed outside.

"Can I go home now?" I asked quietly. I could hardly hear my own voice.

"Yes," Tori said. "Except . . ." She trailed off, making my brow wrinkle.

"Except what?" I asked. Now my voice was shaky. I needed to get away; my tears threatened to erupt again.

Shannon licked her lips as if struggling with what she was about to say. "As a medical professional, it's my duty to report . . . these kinds of things."

My eyes widened. "Please, no. I'm going to stop. I swear."

"I can give you a week," she said. "You have until Monday to find help on your own. If you don't, I'll have no choice but to go through professional channels to enforce the law."

I wanted to yell that she was threatening me all over again, that this wasn't fair, that this was my life and she should just butt out. But I couldn't say those things, no matter how much I wanted to; my mouth wouldn't form the words. All I could do was nod dumbly, then go with Tori as she led me to her car like a small child.

She didn't speak during the drive back to my apartment, and she didn't offer to walk me up either. I think she knew I couldn't handle either. I spent the entire drive with tears streaking down my cheeks. Half of the time I tried to figure out how to get help without Ethan knowing, and the other half I tried to decide how much help I had to get to satisfy Shannon's demands.

Seven days. One week. But only four business days. What could I possibly do in that time?

For a fleeting moment, a horrifying thought crossed my mind—I could take all the pills I still had in one fell swoop. Get rid of them all at once. And hope they took me away forever.

Because life as I knew it was over anyway. Ethan might never forgive me. I'd never be allowed to adopt. Probably wouldn't be able to get a job.

I might as well die.

Chapter 20

AT MY APARTMENT BUILDING, I stumbled my way to the elevator in a haze. My hands shook so much that as I rode the elevator, at first, I couldn't find my keys in my purse, and then when I reached the apartment door, it took me half a dozen tries to get the key into the lock. I hurried inside and slammed the door shut behind me. After tossing my purse onto the kitchen table, I collapsed on a chair, forehead on my right forearm, my somewhat-healed left arm resting protectively in my lap. Of course, it was throbbing, which only ticked me off more.

What now? I had four days. Fine, a week, Shannon had said, but it wasn't like I could "get help" over the weekend . . . Or could I? Drug hotlines were probably available 24/7. I glanced at the phone, which rested in its cradle on the counter. The idea of calling someone—someone who would be able to tell from the caller ID who I was, so I had no anonymity—didn't sit well with me. But if I could find a way to call and keep it private, maybe that would satisfy Shannon's demands. If I called regularly and kept a log.

But how could I survive the pain when they insisted I go off medication? The thought was downright terrifying. I bit my lip in thought, my heart beginning to race at the idea that maybe I'd found a golden loophole. I could call a support line and keep my privacy, and no one would ever have to know about it—including and most especially, Ethan. What if I bought one of those pay-as-you-go cell phone plans? I'd have to research those. Surely I could get one activated that wouldn't show my name on the caller ID, just the number. If I didn't see anyone in person, they couldn't do a drug test, and I could still take a *little* medication, enough to take the edge off so I didn't lose my mind.

I headed over to the bedroom, where my laptop lay on the comforter. I flipped it open and sat down to write an e-mail to Shannon and Tori to tell them about my plan to call a help line and report to them regularly. *I'll call first thing in the morning*, I'd tell them. And I would call in the morning, after I'd gone to the store to buy an untraceable phone. Then I'd call from a park or other place where I wouldn't be seen or heard. I could even take a walk while talking. If I ever needed to call from home, I'd do it in the living room while Ethan slept after a long night in the ER. I could talk quietly on the living room couch, with the bedroom door closed. He wouldn't hear a thing.

This could work. I brought up my e-mail program and began drafting the message when a new e-mail arrived. I clicked over to look at it, expecting a newsletter from the craft store or a coupon for Kohl's. Instead, I found an e-mail from Shannon. It was brief.

Ilana,

I hope you understand why Tori and I brought you to the NA meeting. We're concerned, and we care. Below are some names of rehab centers that are relatively close. One is for women only, and it was featured on the Dr. Phil *show, if that interests you. Let me know where you'll be going for help as soon as you make a decision. I don't want to take action on Monday, but I will if I have to. You can do this.*

My mouth went dry, and it was all I could do not to throw my laptop across the room. She expected me to go to a rehab center? We couldn't afford that. I scrolled down to look at the different centers she'd listed, hoping to find one that was out-patient. That had to be cheaper.

I'd still have to deal with Ethan's reaction though. No way could I hide a treatment center from him, no matter what kind it was.

Groaning, I abandoned both Shannon's e-mail—which I noticed she'd copied Tori on—and the draft of my own e-mail, then slammed the cover shut on my laptop and fell onto the bed. Holding a pillow to my chest, I screamed into it. The tears that had started earlier sprang to my eyes again, and I sobbed into the pillow.

I'd been looking forward to book club on Saturday, where we'd talk about Ruby's new favorite book, *Zen and the Art of Motorcycle Maintenance*. I'd choose the title for June—I was leaning toward *Love in the Time of Cholera*. I hadn't read it, but I'd heard great things about it. But now . . . would I make it to book club this week? Could I face Shannon and Tori?

What about next month? How long would rehab last? Would I be around to lead the group discussion about my book choice?

And why did book club suddenly matter so much?

After I didn't know how long, I wiped the last of my tears, being all cried out for the night. My head pounded so hard, the pain in it almost overshadowed the pain in my arm. I sat up and steadied myself on the mattress. The headache made me instinctively turn toward my nightstand, where, in the top drawer, I had three bottles of narcotic prescriptions—two mine, one Tori's. I could really use two or three pills. It would soften my headache and ease the ache that had crept into my chest ever since I'd first sat in the NA meeting.

My hand reached toward the drawer and opened it, but as I reached for the closest bottle, I stopped and stared at my hand, suspended in midair. I was about to take more pills to deal with the emotions brought up because of how many pills I was taking? Yes, I still had physical pain, but that wasn't the reason I'd opened the drawer. My eyes widened, and I forced my hand to my lap. I kicked the drawer shut with my foot and leaned back on the bed, raking the fingers of my right hand through my hair.

How had I gone right back to the idea that a little pain meant a justification for opening one of those bottles within minutes of returning home? For a moment, David's speech had made me want to commit to never taking another pill again. I'd said good-bye to him not an hour ago. But I'd reached for the bottle again without a second thought.

I do have a problem. I mentally swore.

I'd known I had a problem—of course I had. But now the reality smacked me across the head like a baseball bat. My arm wasn't hurting much. I'd been reaching for drugs to treat a headache, something ibuprofen could handle. But I was emotionally volatile. And I'd reached for Vicodin to make it better.

I thought of the moment when Shannon had taken my hand in hers, and Tori had done the same with my other hand. How we'd sat there, all three of us crying, united for a short moment. They cared about me. Really cared. I couldn't quite fathom why when they didn't know me that well.

A picture came to my mind of me standing at the podium, telling a similar group my story. About how the pills had dulled the pain. How I'd justified the need to take them. How I was terrified of pain—physical and emotional, both. How I'd overcome my addiction one day at a time and that I was clean.

Clean.

That word sounded good. And the opposite of what I was now—a criminal. I'd broken some serious laws. I *wasn't* any better than a junkie on the street; I just had better shoes.

I took a deep breath and voiced a promise to myself. "I'll go to rehab."

The words seemed to echo in the room, making me feel horridly alone once more. I wanted Shannon and Tori to be here to literally hold my hands again. For Ethan to be here to assure me that I wasn't an evil person and that things would get better.

Forcing the words out again, I said—slower this time—"I. Will. Go. To. Rehab." Then I let out a long breath, inhaled deeply, and let out another. The tremors in my body gradually eased. I closed my eyes and tried to relax.

For some reason, a face appeared in my mind—Paige, from book club. My eyes opened, confused. Why would she come to mind right now, of all times? Why would she *ever*?

Because she has faith. She believes in God. She's had some awful things happen to her, but she still prays and reads scriptures and goes to church. To get through rehab, you'll need to believe in a higher power too.

I sat up and flipped open my laptop a second time. I discarded my other e-mail draft and began a new one.

Paige,

We don't know each other that well, but I was wondering if you'd be willing to answer a question for me.

My fingers hesitated on the keyboard. How to phrase this? How to not sound like an idiot? I pressed my lips together in concentration, biting the bullet and just doing it.

Where does your faith come from? How do you keep believing in God when you've had so much garbage heaped on you? This isn't a theoretical question; I really need to know. I lost my faith some time ago, and I think I need to find it again. I just don't know how.

Before I lost the nerve, I hit send. Then, looking up at the ceiling as if I could see straight to the heavens, I murmured, "I'm moving on my end. You'd better be there to catch me. I can't do this alone."

Chapter 21

Closing my laptop, I decided to stay up until Ethan came home so I could tell him, well, everything. First, I grabbed the remote in hopes of distracting myself with television, but I found little to watch on live TV that interested me, and an ad for the next episode of *Vows* only made me remember Tori and the evening I'd had.

I clicked through channel after channel, pausing here and there. Eventually, I paused at a news magazine show; they tended to have interesting stuff. But then I realized it was a story about a woman my age who'd driven while on high doses of both Percocet and Vicodin.

I'd never do something that *bad.*

She'd crossed the median and crashed into a minivan head-on, killing a family of four, including their three-week-old baby. She was in prison serving time for vehicular homicide.

With a shudder, I clicked off the television. Time to find something to distract myself from the pain in my arm—and heart, now that I was trying to be honest—and from the crushing fear of how I'd tell Ethan, what his reaction would be. The worst-case scenario hung over my head like a storm cloud threatening to strike me with lightning: what if he called the cops, had me arrested, and filed for divorce?

I got up and paced the apartment to keep my mind off both Ethan and the three different painkiller bottles I had with varying numbers of opiates inside, all whispering that they'd calm me down, help me think, make it all better.

After hearing David's story, I saw those thoughts for what they were for the first time—outright lies. The brief feeling of relief was only that—brief and fleeting and not a solution to anything. The pain always came back. I needed some other way to cope. But I knew that I could acknowledge the facts and still crave the pills. Still be weak and take more when my body needed them.

I walked around the apartment and picked something to focus on. First I cleaned up clutter—a pair of socks by the couch, a stack of junk mail. A takeout box left on the counter. A pair of Ethan's shoes kicked off in the hall. The clutter didn't take me long; Ethan tended to be a neat freak, so the place looked pretty good, with the exception of the master bedroom, where I spent most of my time. And where I didn't want to go right now.

So I unloaded the dishwasher and folded socks in a basket of clean laundry, which Ethan had run through the wash. Every activity helped keep my mind occupied for a few minutes, but inevitably, my thoughts returned to Ethan's pending disappointment—disgust?—in me when he learned the truth, which meant that my mind next went right to the bottles in my nightstand drawer. And the one in my purse.

Up and pacing again. My arm throbbed from the extra effort of doing chores, and my mind turned to the bottles again. I shook off the thought with a groan of frustration and found my way to the kitchen again, staring into the open fridge for something to snack on until my eyes tracked over to the counter, where my purse sat. I could almost see the bottle inside where I kept ibuprofen . . . and some of Tori's pills. I knew just where it was, which pocket I'd put it in. Which side of the purse it was on. That the bottle was lying sideways. And that it had seven glorious pills in it. I could take three of them without worrying about scary side effects. I'd be able to get a brief release from all of this anxiety, and I really had overdone it with my arm when I put away dishes and sorted laundry . . .

No! I ordered myself. *Not anymore.*

I grabbed a Diet Coke from the fridge to help keep me awake, then marched to the bedroom after all. *It would be a brief release, stupid,* I chided myself. *It doesn't last.* Determined to clear my head and find something else to keep me awake until Ethan got home, I popped the soda can open and flopped onto the bed. No TV. And I didn't want to open my laptop to surf the Internet. I knew it was unlikely that Paige had answered my e-mail yet, especially when it was late, and I didn't have the guts to check anyway.

Scanning the room, I tried to find something else to keep my mind occupied and half wished I'd asked Ruby for lessons on embroidery so I could keep my hands busy. Or, rather, my hand. She had several beautifully embroidered pillows and other items in her house. My left hand could hold the work without much trouble, and my right would do all the big movements. Maybe lessons would be a way she could help me cope. I was sure she'd be willing; she seemed to always want to help me out somehow, and I always turned her down. But would embroidery only aggravate the pain in my arm? If sorting socks hurt, I didn't see how I could do needlework.

My eyes landed on my dresser, where a thick pink paperback rested—May's book club pick, which Ruby had selected. It was one of the few book club titles I'd gotten in what I'd heard some people refer to as "dead tree" form instead of as an e-book. I'd started it, but I hadn't gotten very far, only about a hundred pages out of nearly four hundred. The story, such as it was, felt vague and required a lot of thought—something I was finally able to admit to myself that I couldn't do when drugged up. No way could I devote brainpower to a philosophical memoir when I lived in a hazy cloud.

But right now, my mind was clear. The last pills I'd taken over dinner with Tori had mostly cleared my system, and although I wanted desperately to take more, I hadn't. Which made every thought about Ethan that much clearer and more painful; I didn't have anything to dull the frightening what-ifs of that conversation, which would take place in about—I glanced at my alarm clock—three hours or so.

I'll read, I decided, and before I let myself argue the thought, I snagged the book from my dresser, settled into a pile of pillows on the bed, and began reading, fully expecting to be bored to tears and to be fighting sleep as I waited for Ethan.

Opening the book, I grimaced at my makeshift bookmark—a receipt from a pharmacy where I'd purchased yet another bottle of pills. I crumpled it in my hand and threw the paper ball across the room. And I began to read. Thirty or so pages in, I found myself engaged in the words of the narrator and his journey to find his old self—Phaedrus, he'd named him—from before his electric shock treatments for some type of mental illness. This time, the journey, even the philosophical stuff, fascinated me and drew me in.

How could I have thought this was boring?

One section discussed dedication, something I'd never thought I had an issue with. But the words seemed to turn a light on in a part of my mind that had been dark.

You are never dedicated to something you have complete confidence in, I read. The text went on to point out that everyone knows the sun will rise, so you'll never see people shouting that fact from the rooftops. Only things in doubt are argued over vehemently. The book wilted in my hold, falling onto my lap as I remembered Ethan's concern that I was playing with fire when it came to the pills, even though he knew about only a fraction of what I was taking. How I'd insisted that I was *fine,* that there was no reason to worry, and to get off my back already. I might as well have been shouting it from the rooftops . . . because I wasn't sure myself about whether I was addicted. Or not.

The idea of my being okay, of not playing with fire, *was* in doubt. I didn't have the confidence in my health that I had in the certainty of the sun rising the next morning.

Which meant that I'd known, on some level deep inside, that I had a problem. I'd known it, even in a tiny way, well before tonight's NA meeting. The idea made something twist in my chest. I'd been lying as much to myself as to Ethan. I, who prided myself on honesty. How many other half-truths and outright lies had I told to others? To myself?

I sighed, trying to quiet my thoughts and return to the book. I managed another twenty or thirty pages, when another passage jumped out.

Most people stand in sight of the spiritual mountains all their lives and never enter into them, being content to listen to others who have been there and thus avoid the hardships.

I reread the entire paragraph, from before that passage to after. Something in it niggled in the back of my head. I'd been through plenty of hard things, meds aside. It wasn't like I'd avoided struggling through "mountains" of life.

Except that I never walk through my problems.

The thought made me furrow my brow as I considered it. No, I hadn't gone up and over my problems. I'd found a great way to skirt them, avoid them, watch them from afar like a lion circling a rival, knowing the other was dangerous. This passage was meant for me: I might have stepped onto a mountain path at some point, but I hadn't kept going through the passes, climbing the cliffs and finding my way through to the other side.

Instead, I'd gone back to the valley, where I'd turned my back to the mountain, not wanting to admit that the peak was still there, rising high into the sky. I tried to find a way to forget it and the sharp stones and thorns along the path that had cut my feet. Doing so gave me a false kind of relief—before the drugs too—but no solution. And I'd kept myself stuck in the valley. At this rate, I'd never get out of this low place or progress past this point. My life in five years would be just as dark—or darker—than it was now unless I turned around, faced the mountain, and took every painful step up and over it until I found something better on the other side.

The one question I had now was whether Ethan would be climbing beside me and whether we'd reach the other side together.

I kept reading, now and again massaging my left arm with my right hand. I no longer felt tired and, in many ways, I felt less anxious. Oh, I worried about what Ethan would say when I laid out the truth for him, but the words in *Zen* calmed me in a way I couldn't explain. Not everything in the book applied to my life right now. Most of it didn't. But in its pages, I marked sections with a ballpoint pen and scribbled thoughts in the margins.

I read faster than I ever had, passing the halfway mark, when I came to a section about something the author discussed a lot: "romantic" versus "traditional" thinking. He defined them in a way that took me aback for a second. I'd always dismissed the so-called "romantic" way of looking at things—not something out of a Harlequin novel but what Professor Keating talks about in *The Dead Poets Society*—an almost religious devotion to emotion and living life through feelings. I'd always preferred to listen to reason and logic. Emotions were dangerous. They led to disappointment, especially if you let emotions lead to spirituality and God.

But here, Pirsig insisted that my old friend, traditional thinking, which was logical, reasonable thinking, led to chaos and confusion. He insisted that such chaos existed only without romance, the emotional side, leading the way. Again I stopped reading and pondered. This applied to me—I knew it did, but I wasn't sure in what way until I thought about what the drugs did for me: they masked my emotions. They prevented me from *feeling*.

They kept me in the stupid valley, never experiencing or learning or growing. Anger welled up in my chest. Why had I done this to myself? Why had I purposely cut off the one way to learn and grow? I had to *feel* to do any of that, but I'd practically numbed myself right out of existence.

I couldn't read anymore tonight; I was too upset with myself. I looked around for my bookmark before remembering what it had been and looking at the discarded ball by the dresser. The receipt for more drugs sent me into a greater rage at myself. I slammed the book closed and threw it against the wall.

That's when the apartment door opened. I sucked in my breath as the book slid to the floor. Had Ethan heard it? He stepped inside and closed the door behind him. Then he called out. "Babe? You okay? I expected the lights to be out."

I hopped off the bed, then glanced at *Zen* lying on the floor. My toes slid it to the side so I wouldn't step on it. Then I took a deep breath and headed for the kitchen.

Here goes nothing.

Chapter 22

Ethan and I came short of running into each other in our bedroom doorway.

"Whoa!" he said, backing up a step, then, after making sure I was okay, opened his arms for an embrace. I stepped into it and breathed easily for what could possibly be the last time. I rested my head against his chest and listened to his heartbeat as tears threatened to well up again. I tamped them down, closing my eyes, hard, to give them the message that tears weren't welcome.

Ethan ran his fingers through my hair. "It's so good to see you up, but don't you need your sleep?"

"Yeah," I said, not lifting my head.

"Didn't you go out with one of your book-club friends? I thought you'd be exhausted after that."

For an answer, I nodded into his chest. "Spent the evening with two of them. Tori . . . and Shannon."

Part of me hoped he'd ask the questions, lead himself to the answers so I wouldn't have to broach the subject. He'd known my plans had been to go out to dinner with *one* friend. But he didn't question my mention of two.

"Did you have fun? How's your arm?" Still, he stroked my hair. If my future hadn't been hanging in the balance, I could have fallen asleep right there and died happy. When I didn't answer right away, he tried again. "Was it a nice night?"

My arm still hurt; it always did. And had it been nice? Dinner had been nice. Tori had been nice at the restaurant. I supposed you could say Shannon had been nice in the sense of being polite and doing her duty, what she thought needed to be done.

Okay, what still needs to be done.

But the rest of the night . . . I couldn't call it *nice*. It was merely necessary.

"It had its moments," I hedged, then forced myself to go a step further. Before I dared speak, I reached around his neck and let my fingers play in the back of his hair. The feeling was a comfort, a security; I somehow felt like holding him this way was like clinging to my favorite doll when I was six.

After clearing my throat, I tried again. "Dinner was great. Tori took me to a fun bistro. You'd enjoy it. But after that . . ." My voice trailed off, and again, I hoped he'd clue in and ask about what unpleasant thing had happened next. He didn't; he just hugged me back, and soon we were swaying side to side, almost dancing. Somehow it hurt less that way. That was the closest I'd felt to Ethan in weeks, possibly months. I wanted to enjoy the feeling, especially knowing I was about to destroy the intimate moment.

I also knew my cowardliness was standing in the way.

Be bold. Do it.

I stopped swaying and looked up at him. "I wanted to wait up for you tonight because of . . . because of what happened after dinner."

He leaned back, worry pulling on his face. "What happened?" He lifted his wrist to check his watch, as if he didn't already know how late it was. My staying up must have alarmed him. He took my shoulders in his hands and looked me over. "Are you hurt?"

If only.

"No," I said wearily. Hours of on-again, off-again adrenaline rushes had worn me out.

"Then what is it?" Ethan wrapped his arms around me. For several moments, I just stood there and drank him in—his strong embrace, his heartbeat, his scent that belonged to no one else. Would I lose all of that? "What?" he repeated, gently stroking my back.

I shook my head. "I'm just tired. It's nothing." I'd tell him later, not now. I wasn't strong enough.

"You sure?" He pulled back to look me in the eye. I couldn't quite return the gaze. I lowered my eyes and nodded.

"I'm sure. It can definitely wait until tomorrow."

Ethan kissed me. "Then let's get you to bed." He put an arm around my waist and led me to our room. As we walked away from the kitchen,

I wanted to make some excuse to go back so I could slip a pill or two from my purse. But I refused to be that person, no matter how bad the pain was.

I could have let the whole thing go, crawled into bed, kissed him good night, and fallen asleep as if nothing had happened.

But something had happened. A lot had. And the clock was ticking even faster toward Monday. If I chickened out tonight, I'd still have to face him, and soon, before Shannon turned me in. The image of an orange jumpsuit and shackles convinced me to speak up. I sat on the bed and motioned for Ethan to do the same.

"I stayed up because I wanted to talk. To tell you something. Something important."

He looked at me expectantly and settled by my side, reaching for my hands, which he held in his. "What is it? You look like you've seen a ghost."

I licked my lips, aware of how dry my mouth felt—another side effect of Vicodin, I'd learned. The drug had managed to seep into every aspect of my life. I couldn't even swallow without being reminded of its iron grip. I was sick of it.

"After dinner, Tori took me to a place where Shannon was waiting for us. They had me attend a meeting . . ."

Why couldn't I just spit it out? *Narcotics Anonymous. There. Just say it.*

He chuckled, then, "Let me guess. They're trying to use your friendship to get you signed up with one of those multi-level marketing companies. Is it magic health juice or makeup?"

"Nothing like that." I shook my head. "I wish."

"Did they hurt you?" Ethan's voice was sharp, protective. It felt so good. But would he feel the same when he knew who his wife had become?

I hadn't thought it possible to develop an addiction in such a short time. David from the NA meeting had dealt with his issues for years before getting clean. Maybe I'd be able to kick this thing because I had friends who'd pushed me to get help sooner rather than later. I could hope.

"Remember that fight we had the night I came home from hanging out with Tori?"

"Yes . . ." Ethan's eyes narrowed, and his voice lowered. "What does that have to do with whatever meeting you went to tonight?"

Deep breath. "Shannon and Tori figured out that I have a problem." My voice was going tinny, higher pitched. I took another breath to calm myself.

"A problem," he repeated. "Babe, you're confusing me. I worked twelve hours straight today. Had a guy come in with five gunshot wounds. Another patient died on the table—internal abdominal bleeding we didn't catch soon enough. Can you just tell me straight? I need a shower and some sleep."

"Of course. Right. I'm sorry." This was it. Nothing to do but plunge right in. "They took me to an NA meeting." He didn't seem to register understanding at first, as if "NA" were some company's initials. I kept talking before I lost the nerve. "You were right; I have been taking too many pills. I've been in denial. But you're absolutely right, and so are Tori and Shannon. NA means 'Narcotics Anonymous.' Ethan, I'm . . ." Soon I would have to get used to saying it. Might as well say it to my husband the first time. My eyes filled with tears. They spilled down my cheeks as I tried again. "I'm an *addict.*" My throat choked off anything else I could have said. My face lowered into my hands, and I wept, miserable and disgusted with myself. Terrified of looking up and seeing the same disgust in Ethan's face.

I felt the mattress move; Ethan was getting up. I heard him walking away from the bed, and I cried harder into my hands. But then the bed shifted again. Ethan had gone to his side and was lying down. He reached for me and enveloped me in his arms as he gently urged me down beside him, facing the other direction so our bodies spooned like they belonged together. He didn't say a word.

After a moment, I mustered, "You must hate me." I was grateful he'd spared me the experience of seeing his face. I could look at the wall and cry while he rested behind me, nostrils flaring. Ethan had always been kinder than was necessary. He wouldn't yell or scream or call me names. But he had to think I was a monster.

He brushed a lock of hair behind my ear. "How could I hate the only woman I've ever loved?" He leaned in and kissed my neck.

A shiver went up my spine. I wanted so badly for this to be true, for Ethan to still love me, to find me attractive, to stick with me on this journey. I had to wonder whether I was hallucinating all of this or misinterpreting it all. Maybe I was seeing things as part of withdrawal. He seemed so gentle, so kind . . .

I tried to tell more of the story. "Shannon is a pharmacist. She found some records." I didn't need to explain what kind; I was sure a doctor could infer that much. I could tell him the details another time. "She'll contact the authorities if I don't get help before Monday."

Silence. No response from Ethan at all for several long moments. I finally shifted my position and turned just enough to look over my shoulder at him.

He was crying. This man of men, so strong and unwavering, had silvery tears streaking down his cheeks. What did they mean? A million possibilities—most of them negative—flashed through my mind, one after the other.

With the back of his hand, he swiped at both eyes, then said, "I'm so sorry I failed you."

"You?" I asked. Hadn't he heard what I'd said? *I* had screwed up. *I* had failed *him*. I'd done everything he'd cautioned me not to. It was all me. "You didn't fail me. I did this to myself. It's my problem." My lips trembled. "It's all my fault."

He shook his head vehemently. "I saw the signs." He reached out and traced my arm with his fingers, making warm goose bumps break out across my skin. "Somewhere in my head, I think I knew, but I didn't want to face it. And here you've probably been torturing yourself about it when I could have gotten you help weeks ago if I'd had the guts. I'm a coward." His voice was husky with emotion.

I rolled to my other side so we faced each other. The movement sent stabs through my arm, but I tried to ignore them. I wasn't about to argue over whose fault this mess was; I knew the answer to that one, and I was the only person who needed to take responsibility. Putting a hand on one of his cheeks, I said, "I can't believe I'm saying this, but I think I need to go to rehab." Needles seemed to prick the backs of my eyes as I forced myself to keep talking through the emotions building inside me—fear and anxiety of the unknown. I was about to step into a dark tunnel with only the vaguest hope for a light at the end instead of an oncoming train. A tear slipped out of one eye, and I found my face pulling into a tight knot. "I just hope you'll want me when I come out."

Ethan opened his mouth to protest—surely to say he loved me and he'd always be there—but the truth was, neither of us had any idea what the future would bring. I pressed my fingers against his lips and shook my head. I just couldn't hear his words now. I wanted them to be true more than anything. But I didn't want him making a promise he couldn't keep.

There was every chance he wouldn't be able to handle an addict as a wife—and while I didn't know much about this situation, I'd seen enough *Dr. Phil* to understand that I'd always be an addict. Clean and sober or not, I was an addict now. What if I relapsed? Most addicts did at some point after rehab. I wanted to beat the statistic, but I feared I wouldn't have the strength to. Chronic pain of any kind created huge fear of more pain, in a vicious cycle.

"It'll be expensive," I went on. "If we need a loan, I'll get a job to pay it off when I'm out. And—"

"And we'll get the best treatment available," Ethan interrupted. "No matter how much it costs. And I'll be waiting for you when you're done, with open arms. I'll be the one waving the pompoms."

I smiled in spite of myself and combed my fingers through his hair. "You're amazing, you know that?"

"No, you are." He leaned in and kissed me softly. He was so much more than I deserved. I was the weak one, not the amazing one. Yet he loved me, really loved me, warts and all.

Would his love last? I prayed it would.

In that moment, I really did pray—I'd looked up the twelve steps to recovery, and one of the first ones was accepting a higher power. I didn't have to go to my local synagogue or read the Torah to believe in something greater than myself. I was starting to believe one small thing— that there was something out there, maybe a general force in the universe, maybe more.

So I prayed to that force—whatever it was—that Ethan would be here for me when I was out of rehab. That he'd stick by my side through thick and thin—through lots of thin in the near future. That he wouldn't give up on me even though I'd been so close to giving up on myself. Had he factored in all the repercussions of what this meant? I doubted it. I had to know if he'd thought through some aspects.

With my head resting against his strong chest, his heart thumping in an even rhythm, I asked, "What about your professional reputation? What about our chances of ever adopting?" I had to ask the hard questions, but I wouldn't ask them while looking into his eyes; that would be took much.

He made that happy sound of his, so I knew he was smiling. "You're considering adoption?"

"Maybe." I hadn't been thinking about it, not in concrete terms, anyway. But it was one more thing my situation could affect.

He didn't mention his career.

He kissed my forehead. I tried to let my worries go, to let myself rest in his arms. To not think of what it would mean to be away from him for weeks on end. To be alone save for a bunch of random strangers who were also going through their own personal hells, to have every minute of my day planned by someone else, and to be expected to open up my deepest, darkest thoughts to those same strangers.

Rehab. The details would need to be worked out soon, and I'd be checked in, probably within the week. But I'd need to tell Shannon my plans before Monday, which meant I needed them in stone by then, including my check-in date. I dreaded going through detox, and I couldn't imagine how I'd survive day after day in pain. For now, all I could think about was today.

And today, relief and exhaustion washed over me in waves because Ethan held me. I held him back, and we fell asleep in each other's arms for the first time in far too long. My body relaxed against his, and I drifted off, not into a dreamless sleep, but into a sleep with the first happy dreams I'd had in months.

I sat on a porch swing of a house—our house—while Ethan washed a car with a big, soapy sponge. In my arms was a chubby little baby with little fat rolls on his legs and arms. He bounced on my lap, grinning and laughing.

I knew it was a boy; how, I didn't know, because the only thing the baby wore was a white Onesie. But I knew. He didn't look anything like me or Ethan. But he was ours.

And his name was Levi.

Chapter 23

I SLEPT SO LONG AND hard that night, I didn't notice when Ethan got out of bed. At some point, the scent of cooking eggs woke me, and moments later, Ethan came into the room with breakfast in bed.

"That looks so good," I said, marveling at the omelet, hash browns, bowl of cut-up fruit, and glass of cran-grape juice on the tray. I breathed in the delicious aromas. "Mmmm. Thank you!" I dug into the meal, heartily enjoying every bite in spite of the raging headache behind my right eye, which I knew had to be rebound pain. "What's the occasion?"

"I took tonight off." His face grew serious, the life and sparkle behind his eyes dulling along with his voice.

"What is it?" I asked, lowering my fork to the plate.

Ethan sat on the edge of the bed. He absently played with my toes under the covers. "I don't know how much time I have with you until . . ." His voice trailed off. The melancholy edge in it made me want to weep.

I hoped he didn't have the same reservations I'd had last night—that I still had—about our marriage not making it on the other side of rehab. Maybe all he meant was that I'd be gone soon, for at least thirty days. I hoped that was all he meant and that he wanted to relish as much of the time together as we could.

He rubbed my leg beneath the covers. He had the strong, steady hands of a surgeon. His touch made me feel oddly safe in the midst of an emotional tornado. "I'm arranging to take off work all of next week as well. You know, to help pack up and get you ready . . ." Again, his voice trailed off, but the word *rehab* hung in the air between us like a storm cloud.

I nodded. We both knew.

"I do have to go in for a few hours this afternoon to cover Ashby. He's taking over some of my shifts next week. But I'll be back for dinner. Anything I can get you before I go?"

Around a mouth of omelet, I said, "My laptop?" I pointed at the floor with the fork.

He picked it up and got it ready to go, propped on his pillow beside me.

"Perfect," I said, smiling up at him. "Thank you."

He stroked my cheek with the back of one finger. "I wish I could do more—that I *had* done more." The regret on his face made me wish I could die.

"This is my problem," I said. But Ethan would be as affected as I would be by this whole change. "Please don't blame yourself. I let myself get dragged down a slippery slope. It's my job to climb back up. I'm lucky we're cutting it off at the pass early, not years down the road."

He nodded thoughtfully and shrugged one shoulder. "Even so." He gave me a kiss and headed for the door, where he paused and blew me another kiss. "Love ya, babe."

His words warmed me from the inside out. He often said those same three words. But this time, after everything he'd learned last night, after he'd had to come to grips with the fact that his wife was one of the junkies he so despised at the hospital, I felt like I was hearing the words for the first time.

Ethan still loved me. He still called me *babe*.

I finished my breakfast, set the tray on the other side of the bed, and pulled my computer onto my lap. I brought up my e-mail first, a habit I'd developed while working at the convention center. My mornings had typically consisted of checking e-mail to address any urgent show needs first thing, over a cup of coffee, before leaving for work.

I still checked my inbox first thing each morning; old habits die hard. I absently wondered if my time on the Internet would also be considered an addiction. Going without for a month—or more—would certainly be hard.

First I'd check e-mail, and then I'd research inpatient rehab centers in the area. The idea sent my heart thumping. I deleted several coupon deals and other random junk mail. And then I noticed one personal e-mail—from Paige.

My mouse arrow hovered over the message for several seconds as I got the nerve to open her reply. Finally, I clicked.

Dear Ilana,

You've asked some great—and tough—questions, ones I can't answer in a sentence or two. In some ways, the answers may be different for everyone. I can only speak for myself.

My faith comes from years of prayer, scripture reading, and trying to live the way I believe God wants me to. That may sound mundane and simple, and on the surface, maybe it is. Like you mentioned in your e-mail, trying hard to do what I believe is right hasn't exactly spared me from hard times. I still have nights when I cry over my broken marriage, my boys who have no decent father figure in their lives, and many other things.

But through it all, I've had moments of clarity and understanding. Times when I feel as if God has whispered to my heart and comforted my soul. That's the best way I can describe it, but words are inadequate. Regardless, the result is that I have a firm conviction that my Heavenly Father is aware of me and my sons and that no matter what storms beat against me in my life, as long as I'm leaning on Him, I'll make it.

I don't remember the man's name, but I once saw a book by a rabbi who tried to explain why bad things happen to good people. I've latched on to the last part: bad things really do happen to good people. What makes them stay good people, I think, is how they respond to the storms threatening to carry them away.

When the storms get heavy and I think I can't take anymore, when I'm absolutely spent, somehow, I get a reprieve. The storm may not end, but the winds let up, if briefly, to let me catch my breath. Or a friend comes to stand with me in the storm. Or I'm given a little extra strength to hang on a bit longer.

When the storm passes—and it always does—I'm a stronger person on the other side. It's as if Heavenly Father knew I needed to learn something hard, and going through that storm was the only way to teach me. I don't believe God creates awful things to throw in our way, but I do believe He allows hard stuff to happen and doesn't stop it because He can see that through the process, we'll go through the refiner's fire and turn into something beautiful, just like gold and silver have to be heated to high temperatures before their true beauty shines.

I can think of several trials I've gone through that I never in a million years would have chosen to walk through, yet later, when I look back, I'm grateful I did because of the strength, lessons, and yes, even blessings the trial eventually brought with it.

I don't know what all you're going through, but I hope something here is remotely useful. I'll include links to some of the scriptures I read regularly, and if you like, I'll send you a hard copy with my favorite passages marked.

Where to start getting your faith back? I'm not sure, but here's one thought: pray. Really, really pray. I've had many experiences through prayer that cannot be coincidence; I know it works. Here's the hard part: often, prayers will be answered but not in the way you expect or hope them to be. God is still listening, even when you think no one is on the other end of the line. Other times, the answer is just no. Others, it's "Not yet," or worse, "What do you think?" But He hears us, every prayer. I think that's probably the best place to start—by praying regularly, morning and night and in between if you need it. Write it out if that's easier at first. But give it a shot—and then throughout the day, try to listen for the quiet voice inside you that can give you answers.

Hang in there, Ilana. A lot of people care about you—I know the whole book club does. I'll be keeping you in my prayers.

Paige

I reread her e-mail several times. By the time I sat back, I was sobbing. And didn't know why. Something inside me felt changed—like my heart had opened, and stuff I didn't know existed in there had fallen out, and something else was growing in its place. Somehow I felt capable of experiencing faith, if only on a microscopic level.

For several minutes, I sat there pondering. I could hear Paige's voice as I'd read her words, picture her kind, shy face, hear her certainty. One thing in particular stood out to me: Paige's explanation that prayer helped her *through* tough times rather than *preventing* them. I closed my laptop and thought through the last year or so of my life and how it related to Paige's e-mail. She had blessings because of trials.

Do I? I sat there trying to think of my blessings. After wallowing in my trials for so long, trying to focus on the good parts of my life was harder than I'd expected. But I was determined to come up with blessings.

I have a husband who is kind and hot and smart. But mostly, I'm glad he's kind.

There. That was a start. What else? I started ticking items on my fingers.

I have a nice place to live. I have a car. Food. Clothes. Indoor plumbing.

The longer I went, the easier it became for me to come up with things I was grateful for.

A talented surgeon. A physical therapist who may be a sadist but who knows his stuff. I have a good computer and a nice cell phone. I have curly hair many women envy. A mother who may be nosy but who loves me very much.

I went on and on. When I ran out of ideas, having exhausted water heaters, sunscreen, chocolate, and shows like *Vows* that helped me through my days, I realized I already felt better, more at peace than I had for some time. Maybe it would help to make a point of looking for things to be grateful for every day. Maybe Paige already did.

Now what? I bit my lower lip. *Here goes nothing.* Having no idea what I was doing, I decided to give Paige's challenge a try. I'd have to do it soon anyway; I needed to acknowledge a higher power.

Still sitting on my bed, I wasn't sure how to go about praying. I didn't know what I believed about God, including what I'd been taught as a child about Jehovah. I didn't feel comfortable kneeling, and folding my arms like I'd seen people do in movies was an impossibility at this point; I'd gotten more range in my elbow but not that much. I opted to clasp my left hand with my right, and then I floundered as I tried to come up with my first intentional prayer in years.

Unsure how to begin, I decided to dive in before chickening out. I cleared my throat and whispered, "Dear God, if You're there, could You let me know?"

Chapter 24

STANDING OUTSIDE RUBY'S HOUSE, I clenched my copy of *Zen,* holding it with both hands, not daring to move up the walkway and ring the doorbell. This wouldn't be any regular book club. This would be my chance to tell the others what I'd be doing for the next thirty days minimum, depending on how much time I needed at the rehab clinic. I wanted to believe I didn't need even that much, but if I'd learned anything over the last six days since the NA meeting, it was that I had a lot to learn, especially about addiction, and that it was too easy to take virtually anything for granted. If I had to stay in rehab for six months, I'd do it.

I just prayed Ethan would be waiting for me—forgiveness and love in his eyes—when I got out. I really did pray now, day and night, and a couple of times in between, as Paige had suggested. I didn't have what Paige called a "testimony" in another one of her e-mails, and didn't know if I ever would. God only knew, literally, whether I'd start going to any church. The quiet prayer I'd uttered after reading her e-mail had given me a welcome peace, one I wished I could keep with me always. That alone made it worthwhile to pray every day—I needed peace.

I wasn't sure of much, but I was sure of two things: that I needed help and that if there was a God, He was the only person who could get me through my . . . *addiction.*

Oh, how I still hated even thinking that word.

I turned my wrist to check my watch, though I already knew I was at least ten minutes late. Chewing my lip, I turned toward the street, counting the cars parked along both sides. In a strange way, I was grateful to be able to say I knew who drove each one. The sleek black one belonged to Athena. The midgrade sedan, which I couldn't put a brand to right away, belonged to Olivia. The dreadful old green Dodge was Paige's—she deserved something much nicer to get around in. I still wondered how she could share some of her innermost feelings with women she hardly knew. I looked for the car I'd ridden in with Tori that fateful night we'd gone to dinner and then to one other place—one that had changed my life. It wasn't on the street, so Tori wasn't inside. The last car, an Acura, I recognized as the one Shannon had walked to in the church parking lot after the NA meeting. I mentally went through the names of the other book-club members, wondering if someone else was missing.

Daisy. I'd resented rather than sympathized with her while I'd still been in a self-absorbed bubble of pity. I wished, as I did several times each day, that I could turn back the clock and go back to November when I'd first come to the book club. I'd get to know the others better. I wouldn't hold myself quite so aloof. I wouldn't resent Daisy, who was genuinely going through a difficult time. It wasn't *her* fault that I was infertile. Somehow I felt like I needed to know what kind of car she drove. I hadn't noticed those kinds of details before. Getting to know each of the women here hadn't been a priority.

The door behind me opened, and I heard Ruby's voice. "Ilana, sweetheart? Is that you?"

I turned to face her and forced a smile on my face in the hope of distracting her from seeing the glassiness in my eyes. "Hi, Ruby."

"Come in, come in," she said, waving me toward her. "I'm so glad you made it!"

She meant it, I could tell. I hadn't done much besides blow her off over the months, but she was genuinely glad to see me.

I walked along the pathway to her door, which, as always, had a season-themed wreath on it. This one had plastic daisies and carnations. It was abominably ugly but homey at the same time. When I reached Ruby, I found myself uncharacteristically putting my arm around her in a hug. "It's good to see you," I said, pulling back. Fingering my keys, I added, "I was wondering if, sometime, you'd be willing to teach me how to embroider."

"Oh, I'd love to!" Ruby clasped her hands the way only she could. She gave me another hug.

"It may have to be in a few months though," I said but stopped myself. The big announcement would have to come later. I couldn't bear to say it more than once, and I *had* to say it in front of Shannon, at least, and Tori, if she came.

"Whenever is good for you," Ruby said, then waved me along to follow her to the family room. At the door, I paused and looked around the circle of women I'd come to know and love. Paige smiled at me hopefully, surely wondering if our e-mail exchange had helped. It had, but I hadn't gotten up the nerve to tell her so in the few more messages we'd exchanged.

Shannon eyed me with a slightly guarded expression, for obvious reasons, but I knew her intentions were friendly and supportive too. Shannon seemed almost desperate. I didn't know why she cared so much about my taking action on my own; maybe reporting me would be difficult for her professionally. Ruby sat on a chair by the couch, a breath escaping her as she went down. At one time, her constant attention with phone calls and more had seemed annoying, but in the end, as I looked back, I was grateful to see someone who had tried to show me friendship when I'd felt so alone. Even Athena had influenced me, although we hadn't connected outside of book club. Her comments were always insightful, and I found her calm confidence and professionalism as a woman inspiring. They'd all impacted me in ways they'd never know.

I found tears threatening to build up again, so I tried to change my thoughts. I lifted the book and waved it as I came in. "Great selection," I said, taking a seat on a folding chair by Ruby. I'd sat in almost the same spot last month when I'd been in a stupor of pain and, later, in a stupor of medication I'd stolen from the upstairs bathroom.

As was my habit, I massaged the aching muscles on my bad arm with my right hand. The physical pain wasn't all gone—not by a mile— but Ethan assured me that a lot of my pain, including the horrid headaches I'd been experiencing, would diminish the longer I was off painkillers. The idea sounded backward, but apparently, I was dealing with a lot of rebound pain. I'd have to take his word for it. As things stood, I really wanted a narcotic of some kind to take the edge off. But I wouldn't be taking any. I'd handed them over to Ethan, and he'd disposed of them somehow—but that didn't mean the craving had disappeared with the meds.

At the same time, in a contradictory way, I didn't *want* a pill—I'd been without one since Monday night. Or early Tuesday, depending how you looked at it, as it had been after midnight when Ethan had gotten rid of them. I was already counting my days of sobriety, even as I pondered other ways of getting relief, like finding a bottle of strong cough medicine or, better yet, hitting a bar. I wouldn't act on those thoughts though.

One reason was that even with the pain, my mind wasn't foggy. I felt more alert than I had since before the hysterectomy. I missed the life I had and the woman I'd been before the fertility treatments made my emotions a battlefield, before both surgeries, when I had the ability to feel happy just because. I missed that.

Ruby explained that Tori was out of the country in Dubai with *Vows* and regretted not being at the meeting. Then Ruby got down to business with leading the discussion because she'd picked the book. Her copy was well worn, yet I could have sworn that last month she said she'd just read it for the first time. Maybe she'd bought a used copy online and didn't enjoy reading a book on an iPad after all. She read a brief bio of the author, which she'd printed from Wikipedia, told us some of her favorite parts, and talked about how she had a dream inspired by the book.

"Someday I'd like to take a motorcycle trip across the country too. Not alone, of course, but definitely taking the scenic roads and avoiding the freeways, as Pirsig and his son did in their journey to learn about Phaedrus." She placed her hands on her copy, which lay in her lap. "Wasn't all of the electro-shock therapy stuff just fascinating? Made me want to learn more about it, though I understand it's a far different creature now than it was in his day. Far more humane."

She gushed a bit more about the book, hinting a second time about a cross-country trip she would someday take. Did she have someone in mind she'd be going with? Maybe that Gabriel guy she'd told us about? Wasn't she still mourning her husband's death? How long ago had he died anyway? I didn't remember, if I'd ever known.

"As you can tell, I loved the book. Anyone else like to jump in?" Her speech had left her flushed. She stroked the cover of the book as if it were a treasure.

Before anyone else could speak, I cleared my throat. If I didn't say something right up front, I'd lose my nerve altogether. "I have a few things I want to say . . . about the book."

Shannon looked disappointed when I added the last bit. Inside, I smiled, knowing she'd be all right with what I was about to say. I had half a mind to tell her *I have two more days, remember?* But I didn't goad her. She wouldn't find it funny.

Everyone's eyes turned to me, and suddenly, my carefully rehearsed speech vanished from my mind. My heart hammered against my rib cage, and my mouth dried up like sandpaper. I reached for my water bottle and took a swig, swallowed, and tried again, opening my copy of *Zen* to a page a bit over halfway through the volume.

"First off, I'll admit that it took me awhile to get into the book. I read about a fourth of it and then set it aside for a couple of weeks. And then a few days ago, I didn't feel good, and I needed a distraction." My eyes flicked to Shannon, and her eyes seemed to smile back as if she knew exactly what I was talking about. Paige nodded encouragingly, and I went on. "So I pulled it out and began to read more. Next thing I knew, I was drawn right in and learning lessons about myself I really needed." I licked my lips; the next bit would be the beginning of the hard part.

"Truth is, I've been living in denial for some time. And I've been angry. Blaming everyone and everything for my miserable life and the pain I've been in, although I won't deny I really was in a lot of pain. But that doesn't make it right. I looked around for excuses and a way to fix everything, to make myself feel better and not be so aware of my problems." The myriad problems I'd experienced just since joining this group flashed through my mind yet again. I hadn't planned on telling them about the first surgery but now realized they needed to know about it to understand the rest. Not even Shannon or Tori knew that part.

"In January, I had surgery."

Livvy leaned forward, her brow furrowed. "Another one?"

I nodded, my eyes burning so much I didn't know if I could hold back tears this time. *Maybe you don't have to anymore*, I reminded myself. *It's okay to feel pain.*

I nodded. "A hysterectomy—after three years of fertility treatments, no less." A laugh, interrupted by a sob, escaped my throat.

Paige, who sat to my left, put a hand on my knee. "I'm so sorry. I can't imagine how hard that would be."

"Thanks." I was so grateful she hadn't jumped on the *Hey, just adopt!* bandwagon. Ethan and I could go there someday. Not yet, but someday, maybe. I had a lot to take care of first. I tried not to think about what an adoption agency would think if they ever found out I'd been to rehab—whether that would keep me from being a mom at all. If I'd be branded as "unfit."

A deep breath later, I went on. "The accident at work was three weeks after that surgery. I shouldn't have been back to work yet, but I was being stupid. Next thing I knew, I was undergoing another surgery while still trying to grasp that I'd never bear my own child." For a moment, I had to cover my face with one hand to hold back the emotion building inside me. One deep breath. And another—my only painkiller now. "Recovering from two surgeries at once was miserable. I was in a ton of pain. But I was also trying to escape a lot of emotional pain, and next thing I knew . . ."

Deep breath. I turned to a page close to where I'd begun reading Monday night. "There's a passage here that talks about how we're not dedicated frantically to things we have total confidence in." I shrugged. "I was frantically shouting to myself, to my husband, and to the world that I *didn't* have a problem with painkillers."

I remembered Ethan's concern that I might be playing with fire when it came to the pills, even though he knew about only a fraction of what I was taking. How I'd insisted that I was *fine*, that there was no reason to worry, and to get off my back already.

"But the truth is, I do have a problem. I'm an addict."

I half expected them to gasp and shun me, but all I found were expressions of love and concern. Shannon smiled wider than the rest and sat back in her chair in a looser position, as if relieved. She probably was. I wasn't, not yet.

I went on, still having the floor, as if this were my own NA meeting and I was David with the microphone. I told them about the spiritual mountains and other passages I'd marked, about how Pirsig hit it dead on when he said that solutions are simple only after you arrive at them.

"Looking back, the answer seems so obvious," I said. "But when I was in the middle of the cycle of pain, pills, relief, I couldn't see beyond it." I licked my lips and struggled to continue. "I'm telling you all this for several reasons." I'd tell Ruby about taking her pills later, privately. For now, the group needed to know the big piece of news. "The most important reason is that I most likely won't be at next month's meeting."

Ruby audibly gasped and put a hand to her chest. "You aren't quitting, are you? Please say you aren't."

"We want you to stay," Athena said with a nod.

"We really do," Paige agreed.

Only Shannon didn't speak up; she knew what was coming and beamed like a proud parent.

"I'll come back," I assured them. "But not until I've done the work to fix this mess. On Monday, I'm checking into an in-patient rehab center, and I'll be there for as long as it takes. It may be a month. It may be longer. I hope to be back for July's meeting, if I miss June." I chuckled. "I *was* supposed to pick June's title, but I guess I'll pass on that, as I won't be here to discuss it anyway."

Paige leaned forward. "I think I can speak for all of us when I say we're incredibly proud of you," she said. "And we'll support you in any way we can while you're there and after."

Ethan had been right all along. I was so grateful he'd taken my phone from me in the ER and texted Ruby to say I was coming to the February meeting. Without that single act, I wouldn't be in this room, right now. I wouldn't have had any friends to notice my problem and take action. By the time Ethan would have been convinced of my addiction—if he ever would have known for sure—it might have been too late. I could have overdosed and never woken up.

I owed these women my life.

"I'll miss you guys," I said. "I'm pretty sure I can't e-mail or make many phone calls while I'm in treatment."

"Can we send letters?" Livvy asked.

I sniffed in spite of myself; I'd wanted to be strong tonight, but I was on the verge of completely breaking down in front of them all. I couldn't believe how much they cared.

"Yeah," I said hoarsely through my tears. "I'm pretty sure I can get letters from close friends."

And you really are close friends.

Chapter 25

Two days later, Ethan and I got out of the car and walked to the entrance of the rehab clinic. He pulled my suitcase behind him while I clutched his hand. My stomach felt like it was on a roller coaster, and my chest squeezed with fear and anticipation.

Ethan paused before the doors. "Ready?"

"No," I said, taking in the building that would be my home for the next month. "But I don't have time to get ready." I took a deep breath. "Let's go."

As I stepped forward, Ethan took my arm. I turned around questioningly, brows raised.

"I'm proud of you for doing this," he said, pulling me into a hug.

I melted into his arms and clung to him, wishing I could stay there forever, but my time with him was short. He'd be able to come on special family days and when the therapist thought it would be good to have him in a joint session, but those would be short visits, and we wouldn't have time just to *be*. The meetings would be all business, and then he'd leave. For all intents and purposes, I wouldn't see him for the next month. And when I went home, I wanted to be better.

All better.

"I'm going to work as hard as I can," I promised, hugging him hard. Maybe if I clung to him now, I'd be able to let go when it was time to say good-bye.

Too soon, we broke apart and headed inside, where a woman met us at the front desk with a clipboard.

"Ilana Goldstein," I told her.

She flipped a laminated piece of cardstock on the top of the clipboard—likely there to maintain the privacy of the patients on the sheet of paper below it—and apparently found my name. With a pen, she wrote something on the page, then lowered the clipboard to her side. I expected a smile of welcome, but instead, she was all business and a bit curt. "I hope you haven't brought any of the items on our banned list," she said. "We'll be searching all of your luggage—and you too, if you know what I mean."

My eyes widened, and I looked at Ethan warily. He gave me a supportive if pained smile and squeezed my hand. "It's okay, babe. I'll be with you."

The woman tilted her head and smiled in a way that said, *Aren't you so cute to think such a silly thing.*

"You won't be with her, actually. This is the end of the line for you. Now go ahead and say good-bye, and I'll take her back." She motioned between Ethan and me, waving her hand almost distastefully, as if she'd been through this process way too many times before. She probably had, witnessing couples give teary farewells and promises. She probably had little respect for junkies . . .

Like me.

I turned to Ethan, hoping against hope that I could ignore the toothpick-like woman who looked like the tall, skinny sister who had raised James before his giant peach showed up. Spiker, I thought was the character's name. She looked just like Mrs. Spiker.

Ethan took my face in his hands. "You'll get through this. You're strong."

I smiled back. "I don't know about that, but no one is going to work harder here than I am." I lifted myself onto my toes and kissed him long and hard. Oh, how I'd miss him.

Spiker cleared her throat, and we separated. Ethan gave me the handle of my suitcase, released my hand, and turned to leave. I watched him go, even though Spiker was tapping her pointy-toed shoe on the tile floor, waiting for me. Ethan had his hands shoved into his pockets as he walked. At the door, he turned around and smiled. Mentally, I took a picture. I wanted to remember Ethan as he was in that moment—perfectly fitted jeans, an untucked shirt, and sneakers. And that smile, meant just for me. This was the man I'd fallen in love with all those years ago. The one I didn't see often enough. Not Dr. Goldstein, but Ethan. My Ethan.

Caring nothing for Spiker and her grunts of annoyance behind me, I pressed my fingers to my lips. He did the same, and we both held our hands in the air so our kisses could meet.

I watched until Ethan had rounded the corner, and Spiker said, "All right, Cinderella. Let's *go.*"

Good thing for me, I'd left my cell phone and every other item I'd assumed was taboo at home. Spiker brought me back to a small room with a table and a cupboard. She locked the door, then motioned toward the table. "Put your suitcase there. Time to be sure you're following the rules." I silently obeyed, knowing that cheekiness would not be welcomed by this six-foot-four iron pole. I hefted my suitcase and set it on the table.

"Open it," she said while opening the cupboard. I unzipped the suitcase but startled as I heard a snapping sound once, then twice. Looking over my shoulder, I realized she was putting on medical gloves.

No way.

Way.

Before going through my suitcase, she ordered me to undress, then conducted a body search—including a cavity search. No wonder she'd locked the door. I braced myself and thought of Ethan holding me until she was done. As miserable as the experience was—she was none too gentle—I found an odd sense of pride when she didn't find any drugs, because there were none to be found.

She snapped the gloves off, dropped them into a garbage bin, and washed her hands. Then she turned to my open suitcase and dug through it. I hurriedly redressed and watched her. The process seemed almost as big a violation as the cavity search had as she rummaged through my personal items. She picked up my diary, and as she thumbed through it, I had to use all my strength to not cry out. I knew that in this place, I couldn't expect privacy, but wasn't my journal different? Maybe my therapist would be allowed to read that, but not Spiker, right?

I breathed a silent sigh of relief when she set the little volume aside and kept looking. She emptied the entire suitcase and rummaged through my toiletries bag. Spiker confiscated my fingernail clippers, tweezers, and razor. I wanted to ask—but didn't dare—how she expected me to be hygienic without those. Maybe by the time my leg hair had grown out to the point that I looked like Sasquatch, I'd be allowed to shave my legs and pluck my eyebrows. The idea made me smile.

But she wasn't done yet. She felt along the lining, making sure, I assumed, that I hadn't hidden drugs in there either. I hadn't. Not in my luggage and not on my person. Not so much as a Tylenol.

She pulled out a dark-blue, softback book. Ethan and I had found it slipped through our mail slot last night—a copy of Paige's Mormon scriptures, with a note inside saying that she hoped and prayed—*prayed!*—that I would find the peace and strength I needed through its pages. She'd underlined several passages with a red pencil, which she'd included in the package so I could mark up my own spots as well, I assumed. Why she didn't ring the doorbell and give it to me in person, I'd never know, but I was grateful that she'd gone out of her way to get me a copy and drive it over to my place, making sure I'd have it before I came to rehab.

Spiker noticed the book and held it up. "Interesting."

By her tone, I couldn't tell whether she was being sarcastic or serious. I felt like she expected an answer from me, but I hesitated, unsure about the policy on books. I knew things like the Bible and Talmud were okay, but what about a Book of Mormon, when I was so far from being Mormon that I didn't even remember the real name of the Church?

When I didn't answer at first, Spiker's lips came together, pursed in thought. She nodded. "We've had some good Mormons come through here. I think you'll do okay."

She tossed the book onto the growing pile and kept searching. I almost let the comment pass—if she treated me better because she thought I was Mormon, that would be great, but it wouldn't be honest, and if I'd learned anything about addiction in the short time I'd been facing it, it was that lies only made things worse. Even lies of silence. "I'm—I'm actually Jewish," I blurted.

"Oh?" Spiker paused in her search and looked over.

"A friend gave that to me before I came. She's Mormon. Said it might help me."

"Well, it might at that. Any kind of scripture seems to be a good thing here. It's why any kind is allowed. We've had patients reading scripture from just about any religion you could name. Yep. Anything spiritual is a good thing all around." She kept talking, almost friendly now, as she piled everything haphazardly back into my suitcase, her search apparently complete.

I had to wonder if a lot of patients tried smuggling things in and if Spiker found a perverse sense of satisfaction in catching them. For a moment, I felt a twinge of pride; maybe I was already ahead of the game, doing better than others here because I didn't try to bring in any drugs.

Just as quickly, I banished the thought. No way could I think that I was better than anyone else, farther along the path to recovery. About the only thing I had going for me was that I hadn't been forced here by the courts or family. I chose to come on my own.

Sort of, I thought, remembering Shannon's ultimatum. I wouldn't have gone to the dark place that made me accept that I had a real problem if Shannon and Tori hadn't done what they had. At the same time, I really *had* decided to come because I knew I needed help. The fact that if I hadn't chosen to come, the courts probably would have forced me to be here—or at another center—was irrelevant for the moment.

To get better, I had to accept that I was nothing—another one of the twelve steps—and that I had to rely entirely on a higher power.

This was it.

Chapter 26

My personal therapist's office felt surprisingly homey.

"Have a seat," Dr. Conley said, gesturing to the leather couch.

Had she not said that, I would have tried lying on the couch like a patient of Freud or something. This was my first experience with any kind of counseling or therapy, and I had no idea what to expect.

I sat on the couch, which had two throw pillows—one blue, the other green—and cleared my throat. Dr. Conley sat on a chair a few feet away, not behind her desk, which looked to be oak or pine, not a deep mahogany like I'd expected. Not cheap but not dripping with money either.

"So, Ilana, tell me about yourself," Dr. Conley said. She did have a notebook on her lap and a pen in hand so she could take notes. So that much was true from what I'd seen on TV and in movies.

I didn't know where to begin—that was a huge question—so I gave the bare bones: married eight years to an ER surgeon, college graduate, formerly an event producer at a local convention center. My voice trailed off, hoping I'd answered the question right.

She nodded thoughtfully but said nothing at first, which made me wonder if I'd gotten it all wrong. "I understand you're here for an addiction to narcotics. Is that correct?"

"Yeah," I said and suddenly found it hard to look her in the eye. I studied the tan carpet instead.

"Why do you think you're addicted?" Dr. Conley wasn't one to waste time or beat around the bush, was she?

I took a deep breath and dove in, beginning with the years of failed fertility treatments, my hysterectomy, going back to work too soon, the accident with the carpet roller, and my second surgery. With the basic facts out of the way, I added, "It sort of just spiraled. At first, I developed a tolerance, and the regular dose didn't help, so I took more, and—"

"And let me guess," Dr. Conley interrupted. "You took more to manage the pain, but eventually upping the dose a little wasn't enough, and you needed more and more."

I turned to look into her eyes for the first time. "Yeah. How did you—"

Dr. Conley shook her head with a sad smile. "Because that's how it always starts. I've seen it a thousand times if I have once." She leaned forward, an intent look on her face. "But that's just the surface-level stuff. Why *really* did you get addicted? What's the real reason we're here today?"

My brow furrowed. Wasn't that why? I wasn't making up all of the medical issues I'd dealt with. And I most certainly wouldn't have developed a problem without trying desperately to manage my physical pain. I didn't know how to answer.

She leaned back again, studying my face. I felt like I was on a slide beneath a microscope, and I shifted in my seat.

"Is there a possibility . . ." Her voice trailed off, then lowered as she went on. "Is there a chance that maybe you thought you weren't worth much? That maybe you'd let people down? And maybe the pills helped block out your feelings, even for a little while?"

I nodded, my eyes lowering to my hands in my lap as emotion crawled up my throat, making my voice husky as I spoke. "Yeah. Maybe."

But I knew it was more than "maybe." It was definitely, absolutely, an arrow in the bull's eye. The physical pain had been real—oh, so real. Yet there were times I'd justified taking more pills because the buzz softened my emotions and made me a little bit less miserable. I *had* let down so many people: my husband, my parents, my employer . . . any future children I hoped to have. Every pill signified another disappointment, but I lived in a very dark place, and every pill helped me feel a little less like I was in that dark place. It made the burden easier to bear—but only for an hour or two, after which the pain always returned, crashing down as hard as before. Sometimes harder.

"How did you guess?" I looked into her kind eyes. She didn't say anything, but in the space of two beats of silence, I understood. "That's how it happens."

Dr. Conley smiled in a way only a mother could. I wondered how many kids she had and how old they were. "The triggers and issues vary from person to person, but yes. At the root of every addiction is the need to escape the present, to escape feeling emotions and dealing with them, to—"

"To hide," I finished, understanding, feeling lighter already.

"Exactly." Dr. Conley rested one arm on her crossed leg. "Tell me about it—about what you've been hiding from."

A sardonic laugh escaped my throat. "It's a long list," I said. Tears stung the backs of my eyes. "And a painful list."

"Tell me," she said. "That's what I'm here for. I can listen for as long as it takes."

This woman understood me and where I was in a way I hadn't known I needed to be understood. She didn't judge me for what I'd done, and she wanted to help.

Thank you, Tori and Shannon. This is where I need to be.

I reached for the tissue box on a side table and pulled out three. I'd need them—likely more—before I was done.

"I've wanted to be a mother my whole life," I began.

Chapter 27

I walked the grounds of the gated center during my brief solo time. In my hands, I held four envelopes, letters I'd be able to read during my one hour before group therapy.

It was Monday again. I'd arrived last Monday. But I didn't like thinking I'd been here a week, or a full seven days. I was starting my eighth day of sobriety, which sounded much longer than the seven I had completed. Everyone around me celebrated each day, and that was the number I counted. I'd been without my pills for five full days before checking in, but I couldn't count those days as sober. For starters, on each of those days, I'd indulged in an evening glass of wine to calm my nerves; I'd needed *something* to take the edge off the pain, and ibuprofen just didn't cut it. I'd been terrified about what rehab would be like—would I be curled into a ball, shaking and wailing in agony from withdrawal? I fantasized about doctors putting me under and letting me sleep off the physical addiction so that when I woke up I'd have only the psychological issues to deal with.

Only. The psychological aspect was proving harder than the physical. The longer I was at the clinic, the more grateful I became for Shannon and Tori kicking me in the pants to get me here. I could have fallen so much farther, become so much worse off. Many residents here had been through rehab multiple times, had nearly died from overdoses, had tried to commit suicide, or had been to jail. One nineteen-year-old who looked no older than fourteen had been to jail, starting with juvenile detention, at least five times. I couldn't even imagine.

She talked about crushing Vicodin and Percocet pills and snorting them or injecting them for a quicker, stronger high. Several heads in the circle had nodded in understanding. I was so glad I hadn't gotten that far; I easily could have. Another month, and I may well have been desperate enough to pulverize the pills so they'd work faster—if nothing else by chewing them up and swallowing them, something a fifty-year-old man said he'd done to get a quicker rush.

At one point, the therapist read off a bunch of facts, and some of them blew my mind—like how prescription painkillers were the number-one addiction in the United States, above even alcohol and cigarettes.

Now, as I walked along the winding path, I held all four envelopes in both hands, clutching them as my only connection to the outside world. I hadn't yet earned the privilege of a phone call from the center's landline, so I couldn't call Ethan. At this point, I had no desire to call anyone but him, with the possible exception of Paige, and I could wait on that. I desperately wanted to hear Ethan's voice. Today, a letter in his words would have to be enough.

The path was paved with stones, and palm trees swayed in the warm breeze as spring gradually surrendered to the coming summer. I lifted my face to the sun, pausing in my step and closing my eyes to feel its warmth on my face. My senses were alert in a way they hadn't been for a long time. My arm still hurt, as did the muscles in my neck, shoulder, and back from the sling and splint, but not as much. The headaches were fading but not gone.

Therapy had helped me work through some of my grief over losing the chance to give birth to Levi Ethan or Ilana Rose. Dr. Conley was the only person in the world I'd told those names to. I would have called my son Levi and my daughter by her middle name, Rose, but both would have been named after their parents.

Would have been.

I took in a cleansing breath of outdoor air and headed toward a bit of shade near a grouping of palm trees and other plants. A bench sat off the path there, slightly in the shade. It was as close to a personal private place as I had for the moment. Although the bench was visible, another person would have to cross the grass to get to it. No one could sneak up on me, and other patients knew not to bother whoever was sitting here—it was like an unspoken code at the center.

Sitting on the bench, my back to the path, I flipped through the envelopes again. In addition to the letter from Ethan, there was a thin one the size of a thank-you note from Mom, a thickish one from Paige, and finally, one from Shannon, of all people. I eyed that one suspiciously. Had I taken her ultimatum seriously enough? Was she congratulating me on entering rehab? Or was she giving me a warning that I'd better stay for the full course of treatment, or she'd turn me in?

She didn't know about Diane's refilled prescription. I decided to let her letter wait and face the letter I dreaded most: the one from Mom.

All of the envelopes had already been opened by the staff as a precaution. I slipped a small greeting card from my mom's envelope. I prayed it wouldn't say "thank you," which would have meant that Mom had taken a card from a stack without thinking or that she was thanking her daughter, sarcastically, for bringing embarrassment to the family.

The front *didn't* read "Thank You." It was yellow, with two stripes of sky blue and a daisy in the middle.

I braced myself and opened it.

Dear Ilana,

I am so sorry for all you're going through. I had no idea about your hysterectomy; why didn't you tell me? I would have been with you at the hospital and cared for you at home during such a difficult time.

The words made my eyes water. I did tend to be overly independent. I sniffed and pressed on.

Ethan says you've had another surgery, this one because of some job injury? I didn't know that working at the convention center was dangerous. If you'd like me to call my lawyer, maybe we can file a claim against the company for violating OSHA standards.

I chuckled at that. Typical Mom, trying to find a solution to every problem. The accident was just that—an accident. Sure the twenty-whatever carpet layer should have been more careful, but I wasn't about to sue Chuck. I could probably tell him to get rid of the guy who'd been the cause of the accident, but I couldn't hurt a friend, and I considered Chuck a friend. I had no desire to sue the convention center or Alexander either. Any kind of case there would go public, and I didn't need the media digging into my life right when I was trying to find myself again and truly heal. Any kind of headline about me and a lawsuit would destroy Ethan. So no, I'd reply to my mother and tell her I was doing better and not to worry. As I slipped the card with her brief message back into the envelope, I realized she hadn't mentioned drugs or the rehab center. And that's when I flipped the envelope over and realized it had been forwarded from home.

I couldn't help it; I smiled. *Thank you, Ethan, for not telling her.*

Maybe I'd tell her sometime in the future. Probably not, unless she tried giving me liquid cough medicine that had Vicodin as an ingredient, and I'd have to gently but firmly tell her no. Once an addict, always an addict. I could never indulge again. That was a lesson I'd learned in one of my first therapy sessions: that I'd have to say good-bye to ever feeling the warm glow, the "high" of my drug. The choice was remarkably hard—maybe harder than for some of the other patients, I guessed, who were addicted to street drugs. Saying no to those long-term was pretty cut and dried. But any surgery or major injury—heck, even a bad case of the flu—risked getting me back into the cycle of drug abuse. It would be a challenge, to put it mildly.

I set Mom's letter beside me on the bench and opened the next one, from Ethan. The practical doctor in him had typed it up, and it was two pages, single spaced. He talked about funny things that had happened at the hospital—a catheter bag that had burst all over a nurse and a new surgeon named Dr. Sambuchino who insisted on blasting Aerosmith playlists as he operated, saying it helped him focus.

I don't know about anyone else in the room being able to focus, Ethan wrote. *I know several of us have been caught bobbing our heads, and I've seen surgical masks moving enough that I can tell the other person is lip syncing to "Dude Looks Like a Lady" or "Don't Wanna Miss a Thing." Then there was the man who came into the ER delusional, thinking he was Moses. He was special. I had half a mind to ask him why the ban on meat with milk because the scripture about it is kind of vague.*

I laughed aloud at that. He finished his letter with sweet words of love and encouragement and then,

I miss you, babe. I really do. Can't wait until we're together again. Praying that you find the help you need. You're strong. You're powerful. You can do this. And I'll be waiting for you with open arms when you're ready to come home.

He'd signed it with a pen. My finger ran across his name as I pictured his smile, the first thing I'd been attracted to. I was one lucky woman to have a man standing beside me during all of this. A lesser man would have walked away when he learned I was barren. Or when I got addicted to drugs. Not Ethan.

I reread the last part and realized that he too was seeking a higher power—he was praying for me. Tenderly, I folded the letter and slipped it back into its envelope.

I could guess that Paige's letter held comforting words, much like the letters from Olivia and Ruby, which had arrived two days ago. How had

I not realized what a powerful group the book club was? How blessed I was to be led to that specific group of women.

Blessed. I was coming to see the world through Paige's lens, with all my thoughts of *prayer* and *blessings.* I had to admit, I liked how it made me feel—never alone and always with comfort and help in reach. Help I'd be relying on for another twenty-two days at least.

I turned to Shannon's letter next, surprised at how thick it was. It was handwritten, which in part explained its size. But before I had a chance to read it, I heard someone call my name. I quickly tucked the letter back into the envelope, then stood and turned toward the voice—Spiker, who I'd learned was named Penny and who wasn't nearly as crotchety as she'd led me to believe that first day. I'd learned that she'd grown up Mormon, so the connection of the book Paige had given me softened Penny toward me, and she often smiled my way, gave me a hug, or slipped me an extra brownie at meals.

She was coming toward me along the path, walking briskly, her long, thin arms moving forward and back with quick precision.

"Is it time for group already?" I asked.

"Nope," Penny said. "Someone's here to see you."

My heart leapt in my chest. I had no idea who would be here, especially as I wasn't supposed to have visitors for another week at least. "Who? Why? How?" The three words tumbled out of my mouth as the last two letters dropped to the bench.

Penny smiled, a warm, tender smile I hadn't known she was capable of a week—no, eight days—ago. "Dr. Conley thought that after all the hard work you've done, she'd reward you with a visitor." She turned around and beckoned someone behind her to come.

I gazed steadily at the path, waiting to see who it would be, hoping, yet trying *not* to get my hopes up that it would be . . .

"Ethan!" I abandoned the letters and ran across the grass to him.

He dropped a blanket and a picnic basket to the ground, then enveloped me in his embrace, holding me so tightly I almost didn't know where I ended and he began.

"I've missed you," he whispered.

"I've missed you too."

He kissed me soundly. Penny gave a little harrumph at that, but I didn't care; this was my husband, the best reward Dr. Conley could have given me.

Penny interrupted our kiss. "You only have an hour."

"What about group?" I asked.

"Dr. Conley has excused you from group today." She smiled knowingly. "Enjoy your hour."

We did. After Penny left, we looked around and saw no one on the grounds, at least in the immediate area. I took Ethan by the hand and led him to the grassy spot beside the bench. He spread out the tattered blanket, and we lay on it, looking up at the bright blue sky and cumulus clouds slowly floating past. We could eat our picnic later; I was more interested in soaking up as much of Ethan as I could.

He held out one arm, and I scooted in close. He wrapped that arm around me as I rested my head on his chest. There it was again: the steady thump, thump, thump of his heart. His good, good heart. I'd never known a man with a heart like his. I rested my arm across his chest and thought I might be able to lie like that quite contentedly for the rest of my life.

After several minutes, Ethan spoke up. "I have a thought."

"What's that?" I asked, only half listening. The joy of cuddling with my husband under the sun was so much better than any drug buzz. I felt myself almost vibrating with happiness.

"What's the name of the old lady from your book club? She keeps calling to ask for updates on you."

"Ruby," I said with a laugh. "She's a dear."

"The one I texted in the ER? I remember now."

"She also brought us dinner the day before my elbow surgery."

"Then I love her on principle." Ethan laughed. "She sure likes to talk. I swear, every time she calls I'm on the phone for twenty minutes, and I'm not doing the talking—it's all her—but I hang up smiling every time."

"Sweet woman," I said.

I reached up and started playing with the hair behind his ear. He'd be getting a haircut soon, I knew, but I liked it this length—just long enough that I could thread my fingers through it. "So you came here and decided to talk about Ruby?" I asked, teasing.

He laughed. "During one of our long conversations, she told me about something that might be really fun."

At that, I lifted my head. "What would that be?" Ruby wasn't exactly known for her wild and crazy fun times.

Ethan put his other arm behind his head to prop it up and looked right at me. "I think it's time we take a second honeymoon. I'll take off a few weeks from work, and we can go anywhere you want."

My eyes widened. "You're kidding."

"Not kidding. The wife of a friend at the hospital works at a travel agency and can get a screaming deal."

"Wow." I had one more reason to do well here and get home soon.

Ethan leaned in and kissed me softly. Butterflies erupted in my middle as they had the first time his lips had met mine so many years before. Maybe being apart had sparked a greater attraction. Or maybe we'd both grown up a bit and learned a few things, realizing we had to rely on each other. And *that* was pretty darn sexy.

Another peck, and then he added, "I'll never let you down again. It's my job to remind you every day that you're a queen. To be there for you so you never feel less than you are, so you never have a reason to go back to pills."

Afraid I'd burst into tears, I rested my cheek against his. I still couldn't understand how he could look at me and not be disgusted by what I'd turned into. Yet he *did* love me and saw me as something wonderful.

A breeze knocked the letters to the ground beside us. I glanced over, making sure none flew away. Four letters from four people who cared. They'd taken their time to write the old-fashioned way, sending their message with a stamp and everything.

I would show them all, from Ethan and my mother on to Paige, Ruby, Tori, and Shannon, and all the other book club ladies, that their love and kindness made a difference.

And I'd do my darnedest from here on out to act as Ethan saw me: a queen.

Ilana's Comfort Snack—Snickerdoodles

Cookie Dough:
1 ½ C. sugar
2 sticks of butter, softened
2 eggs
2 ¾ C. flour
2 tsp. cream of tartar
1 tsp. baking soda
½ tsp. salt

Rolling Mixture:
¼ C. sugar
2 tsp. cinnamon

Preheat oven to 400 degrees. Mix sugar, butter, and eggs. Add the flour, cream of tartar, baking soda, and salt. Mix well. In a separate small bowl, combine the sugar and cinnamon for the rolling mixture.

Shape 1½ -inch balls by rolling dough between your palms. Roll the dough balls in the cinnamon-sugar mixture, then place on an ungreased cookie sheet, about 2 inches apart—the cookies will spread.

Bake 8–10 minutes. Cool. Enjoy with a glass of milk while you read a good book.

SHANNON'S HOPE
NOW AVAILABLE

JOSI S. KILPACK

A NEWPORT LADIES BOOK CLUB NOVEL

SHANNON'S HOPE

Preview

Chapter 1

THE PHONE RANG, AND MY brain and body reacted as only a brain and body can react to a phone call in the middle of the night: sheer panic.

I shot up in bed, scrambled across John's still-snoring form—causing him to grunt—and fumbled for the phone on his nightstand. "Hello?" I said, not yet fully awake but alert enough to wish I'd taken just one full breath so it wouldn't sound like I'd just been pulled out of REM sleep.

I could hear noise from the other end of the line—traffic, and a man's voice shouting in the background.

"Hello," I said again as I finished crawling over John, who was awake now, or at least not snoring.

"Can you come get me?"

My heart pitched, and I let out a breath as my grip tightened around the phone. "Keisha?" I asked, though we both knew I knew who it was; Keisha was my twenty-one-year-old stepdaughter, John's daughter from his first marriage. "Where have you been? Where are you?" She'd fought with her mother two weeks ago and had left the house with nothing but her purse and her phone, which she hadn't answered since then. I'd called her at least once a day.

"Please come get me. I don't have anywhere else to go."

I adjusted my position so I could sit on the side of the bed. John sat up behind me, listening. "Is it Keish?" he whispered.

I nodded and covered the mouthpiece of the phone. "She wants us to come get her."

John fell back on the pillows, worn-out by one more crisis following the years of crises involving his daughter. Drugs, rehab, drugs again. Living with her mom, living with us, living with friends, living with her mom again. But, despite the chaos, we had always known where Keisha was at any given time. Not knowing during these last weeks had been horrendous.

"Where are you?" I asked into the phone.

"Compton. By the airport," Keisha said, sniffling. "Can you come?"

"Of course I can come," I said. John's grunt from behind me communicated many things—disappointment in me, annoyance at this situation, and frustration with his daughter. I hoped, however, that within all those negative feelings was also relief that she had called, that we knew she was okay. I knew he'd been as worried about her as I was. I pulled open the nightstand drawer and found a pen and an envelope I could write on. "What's the exact address?"

She gave it to me and asked me to hurry.

"I will," I said. "I'll have my cell phone with me, so call if you need to, okay?"

John climbed out of bed and turned on the closet light.

"I don't know your cell number 'cause I lost my phone," Keisha said, still crying. "I found some guy who let me use his to call you guys."

The need for urgency was building in my chest. "Let me give you my cell number, then. Do you have something you can write it down with?"

"No, just come," she said, sounding frustrated. "Please hurry, there's some really creepy people down here."

"Okay," I said, standing up. "We're on our way."

I hung up the phone and relayed the information to John, who was buttoning up his jeans. "We should be able to get to Compton in about forty minutes this time of night, don't you think?" I grabbed the hem of my knee-length nightgown and fluidly pulled it over my head as I crossed the room to my dresser to get some clothes. Keisha was okay. She was coming home.

"I'll go," John said. "You stay here with Landon."

I stopped, holding up a pair of jeans and looking at him. Oh yeah, Landon, our twelve-year-old son. "I told her *I* would come," I said. "Maybe you should stay with Landon."

"And send you to Compton in the middle of the night by yourself?" He pulled a T-shirt over his head, sending his sleep-mussed hair even more out of control. His hairline was nearly halfway back on his head these days, and though he kept his remaining hair short, the half-inch strands stood up in fifteen directions.

He was right about me going alone, of course. It was bad enough that Keisha was there; to send me there too was ridiculous. But . . . "Go easy on her," I said.

He gave me a look that bordered on a glare and went back into the closet to get his shoes. It was an old argument between us—tired, worn-out, and threadbare. I was too soft on his daughter, and John was too hard. When she'd gone to rehab the last time, he'd become a big proponent for "tough love" and saying, "She's an adult." I wanted to believe that if he'd been the one to answer the phone he'd have agreed to get her like I had, but I didn't know. The poor choices Keisha had been making the last four years had sent us on an emotional roller coaster as we tried over and over again to help, only to have her fall further down the pit of addiction. Maybe for John anger didn't hurt as much as hoping did.

"We just want her to be safe," I said, reminding him of our shared alliance.

He nodded, though reluctantly, and kissed me quickly on his way to the door. "Try to sleep."

"I won't be able to sleep," I said, shaking my head at the idea. "Call me when you get there, okay? I want to know she's with you."

He nodded again and disappeared through the doorway, leaving me standing in the middle of our bedroom. I listened carefully for the sound of the garage door closing before putting my nightgown back on and puttering into the living room. It would be at least an hour and a half before they got back, but if I stayed in bed, I would just stare at the ceiling. I'd rather clean to pass the time; heaven knows with both John and me working more than full-time, and with John coaching whatever sport-of-the-season Landon was playing, there was always something in need of cleaning, but then I saw the yellow-and-purple book cover peeking out from beneath a pile of mail and newspapers on the kitchen table.

I'd bought *The Help* last week at Walmart after Aunt Ruby told me it was the title for next month's book group. We'd been meeting for four months now, and I had yet to finish any of the other book club books. I'd seen the movie for this one, though, and liked the idea of comparing the two formats. I glanced at the clock. It was 2:14. Was John to Anaheim yet?

I sat down in John's recliner and pulled back the stiff pages of the book. An internal hesitation almost stopped me; I'd developed a prejudice toward fiction many years ago. Why read fiction when there were so many fascinating truths out there waiting to be learned? I pushed away the thoughts and honed in on the first page, determined to make this work. I was thirty-eight years old and in most ways I was well-rounded, but I could use some more things to talk about and think about. Landon was almost thirteen and more independent than ever before. John was extremely involved in Landon's athletics, leaving me with time I didn't know how to fill. Hence, I'd accepted Aunt Ruby's invitation to join her book group and yet hadn't finished a book. This time would be different.

I looked at the clock again and hoped this experience with Keisha would be different too. She'd lived with us half a dozen times since she'd turned seventeen and first starting hitting serious turbulence. Once she stayed with us for five full months; all the other times were just a few weeks here and there until she got back on her feet or repaired things with her mother. These last two weeks when she'd been gone were the longest weeks of our lives. We'd filed a missing persons report with the police, we'd contacted all of her friends we knew, and we'd called the local hospitals more than once. And now she'd called us. Thank goodness. I hoped that her calling us was a sign that she had finally hit the bottom of her trials and was ready to build her way up. I had always been able to see incredible potential in her, and I was determined to help her see it too.

But right now I needed to stop obsessing about her. I needed to get lost in something else and prepare for whatever tomorrow might bring. I smoothed my hand over the first page of *The Help*, took a breath, and started reading.

About the Author

ANNETTE LYON IS A WHITNEY Award winner, the recipient of Utah's Best of State medal for fiction, and the author of several novels. She loves exploring the power of female friendship in her work. When she's not writing, editing, knitting, or eating chocolate, she can be found mothering and avoiding the spots on the kitchen floor. Visit her online at blog.annettelyon.com and on Twitter: @AnnetteLyon.